Champagne &
Lemonade:
A collection of Short
Stories, of Mixed Genres,
for Young,
Middle & Old.

John AD Hickling

Clink
Street

London | New York

Published by Clink Street Publishing 2016

Copyright © John AD Hickling 2016

ISBN: 978-1-910782-14-9
Ebook: 978-1-910782-15-6

STORY LISTINGS

A Golden Tail

It was a red hot summer's day and the lovely little fish pond in the Brannings' back garden glistened in the morning sun. The pond was filled with Koi carp and one of them, a small orange fish with a distinctive white stripe across his back, called Nibble, was doing his daily moan routine to a big black fish named Lucky.

"Bored, bored, bored — mmm just bored."

"I take it you are bored, Nibble?" Lucky snapped.

"There must be more to life than swimming round in circles all day with you boring old lot."

"Why, what's up with this place, Nibble?" Lucky questioned, swimming angrily around him.

"Well, let's see…there's never any action, there are no young female fish and most of you may as well be floating belly up," Nibble replied sarcastically, ticking each point off on his fin.

"I've told you before, this appetite for action will get you into trouble; and a female definitely will," Lucky replied with a smile.

Nibble was about to make a retort when a chorus of 'Yippee' sounded around the pond. A silence followed as the fish huddled together, remaining as still as possible; their tails swishing back and forth in the water. All eyes were firmly fixed on the human shadow that loomed over the pond. A handful of food dropped down; breakfast had arrived.

"Attack," yelled a white fish named Bob as he shot towards the food. He opened his mouth wide to gobble some up, but another fish butted him out of the way. Another fish was also about to indulge when a multi-coloured fish pulled him back by his tail. Yes, feeding time in the Brannings' fish pond was, as always, chaos.

"There, that's exactly what I mean — the highlight of your day," Nibble said, smirking.

Lucky swam back down to Nibble. "Well — chomp — you have to — chomp — eat."

"Yeah, fair enough, but look at 'em; it's like a pack of them humans bringing down a spit roast pig at a barbecue."

"You had better hurry if you want some, there's hardly anything left," Lucky said.

Nibble shook his head. "I know; a pack of pikes would leave more than this lot."

"You joke, but I was lucky to get away." All down his sides Lucky was covered in scars.

"Not that story again please," sneered Nibble.

"It's true."

"Yes, you were in the river when three pikes grabbed ya, but you got away and you were rescued; hence the name Lucky."

"It was four," Lucky snapped back.

"Four? Four what?"

"Four pikes."

Nibble was swimming along shaking his head when a dark shadow fell across the surface of the pond. "Wow, they're feeling generous today; two lots of food," yelled Nibble as he shot up towards the surface.

"No, Nibble," shouted Lucky.

There was a big splash and a dazed Nibble found himself hanging upside down. He saw Lucky with his head sticking out of the pond, but he was getting smaller and smaller. Nibble looked up to see his tail in a great bird's mouth.

"Arrgh, oi let me go," Nibble yelled.

The bird tossed back his head, which sent Nibble spinning in the air. "Don't think so, mate," he screeched.

He opened his mouth ready to catch Nibble, but at that moment another bird knocked Nibble away; also wanting to eat him for dinner.

"Here, I'm not a tennis ball!" Nibble cried as he started to fall. He was flapping his fins up and down, hoping to stop himself, but it was to no avail as he continued to plummet. He looked up to see the birds fighting high above him. *Well this isn't good*, he thought.

Splash. A confused Nibble landed back in the water. He was slowly swimming around, trying to regain his bearings, when out of the corner of his eye he saw something. "Lucky, i-is that you?" he nervously asked as he slowly turned around. "Arrgh," he screamed; a lot of big teeth were heading towards him. Before Nibble could react there was a shout of 'Chaarrggge' and a fish as big as himself head-butted the big fish with all the teeth in the side.

"Quick, chum, follow me," shouted the fish; he was greenish in colour and had a fin with spikes on his back. Nibble followed him as fast as he could, but the murky water made it hard for him to see where they were heading. He swam past tall reeds and lots of human rubbish; he even saw a wellington boot like the ones the Brannings left outside their back door. There were a lot of different fish swimming about; fish that Nibble had never seen before. They swam down a narrow trench and lay there. "Sssshh," the fish said to Nibble as they lay there in silence waiting for the big fish to swim by. It felt like a lifetime waiting in that murky water but eventually the coast became clear.

"Hello, me ode pal, I'm Muncher," said the fish with a smile as he stretched out his right fin to shake Nibble's.

Nibble grasped the proffered fin and shook it. "Erm, hello, my name's Nibble," he replied looking cautiously around him.

"Ha, Nibble, ya nearly got nibbled. Mind you, I'm not surprised with you being that colour; you don't camouflage very well, do you?" Muncher said with a smirk.

"What was that thing? And what's it doing in a pond?" asked a puzzled Nibble.

Muncher rubbed his gills. "Pond, ha! That was Bruiser, he's a pike, and this ain't no pond, me ode pal, it's a river," he blurted cheerfully. "The coast is clear now; we should go."

Nibble froze, "A river…b-but…"

3

Muncher swam up to Nibble and urged him to follow. "Anyway, where you from?" They swam off and Nibble filled him in on the day's events.

*

A little later on and a bit farther up the river, Nibble's rumbling stomach prompted him to say, "I'm starving; where do you eat around here, Muncher?"

"That's a good question," he replied, scratching his brow. Nibble was about to speak when, "Rats," Muncher yelled.

Nibble hid behind him. "R-rats, where?"

"Don't be daft, Nibble, what ya hiding from? What I mean is the water rats; they've always got food," chirped Muncher. Nibble looked at him confused. Muncher grabbed him and said, "Oh come on, I'll show ya."

A couple of minutes later Muncher uttered another 'Sssshhh' as they swam through some weeds towards the rat nests on the bank. Their hearts sank; there was something skulking towards them through the weeds. Muncher wondered, *is it Bruiser the pike or the rats?* He hoped it wasn't Nuggets; he was a large rat with one eye — a nasty piece of work.

"W-what is it?" stuttered Nibble.

"Quiet," Muncher whispered. They huddled up as it got closer, and closer, and —

"Muncher, me old china." A fish jumped out at them.

"My heart, are you plumbed in woman? Dear me, how's it going, Poppet?" snapped a relieved Muncher.

"Who's this?"

"Oh sorry, Poppet; this is Nibble from the pond."

"Oh, hello," said Poppet, smiling as she looked into Nibble's eyes.

Nibble couldn't take his eyes off this beautiful small silver fish with red fins. "Erm, hello."

"Shush," interrupted Muncher, worried that the fish with the teeth were still lurking about.

"What are you both up to anyway?" asked Poppet, unable to take her eyes off Nibble.

"We're going to borrow a bit of grub from the rats," replied Muncher.

"Are you mad?" snapped Poppet.

"No, just hungry; well, see ya then, Poppet." Muncher made to swim away.

Poppet looked at Nibble who still hadn't taken his eyes off her. "Well, I'm hungry too so can I come with you?"

Muncher was just about to answer when Nibble jumped in, "Oh, yes, can she Muncher?" he begged, smiling at Poppet.

Muncher smirked, looking at the two lovebirds. "Come on then, but be quiet."

They swam slowly towards the nests, but the first one they got to was empty. They continued and swam up to the next one along and were just about to enter when they heard something coming up behind them.

Muncher, with a lump in his throat, slowly turned around. As he did so a loud, cackling laugh surrounded him. They all turned to meet Nuggets, the one eyed rat, who was flanked by two other river rats. Nuggets put his paws on the two rats' shoulders and with a sly grin shouted, "Lunch, boys, hehehe."

The rats leapt for the fish; Nibble and Poppet shot off with the two rats in tow while Muncher was being chased by Nuggets. Muncher smirked to himself and swam down the dark trench.

Poppet grabbed Nibble's fin and they exchanged a smile as they swam as fast as they could with the rats giving chase.

"Oh no," yelled Poppet; the cackling rats had them cornered. Nibble leapt in front of Poppet, protecting her.

Elsewhere, Muncher was swimming down the trench singing, "Too many fish in the sea."

Nuggets, however, had gained on him. "There will be one less in a moment, ha," he yelled.

Muncher stopped dead. "Food, boys," Bruiser the pike yelled as he lay in wait at the bottom of the trench with his mouth wide open. Muncher swam under him and headed back out of the trench again.

"Teeth," screamed Nuggets, jumping over Bruiser. He then shot after Muncher with Bruiser and two other pikes giving chase.

Nibble gave Poppet's fin a squeeze and couldn't stop thinking about the pond and Lucky. The rats were about to strike.

"Swim for your lives," screamed Nuggets.

The rats turned to see lots of teeth. "Arrrgh," they yelled and swam as fast as they could with the pikes hot on their heels.

"Yee-ha," yelled Muncher, bringing up the rear.

Nibble, Poppet and Muncher embraced. "That was great, Muncher," cheered Nibble, grinning with relief.

"Yeah, not bad for a genius like me." He smirked. Behind him Poppet and Nibble were cuddling.

Nibble thought to himself, *well I wanted action and a girl.* Poppet held his face and kissed him. "Yee-ha," he shouted as he shot up to the surface. He jumped out of the water and was about to shout again when he felt a thud. He shook his head and looked down to see Muncher and Poppet getting farther and farther away. He then looked up to see wings and yelled, "You're having a laugh!"

The Monster Hunters

The Prime Minister's, James Barrowman's, flustered face was the talk of the day amongst his house staff and a handful of reporters as he raced inside Number 10 for an emergency meeting. It had been arranged as a last minute thing and Barrowman had been forced to cut short his appearance at a charity function.

The red, flustered face of the PM was stared at by all in the room as he bounded in. His hair was uncombed, his right trouser leg was tucked into his sock, his tie was loosely fastened and he was still tucking his shirt into his trousers.

"Can't even have a number two in peace," he mumbled to himself as he sat down and threw a dossier on the table.

At this moment in time, England had eyes on her from all over the globe. There had been numerous rumours for years, of course, but these last few months had caused them to go through the roof. Various stories from conspiracy theorists were dominating the news channels and newspapers; they were all adamant that the government was hiding the truth from the nation. According to the theorists, the governments from all over the world had been working together to keep the public believing that any stories of mythical creatures were untrue. In the last couple of weeks, however, stories and sightings had quadrupled and it was becoming harder and harder to shield the truth from the public. UFO and Bigfoot sightings had come in from all over the globe, the Loch Ness monster had re-emerged and had been reported to have sunk a boat in the loch; one of the survivors had taken a photograph, but his camera had been mysteriously taken (by the government was what most of the theorists were saying). There had been stories of unicorns running around the National Park in Dartmoor, Devon; trolls were causing mayhem in the Hartsop area of the Lake District. And there was more: last week, London came to a standstill when Tower Bridge was wrecked; one half of the drawbridge had been left hanging down, bent and twisted, while the other half was at the bottom of the Thames. The reports that came in said that it was down to a large, troll-like creature which had been causing havoc. A handful of the public and a couple of reporters had borne witness to this. The government's official explanation had been that it was an earthquake and any witnesses that said anything different were quickly silenced in one way or another. Any reporters in the area at the time had been sent on a faraway exclusive with bonus payments that amounted to enough for an early retirement.

Only a select handful of people had been chosen to attend this meeting. There was George Bent, Secretary of State for Defence; Neville Green, the Deputy Prime Minister; Shirley Sherburne, Mayoress of London; General Frank Peace of the army, Admiral John Lincoln of the navy and Stephanie Brown, aide to the Queen whose job it was to keep the Queen up to date on the situation.

Also in attendance at this meeting was a new member of the cabinet, a military commander, Jack Durnham. He was a strapping, six foot, muscular man who took pride in everything he did — his cuffs and collars were pressed to perfection. He had short brown hair, a thin, brown moustache, brown eyes that glinted when he smiled and on his left cheek was a two inch scar that he had obtained during one of his tour duties. He sat, looking at the various members that had gathered, wondering what the meeting was all about.

The PM was sat across from Jack and Jack found himself staring at the PM as he flicked open a page in Jack's file and said, "I have been going through your files; you have had a remarkable career." The PM flicked over another page and tapped his finger on it. "One tour of duty in Iraq...two tours of duty in Afghanistan." The PM smiled then ran the fingers of his left hand through his uncombed hair; he turned to another page and said, "Plus thirty-two successful missions — without a scratch." He snapped the file shut. "You get the job done, no matter the odds or consequences, Jack; I like that. I think you are just the man we need." The Prime Minister suddenly turned graver. "Tell me, what do you know about the Tower Bridge incident?"

"Thank you, Sir; it's an honour to be here. Only what I saw on TV; it was an earthquake, I believe."

George Bent stood up, looked at Jack and said, "What have you heard about the troll story?"

"Rumours, like the rest of the stuff going round; just rubbish." Jack started to laugh, but soon stopped when he realized he was the only one.

"They're not rumours, Jack; read this," said the Prime Minister as he slid the top-secret dossier across the table to Jack.

Jack flicked through the dossier, grinning at first as he thought it was all a windup because all the pictures of different creatures (trolls, dragons, werewolves and much more) couldn't possibly be real. Then, as he was shown some video footage, his happy expression started to fade. First, there was an old black and white video of some sort of dragon creature in Mexico snatching people up from the ground, none of which were ever seen again. Some other footage showed what was known as a mountain troll being experimented on in a secret, underground facility in the USA. Jack watched the next clip open-mouthed as a man transformed into a werewolf, and his mouth opened even wider when a very fuzzy piece of film showed a goblin troll being experimented on in the Lake District. Another image flashed up on the screen and Jack piped up, "I remember that; it was the gas explosion at Chippenham Power Plant, two years back." But after watching the clip, Jack realized it was no gas explosion as he saw a twenty foot troll smash and destroy the building. The lights came back on as the videos finished and Jack was sat as silent as night as it dawned on him that everything he had always believed to be nothing more than myths, fiction and tales, was actually real.

He gulped as he looked at the Prime Minister, who then patted Jack's shoulder and said, "For years, we, and members of other governments, have kept these creatures contained. In the past we could just pay people off to keep quiet of any sightings, but now it's getting worse. There are far too many to pay off as the creatures seem to be more each day and our pockets are no longer deep enough. That is why I am putting you as Head of Operations, Jack; you have forty-eight hours to come up with a plan; report to George."

"Yes, Sir," whispered a shocked Jack. The Prime Minister shook his hand once more and left to broadcast to the nation about ridiculous hoaxes.

*

Somewhere in London, in his mate's Dad's garage at 5.30 a.m., Jake Birch, a 22-year-old lifeguard, 6 foot in height, crew cut hair, stocky build, was helping his mate Greg Polanski, a polish 23-year-old who was an inventor with long, blond hair tied back in a ponytail, pack for their camping trip to Hartsop in the Lake District. Greg and Jake were putting the finishing touches to Greg's campervan; it was chrome, could sleep six, had a brilliant GPS tracking system — all the mod cons. Jake was putting in fishing tackle and guns as they liked to go shooting. In fact, one of the reasons they were going to the Lake District was to see if they could catch the so-called beast of the Lake District; which was supposed to be some sort of a great, puma cat thing that had been spotted there.

It was an hour later before the rest of the gang turned up. There was James Hall, a 21-year-old, black Jamaican, 5 foot 9, dreadlocks; he was an animal catcher for the RSPCA; and Mollie Spindle, a 24-year-old, white, toned girl, 5 foot 7, short, brown hair; she was studying for her Computer Science degree at Birkbeck, University of London. She was also a black belt in mixed martial arts. She had always been a tomboy and felt more at ease having the lads as her mates.

"Morning all, the van's looking well, Greg — I can't wait for this trip," said an excited Mollie.

Greg wiped a side window on the van and said, "Thanks, Moll, yeah me too. We're just about ready to get off — oh, is that your new sheath knife you were telling me about? Let's have a look."

"Yeah, it's a good one, got it from Marshalls."

"How are ya, James, pal?" asked Jake, smiling as he patted James on his back.

James rubbed his eyes and yawned. "Well, I could think of better places to be at this time in the morning."

Greg laughed as he picked up a box of food to put in the van. "Stop whingeing, Hall, and come and help me — grab that box near the garage door."

James smiled then went to pick up the box. "How long do you reckon it will take to get there, man?"

"About five and half hours I reckon, that's why I wanted to get off earlier than this."

"You must be mad, man, it was hard work getting up and ready for this time," James replied with a smirk as he took some of Mollie's gear off her and passed it to Greg to load into the van.

"Oh, stop moaning, James; you can sleep in the van," smirked Mollie, jabbing James in the ribs.

"Yeah, come on, let's get cracking; have you put all your stuff in, Jake?" Greg asked as he got himself set in the driver's seat.

"Yes, mate; right, all aboard that's coming aboard," grinned Jake and the gang all clambered into the van and set off on their long journey.

*

The Prime Minister jumped up and kicked over the coffee table. He watched the news reporter explain in graphic detail how out of four climbers tackling Everest, three of them had been killed. The shook-up fourth climber, who was in intensive care, had reportedly mumbled something to the paramedics about how an 8 foot tall, white, horrible faced and sharp teethed thing with straggly fur had attacked and killed his friends. Bigfoot was what the reporter had deduced. Then, in the next report, two fishermen had been dragged to the bottom of Loch Ness; no bodies had so far been recovered. The locals were saying that it was the work of the monster.

The Prime Minister kicked the coffee table further across the room, this time breaking it in two; carefully tiptoeing around the broken glass he then answered the phone to the President of the USA.

*

Greg was making good time in his campervan, hitting 70mph most of the way; he was oblivious to where he was as he was singing full-bore to Queen's *Don't Stop Me Now*, which was blaring out of the radio. Mollie was making hot drinks for everyone, two teas (no sugar, very little milk) for Greg and James, a coffee (black, one sugar) for herself and a milky coffee (four sugars) for Jake, while James was explaining to Jake the best way to catch a big cat. This had now become the gang's top priority since it had been announced on the radio that there was a £1000 reward for its capture.

"What you gonna do with your money after we catch the thing, Moll? You know, your hundred quid after it's been split four ways," said James with a laugh.

Mollie passed out the drinks. "Ha, ha, very funny — woah, slow down, Greg, or I'll karate chop you; I nearly had coffee all over me."

Greg looked at Mollie in the rear-view mirror, giving her a sheepish grin as he carried on nodding his head to the radio.

"I'm not sure, James…probably clothes or put it towards the new iPhone; what about you?"

James rubbed his lip after nearly burning it off from taking a sip of his hot tea. "I'll just put it towards my nets and animal catching stuff, I'd imagine."

Greg took another corner a bit too sharpish, which left Jake, who was in the back, hanging on to his seat with one hand while trying not to slosh his drink everywhere with the other.

"Sorry, guys! I'd do the same with the money, I think, put it towards some invention; probably the jetpack I'm working on," said Greg.

They all went silent as they drank, but it didn't last long when Mollie piped up, "What about you, Jakey? What would you spend it on?"

Jake put his empty cup in the sink. "Well, providing we catch the thing, I don't know…probably swimming lessons," he said, laughing.

"Yeah, man, that might help, what with you being a lifeguard and all," James said and they all joined in the laughter. But the laughter soon subsided as Greg quickly shushed them, when a breaking news report came over the radio.

"This is an emergency broadcast. People are being told to keep away from the Saddleworth Moors in Greater Manchester as there have been mysterious sightings of what are being described as wolf-like creatures. There are fatalities, the roads are being blocked off and the army have been called in."

"What on Earth is happening? What is it with all this stuff going on?" asked Mollie.

"Tell you what, we'll go and catch this big cat then go to the moors and catch whatever those things are and then we can make a quick left to Transylvania for a spot of vampire hunting." The other three laughed at Greg's comments. The laughing soon stopped again, however, when they saw the sight in front of them. As they were nearing Stoke people were screaming and had all stopped their cars to point towards the sky. Greg pulled over and they all got out of the van.

"What the hell is that?" shouted Jake pointing upwards.

Mollie stood shaking her head, watching the creature fly away. "It looked like it was a dragon thing...what was in that coffee?" They all looked at each other, their faces ranging from confusion, shock to pure bewilderment.

"Come on, let's get after it," yelled Greg as he started up the van. They jumped in and sped off.

*

"Quiet, Chez," whispered her brother Brett Hollis as they sneaked through Grizedale Forest in the Lake District, trying to photograph the mysterious creature that was roaming around. Brett and Cheryl Hollis were 24-year-old twins from Manchester, who were on a camping trip in the Lake District. They were both firm believers in the untold, conspiracy theories and myths and were determined to catch something to prove that their beliefs weren't a waste of time. They wanted to show people that they had been right all along, but most of all they wanted to prove that they weren't crazy for believing in such stuff.

RRRRooooaaarrrr.

"What was that?"

"It was no puma cat, that's for sure, Chez; come on." Cheryl checked her camera to make sure it was set up properly so she wouldn't miss the photo that would definitely prove they weren't crazy. Brett was carrying a trap he had made; it was housed in a rucksack and made out of old fishing nets that he had tied together. The idea was to put some bait down near a tree, on top of the nets, which would be attached to the tree by pulley ropes.

As soon as the beast walked onto the nets it would be hoisted into the air then they would photograph and catalogue it for their records before calling in the authorities — well that was the theory anyway. They were really deep into the forest now and it was becoming damp, dark and claustrophobic. There were so many trees and they were all around them; they stretched so far upwards that they appeared to touch the sky. Straight ahead of them several trees shook and birds screeched and squawked as they flew away.

"Sssh, Chez," whispered Brett as they sneaked up on the very close target. Adrenaline was pumping through their veins at the thought of finally seeing one of the mythical creatures that they had been pursuing for so long. However, there was also some nerves mixed in along with a fear of what their eyes were about to fall upon.

"Wow, whatever it is stinks," mumbled Cheryl with her hand over her nose.

"Whatever it is, it's big; look at the tops of the trees." Brett pointed at what they could just make out to be hands, big hands at that, on top of the trees. They were a dirty, greyish colour, all covered in warts and cuts, the index fingers were bent like bananas and the nails were long and misshapen. The Hollises sneaked through a clearing, hoping for a better view, but they were careful not to attract attention to themselves.

Cheryl's scream was deafening at the sight of the creature that met their eyes. Brett grabbed the camera from his incapacitated sister's hands and managed to take a photo. The creature went mad from the dazzling camera flash and growled as it went for them. "Run, Chez, run," shouted Brett.

*

Greg and the gang were just under an hour away from the Lake District and the roads were getting busier by the second with people trying to flee the areas where there had been reports of sightings; while other people probably wanted to see all the commotion with their own eyes. A report had just come over the radio saying that airports were swamped with people wanting to leave England, while in Dover security had to stop people from trying to force their way onto a ferry.

"I can't see it," said Jake, referring to the flying beast; the others were looking out of the windows.

"I reckon it has come this way," said James, pressing his face up against the glass and looking at dead sheep carcasses on the side of the road as well as the debris from smashed road signs which littered the road in front of them — this was doing nothing to ease the traffic congestion.

Mollie was on her laptop. "Jesus, you ought to see all the various stories that are being reported, there are loads of different sightings. Oh! Here's the flying beast, it's been mentioned and was last spotted up in the Lake District. And all this other stuff is incredible; what I can only describe as some troll creature has been seen near Tower Bridge in London, a village in Sweden has been burnt to the ground with witnesses saying it was a dragon. The list of sightings goes on, ranging from unicorns, dinosaurs and even a Cyclops. What *is* going on?" she said.

"I've been saying for ages things are being covered up." Greg scowled, the tapping of his fingers on the steering wheel getting louder with his impatience at being stuck in the traffic.

"So you believe in these...things that are supposed to be alive then, man?" said James as he looked out the window at the masses of beeping vehicles.

"Yeah, Hall, I do. I tell ya, the governments cover all sorts up; so why should this be any different?" said Greg.

"Well, something's going on; I mean, why is all the traffic like this for a start? And look at this..." yelled Mollie, showing the gang a fuzzy picture and a report of some dinosaur-like creature in Germany.

"Wow, that looks horrible, what is it?" asked Jake as he checked his watch.

"I'm not sure, it looks like a Velociraptor — according to my files — which is impossible; they have been extinct millions of years," said a confused looking Mollie.

"What about Photoshop, man? It's probably a fake," James said, trying to add some logical explanation.

"God knows; keep looking for different reports, Moll, so we can try and make some sense of it all," said Greg. Mollie nodded.

"Yes, man."

"At last," said James and Greg as they high-fived each other because the traffic had started to move again.

*

Jack Durnham and his team were about to board their private jet to go to the Lake District. This was the first point of call because some of the creatures had been housed here in the past due to its vast acres of land that were hidden away from the public. Recently, however, more and more creatures were being spotted here than anywhere else; there were even new species that had never before been documented. One thought on why this was happening was because of the recent building activities of humans; we were building on these areas of vast countryside and forcing the creatures into our habitats.

Jack was deep in thought and wondered what exactly they would encounter. All sorts of things were racing through his head; he took a sip of bottled water, clicked his pen and started scribbling down ideas, hoping to organize his scattered thoughts. How were they going to recapture the creatures that were already free? How, in the future, were they to keep their numbers down?

He scribbled out a section of his notes as he deemed an underground lair in which to house trolls too impossible until he knew how many there were and what they were: did they eat meat? Plants? What? Was it feasible to capture them instead of slaying them? He knew there were acres of the restricted forest areas where, in the past, creatures had been guarded by specially trained military personnel, but they had long since disappeared.

Jack looked out of the window, took another sip of water and carried on with his notes.

*

Greg and the gang had arrived at their campsite and pitched up their van. Jake was sorting food out on the BBQ: he had a selection of burgers, chicken and steak (his chicken burgers were apparently to die for). Meanwhile, James and Greg were sorting out their tracking and catching equipment, which consisted of a black, handheld device that Greg had made which could detect movements along with the range of them. James had invented different sized Hall Spring Nets, which were housed in sport bags and would spring out and snare different animals from a remote control device. These were some of the things they possessed to help them track the cat and flying beast.

"How many burgers, Moll?"

"Just one, Jake, thanks," Mollie replied as she made sure she had plenty of battery for her camera.

James and Greg were still checking over their kit. "What rifle have you got there, Greg, man?"

"It's a Marlin 336xlr, it's a good 'un, got it quite cheap off eBay," Greg replied as he held it out for James to get a better view.

"So what have you been up to at work, Hall?" asked Greg.

"On Tuesday there was a large fox that had wandered into a housing estate. It was pretty cool, actually, because it gave me an opportunity to try out one of my spring nets. It worked too; mind you, that was the easy part, getting the nasty git out of the trap and into the van was the hardest part; it took me and two of my work colleagues at least 45 minutes."

"You've made a good bit of kit there, mate. What's your boss think of them?"

"He thinks they're good, man. He wants me, or should I say us, to come up with a specific one for the job — and a price." Greg smiled as he got some plates and cutlery ready.

Mollie had put down her iPad after checking out more reports of creature activity, while Jake flipped and pressed down some steak on the BBQ and yelled, "Grub's up, you two; do you want some steak and chicken?"

"Yeah, ta," shouted Greg.

"Yeah, that'd be great, Jake, then we'd better get a move on."

"Here you are, Moll, a bit of steak. How are the exams going?"

"Cheers, yeah, they're okay; quite tough but enjoyable. How's the new lifeguard job at the Ironmonger Row Baths?"

Jake hurriedly chewed his piece of steak. "It's good; boss is fine, and my colleagues are great. I had to jump in and assist a teenager the other day; he put his foot in someone else's arm band and nearly ended up drowning." They all laughed as they tucked into their food.

*

It was 6 p.m. and the sky was full of sunshine as Jack and his troops landed on an unused airstrip. Jack surveyed the view as the jet landed. There were old huts and sheds which he supposed was where the creatures had previously been housed, but they were now abandoned; the facility had become overcrowded and had not been updated as more species had come to fruit and become smart enough to figure out ways to escape.

He noticed a few old, battered, brick built offices and barracks that looked like they had been around since the Second World War. There were also three aircraft hangers, two of which were badly damaged, and the whole area, which was situated on a bumpy field, was fenced off by a tall, wired, electric fence. The camp was surrounded by trees and Jack noticed an area of them which had been smashed and torn apart, leaving a couple of trees scattered all over the base.

There were already another ten soldiers there, setting up the base, and, as they exited the jet, one of them came running over to Jack. "Evening, Sergeant; I'm Commander Jack Durnham," yelled Jack over the noise of the aircraft, giving a salute.

"Evening, Sir; Sergeant Steven Black at your command." They shook hands.

"How're things going, Sergeant? And I presume you have all been briefed on the mission?"

"We have communications set up, Sir, and we are sorting the accommodation. Yes, Sir, we have been briefed on the mission and what has been happening by the Prime Minister, Sir."

"And what do you think of what you were told?" Jack and Steven smirked as they slowly walked on.

"At first I was waiting for the joke, Sir, but nothing surprises me and you have my full backing, Sir." Jack smiled. "Let me show you around and introduce you to your men, Sir." And off they went.

*

At around 7 p.m. Greg, Jake, Mollie and James left their campervan, hired a Jeep and chucked all their rifles, tracking equipment and other stuff inside, and set off. About twenty minutes into the drive, they were closing in on the restricted area of the forest, travelling along a very narrow dirt track, when a large cat ran out in front of them. Greg, who was driving, swerved so as not to hit the creature and slammed his foot on the brakes, missing a tree by centimetres. Greg looked over his shoulder and watched the cat go through a hole in the fence.

"Is everyone okay?" yelled Greg as the others stumbled out of the Jeep.

"Yeah, I'm fine," said Jake.

"Apart from my heart I'm ok," said Mollie, patting her chest.

"James?"

"Yeah, fine, Greg, man."

Greg checked over the Jeep while the gang checked themselves and their equipment; Mollie had to wipe a bit of blood off Jake's face where he had grazed it on the window.

"Anyway, what was that thing?" asked Mollie.

"Well, it was no domestic cat; that's for sure," yelled Jake as he and James were getting out their rifles and equipment. Greg got his gun and a long canvas bag which housed a trap of his own design.

"Grab your camera, Moll, and let's go; it went through that hole there," Greg said and off they went in pursuit.

"Sssh," whispered James as they sneaked behind some trees. The cat was a few metres in front of them, sniffing around a dead deer carcass. It was the size of a tiger but its paws were huge and it had long teeth protruding from the top of its mouth. It was golden brown in colour with faint, black stripes running along the top of its back.

The gang looked at each other in disbelief before Mollie rummaged around in her rucksack, looking for her camera; she pulled out her compass, a multi-tool, combined Swiss knife, her notebook and an iPad before finally finding it.

"What the hell is that?" whispered Jake.

"Well, I'm no expert, and I believe they're meant to be extinct, but with its long teeth and golden coat it looks like a sabretoothed tiger to me," said Mollie as she managed to take a couple of pictures.

"Right, Jake, you distract it; me and James will snag it," whispered Greg. James and Greg nodded in agreement, while Jake looked at them gone out, not feeling entirely happy with his role in the plan. Greg jumped as a loud roar sounded from high above them. The cat ran off.

"It's the flying thing," yelled Jake and he began to run as the beast clocked eyes on him and gave chase. He was now wishing that he had hidden himself a bit better. The beast was about ten feet long and green in colour with a long tail and neck — like a serpent, but it also had eagle-like talons and a beaklike jaw. It was definitely reptilian though as its mouth was full of razor-sharp teeth. It was trying to get through the trees for its dinner, which just so happened to be Jake.

"That's it, Jake; keep it occupied," yelled James.

Jake was dodging in-between the trees as the beast struggled to get down to him, and with Jake involuntarily distracting the beast it gave Greg the perfect opportunity to lay down one of his bag traps in the open clearing. "Jake, bring it over here," shouted Greg.

"Try and bring it over this way too, Jake, so I can get a good picture of it," Mollie also shouted from behind a tree as she held her camera up ready.

"No problem, and after I've done that I'll nip back to camp and make an à la carte candlelit supper, shall I?" sneered Jake as he shot towards the clearing and the beast swooped down for him.

"Now, Greg," yelled James. Greg responded by pressing a button on a remote controlled device which was strapped to his wrist. This made the canvas trap bag spring open and a net shoot upwards; it spun in the air and snared the beast, wrapping so tightly around its wings that it incapacitated its flight and brought it crashing down. The screeching noise it made was deafening as it smashed through tree branches before finally hitting the ground — Jake only just managed to roll out of the way in time.

Greg and James jumped up and smashed in pegs and tied ropes from the net to nearby trees as the dazed and cut beast made little attempt to redress its situation. It took them little over a minute to secure the net and trap the beast. James high-fived Greg and they both turned to pull a dirty Jake up from the ground. Jake shook his head then smiled as they patted him on his shoulders in gratitude. Mollie was still taking photos of the creature.

"What the hell is it, Mollie?" asked Greg.

"Well, it's certainly no canary, is it?" quipped Jake, swigging from a bottle of water.

Mollie sat down on a tree stump, slipped off her rucksack and put down her camera. She took out her iPad, which was in an army camouflage case, tapped in her password and then she scrolled through her own database — The Spindle Files — in which she had information on living, factual creatures as well as in-depth research on myths and legends. She tapped her right foot continually as she studied the web and her files. "I've come across something like this before, I know I have — ahh, here we are," said an excited Mollie as some files and pictures loaded on her system.

The others gathered round. "What? Have you have seen one of these before?" asked James.

The creature tried to wrestle itself free, but the lads made sure it was secured then went back to Mollie, who continued, "I haven't seen one like this in the flesh before, but as you can see here, these photos are from thirty years ago and were passed off by the government as fake. You can see the similarities — the eagle talon-like claws on each foot...the beaklike jaw." Mollie clicked a button that said 'Archive Files'.

"I think it's not long eaten by the look of the blood and flesh around its teeth," observed Greg.

"Well now we know what all the reports of missing cattle are about," said James.

"Look, mythology records state that these creatures are called wyverns — don't get too close to the barb in its tail, Jake, it's venomous. According to this, they come mainly from Great Britain and Ireland, live in caverns or similar protected lairs which can be easily identified by the bones of their prey which they leave scattered by the entrances," said Mollie, showing the gang all the information.

The gang stood in awe, admiring the creature, which attempted to do a deafening roar, but the ropes and nets put paid to that.

"What we gonna do with it?" Jake asked, but before he got an answer they heard the mightiest roar; it shook the trees and made the birds flee from their nests. It was instantly followed by a girl's scream ripping through the air.

"Oh my God, what was that?" yelled Mollie.

"Quick, come on; it came from over there," bellowed James and off they ran in the direction of the gut-wrenching scream.

Five minutes later they were negotiating their way through some tall, tight trees when Greg fixed his eyes on the treetops, which were shaking.

"Someone please tell me I'm not going mad and my eyes aren't deceiving me because it looks like there are some huge hands on top of them trees," whispered Jake. The huge hands were the reason why the trees were shaking so violently, sending branches crashing down to the ground; leaves were falling and fluttering everywhere and the birds and animals of the forest squawked and squeaked as they fled for cover.

The gang were startled as the sound of voices came from behind them. "Be quiet, trust me, you don't want that thing after you. Hi, I'm Brett Hollis and this is my sister Chez."

"Hi, I'm Jake," he whispered. Jake and Brett shook hands before they all crouched for cover behind some bushes.

"Hi, I'm Mollie, Jake you already know, that's James and that's Greg." Mollie pointed. A roar made them all crouch further down for a few seconds.

Mollie smiled at Brett who was a six foot, gangly figure, dressed all in black; his brown hair was swept over his head to form a ponytail at the back, he had a thin goatee and a warm expression was conveyed through his brown eyes.

"What is that thing? It sounds like King Kong," Jake asked, trying to whisper louder than Greg and James who were busy discussing plans of action.

"You're not far off, mate; it's some kind of troll thing, me and our Chez have been stalking it to prove that these things do exist," Brett replied. The gang looked at each other, bewildered at hearing the word troll, but after what they had already witnessed so far that day it wasn't hard to believe that what Brett was saying was true.

"What are you all doing up here?" asked Cheryl, who was a pretty, petite girl with short, cropped, brown hair, three piercings in each ear as well as a nose stud. She too was dressed in black and, like her brother, carried a small backpack.

"We're here to catch the big cat that there is a big reward for. The locals are keen to stop it killing off their livestock," said James.

"Any luck with that?" asked Brett.

"Not yet," was Greg's reply as he checked his rifle.

"What now, then, Greg?" asked Jake, but before an answer could be given, a growl came from behind them. They all stood and slowly turned around to be faced with the cat. James slowly eased out his rifle and had just cocked it when the cat yelped and ran off.

"That was easy enough," quipped Brett

"Too easy," replied James. "What's that smell?"

"Urrgh," said Chez with a shiver.

"What the hell is that?" asked Mollie as a yellow, greeny coloured, slimy liquid, full of lumps and about ten feet in length splattered onto the ground; it looked suspiciously like drool and some of it splattered over Chez and Mollie. They all slowly turned around, and there, looking down at them from twenty feet high, with bits of grey fur hanging on its grey skin, hands as big as houses, red eyes, a pointed nose and a mouth full of manky, sharp teeth was a —

"It's a troll thingy-me-bob — a big 'un at that," yelled Jake.

"Run," was Brett's command and they did. The troll roared as it started ripping up trees to try to get to them.

"There's no such thing as trolls, Jake," yelped James as he ran alongside him.

"Well it looks real enough to me, pal!"

"Freeze," yelled Commander Durnham. Jake and the rest came to a sudden halt, all of them staring down the barrels of soldiers' guns.

One of the soldiers attempted to grab Mollie, who, after taking a karate stance, swiped his legs out from underneath him, but that was the last display of her karate skills as two soldiers pointed their rifles at her, making her nervously smile and raise her hands.

"Who are you and what are you doing here?" demanded Sergeant Black.

"Well, we were camping and having a BBQ, but now we mainly seem to be finding a host of things that don't exist," sneered Jake sarcastically. A soldier pointed his rifle at Jake, who started whistling as he raised his hands.

"Enough of that. Can you explain to me why six of you are running about in a dangerous, restricted area? Well?" shouted Commander Durnham.

Greg stepped forward. "Well, Sir, we *have* come camping, but we have also come to catch the cat that has been reported in the area."

Jack looked the group up and down then said, "A cat is about right. I believe it was someone's house cat, that is all."

James looked at Greg in bewilderment then spoke, "That's a good one, a house cat, it was nothing of the sort, it was —"

"Quiet, I can't have six young people, who don't understand the situation, running around a restricted area; these men will escort you off the premises."

"We know what is going on here, man, and that thing we just saw was different to any house cat I have ever seen," said James

"Yeah, then there's the wyvern we just caught," said Mollie, waving her iPad.

"And the troll thingy," said Brett, looking at the trees.

Commander Jack Durnham shared a look with Sergeant Black. "What is a wyvern and how do you know all this?" said Jack.

"Because we have caught it, man," said James.

"And *you* are? Exactly what expertise do you have in such matters?" asked Jack.

"James, Sir, and I work for the RSPCA as an animal catcher."

"Mollie, show him," said Greg as another roar crashed through the trees

Jack looked at them with caution; Greg was looking at the hundreds of birds, wondering what was making them flock in the sky. The soldiers were all looking nervous as they had the guns aimed at the rustling, but with no idea what was behind it. They were all startled when a spine-tingling shriek came from what sounded like another creature deep within the forest.

Mollie approached Jack and started showing him her camera images; Jack gulped, looked at Mollie, and then carried on surveying the pictures. Sergeant Black signalled with his right hand, and some of the soldiers slowly moved forward to see what the rustling was.

"I would get your men back and get out of here if I was you, boss man," said James as he started backing away from the shaking trees, but before Commander Durnham could ask why —

"Aaaaahhhhhh," screamed four of the soldiers as the troll burst through, throwing the soldiers to their deaths. One soldier fell in front of the troll and started to fire his L85A2 rifle. The troll roared and trod him into the earth.

The Commander went to pull one of the soldiers to his feet but he slipped and the troll growled and went towards him. Jack took aim but his gun jammed and he thought he was looking death in the eye when...

"Hey, stinky," yelled Jake, throwing a stone at the troll which hit it in the eye. While the troll was distracted Jake pulled the Commander to his feet. Grateful, he shook Jake's hand.

"Run," yelled Sergeant Black even though most of them were already doing so. After a couple of minutes of running and shooting, the Commander, Sergeant Black, Greg, Mollie, James, Jake, Brett, Cheryl and the three soldiers that had survived all hid in a trench.

"Quiet, everyone," whispered the Sergeant, putting his finger to his lips. They could hear the troll, grunting and sniffing about. Greg and James were thinking about the best way of trapping the thing, with Greg hoping the nets he had invented wouldn't let him down. Mollie was wondering where the trolls had come from, wondering about their existence. Durnham's head was full of different scenarios. How was he, firstly, going to sort out the troll and, secondly, salvage the whole operation? Because he, after all, was in charge and the buck would have to stop with him. The others were thinking about their families and whether they would survive to see again, while Jake was thinking about the date that he had been asked out on a couple of nights ago by Tiffany Bishop, a fellow lifeguard at work. She was the prettiest girl he had ever met and he was really hoping that he would still make their date.

"What are we gonna do, Greg...James?" asked Mollie and everyone looked at them for an answer, even the military.

"I wish I could get to the van and get my bag traps."

"They wouldn't be big enough, Greg," said James. He then turned to Jack and asked, "What have the soldiers got in their bags?"

"Rope, food, chloroform, tranquilizers. Why?"

Greg and James whispered a plan, smiles etched across their faces, excited because these were the exact ingredients they needed to put a plan into action.

"Have you noticed it's gone very quiet?" mumbled Cheryl. The Sergeant waved his hand at one of the soldiers to go and investigate. The soldier gulped, saluted and slowly climbed out.

"Right, listen up, we need to sneak out and tie some ropes to the foot of those trees. Next, we calculate the area where this thing is likely to fall and put twigs and leaves there along with some chloroform. That leaves a couple of us to climb up high into the trees with the tranquilizers," James finished with a grin.

"I know you're an animal catcher, James, and you all did a cracking job on the wyvern creature, but I don't think you have caught anything on this scale before have you?" Jack asked.

"Well no, Sir, but it's all the same principle."

"It sounds like we might not need your plan, after all, James; it's gone very quiet. And hey, where did that soldier go?" said Mollie.

"Good point; get on the radio to him," ordered Sergeant Black. It was then that they heard a scream and the body of the soldier, minus his head and with his intestines dangling out from his battered body, landed in the trench. Greg and Brett put their hands over Cheryl and Mollie's mouths to muffle their screams.

"Right, we go with the plan," said the Commander, through gritted teeth, his eyes fixed on the mangled soldier's body, a man he had served with in Afghanistan and Iraq and had much respect for; it was from this respect that Durnham knew they had to try to do something, and he knew James' plan was the best that they had. "How do we get its attention?"

Everyone looked at Jake, who reluctantly nodded his head; James patted him on the back and said, "Jake, take him away and then double back, I can see an area a few yards away that should do; give us five minutes."

Jake stood up and peeked out of the trench; he could see the troll a few yards back, eating one of the soldiers: clothes, helmet, boots and all. The crack of the soldier's bones as the troll chewed on him was stomach turning.

Brett tapped Jake on the back. "I will go with you, mate." Jake smiled at him. The others were slowly sneaking out of the trench and making their way to the trap site; they were going to start setting everything up.

As Brett and Jake were waiting for the others to safely reach their destination they decided to get to know each other a little better. They established that they were both Taurean, which they thought was cool, but Jake supported Tottenham Hotspur while Brett supported their fiercest rivals: Arsenal; but in their current circumstances that didn't seem to matter so much — for the time being anyway. Brett also revealed he liked, and was good at, swimming, which Jake could appreciate. After their chat they felt that they could trust each other that little bit more and their nerves were slightly soothed.

When their comrades were in place they both took a deep a breath and cocked the guns that Commander Durnham had given them for protection. "Some camping trip this," quipped Jake. They both laughed and jumped out of the trench. Jake quietly passed Brett his gun and then picked up a big stick. "Hoh, smelly," he yelled as he threw the stick at the troll, hitting it on its back. The troll roared as he dumped the remains of the soldier down on the forest floor. He then threw a bigger stick back at Brett and Jake which, for the troll, was a huge tree branch; it was a struggle for them both to get out of the way in time.

"This way, Jake; quick, it's coming," shouted Brett.

Two of the soldiers were in the trees with loaded guns and tranquilizer darts. The girls and the Sergeant had laid down twigs and leaves and then poured over the chloroform, while the Commander, James and Greg had tied the ropes around the foot of the trees, in hope of bringing the troll down.

About five minutes had passed with the Commander and everyone else waiting in anticipation to spring the trap when they heard the roar coming towards them. The roar was closely followed by the hurried footfalls of Jake and Brett running back to them. "Get ready, it's coming," yelled Jake. They jumped behind the trees and took cover with the girls as the troll came tearing down to the trap.

"Now!" yelled James and Greg as they pulled the ropes, which tangled around the hairy, wart-filled legs of the troll. The troll growled as he started to fall and tried to grab hold of a tree for support.

"Fire!" yelled Sergeant Black and the soldiers fired the darts into him. After a bit of a stumble, it fell into the chloroform, landing on its side. It roared and tried to get up, prompting the Commander to throw more bottles of chloroform to knock it out. Jake and Brett secured its head by wrapping bungee ropes around its greasy neck and attaching them to a thick oak tree. Greg and James, meanwhile, were roping its legs together when, all of a sudden, the troll roared, startling the four lads. The roar soon turned into a yelp and then silence as it succumbed to a deep, chloroform induced sleep.

"Hooooorraaah," they all cheered, before all jumping as the troll let out the loudest trump.

"Jesus wept, I want to be sick," grimaced Sergeant Black. Mollie, Cheryl and Jake were well ahead of him and already throwing up in some bracken, the odour of the troll making their eyes water.

*

The next day, Commander Durnham had just got off the phone to the Prime Minister after filling him in on the previous day's events. In the end, not only did they capture the troll and the sabre-toothed tiger but also a flying beast, which Mollie had later catalogued as a banshee, and all of them had been impounded in makeshift cages and huts in the restricted area of the forest.

The Prime Minister was sending troops to build a top secret compound for the rehousing of all creatures at that location. When Jack had asked about the cost the PM's reply had been, "We will blame it on the council tax." It was to be a top-secret facility and Greg and the others were to be part of the team; Unit 171 – The Monster Hunters. When the PM needed to talk to other governments, the code word would be Môn strum Venator — the Latin for monster hunter. They were to be sent for training immediately. They would have the best weapons, vehicles and all the state-of-the-art technology there was to help keep the world safe from whatever else was out there.

*

Two months later, the Prime Minister was sat in his office and on his desk was a top-secret dossier. He opened it up and looked at it with a grin; it read:

UNIT 171: THE MONSTER HUNTERS:
Commander Jack Durnham U171MH 101
 Sergeant Steven Black U171MH 102
Cadet Jake Birch UMH171 111
Cadet James Hall UMH171 112
Cadet Brett Hollis UMH171 113
Cadet Cheryl Hollis UMH171 114
Cadet Greg Polanski UMH171 115
Cadet Mollie Spindle UMH171 116
Next mission: Loch Ness, Scotland.

Bernie Broom's Bubblebum Bottles

Dad walked in; 5.15 p.m. on the dot, black as coal (funny that seeing as he is a coal delivery man though, don't you think?). Anyway, I was sat at the table in the kitchen diner, well, it's kind of our lounge as well. Dad's promised to replace the wall, you see, but I'd say that was 6 years, 4 months, 3 days, 10 hours, 45 minutes and 20 seconds ago, but I'm not one for being precise.

Dad walked into Mum's clean washing, tripped over our dog Beetroot, put the kettle on and let out the biggest trump you've ever heard. He then sat down with his newspaper, not even noticing that my complexion had turned green from his recent bubblebum activity. Beetroot had nearly worn his claws down scratching at the back door in an attempt to get out of the stink. I looked at Dad (or Mr Broom to you) and he gave me a quick smile before burying his head in the newspaper. He was oblivious to me punching myself constantly in the nose, trying to stop the dreadful stink. I caught a glimpse of myself in the now steamed up mirror and my nose looked like a badly made jam sandwich.

I was about to ask Dad how his day had been when, not taking his eyes of his paper, he cocked his bottom slightly (and I mean slightly) to the left and let another trump out. Dad's nostrils didn't budge and he also took no notice of me now trying to stuff socks up my battered nose. My head nearly shook off with me shaking it in disbelief at Beetroot who yelped, growled and squeezed through the keyhole, all in one motion, and the keyhole had the key in it at that!

All of a sudden, Mum (or Mrs Broom to you) came in with some washing under her arm. She was wearing her faithful, full of holes pinny which buried her skinny frame. Her blonde hair surrounded by curlers and the smell (which by now had peeled three sheets of wallpaper off the wall) not bothering her. She put the washing down, looked at Dad and Dad looked up. They looked like they wanted to say something to each other, but something was stopping them. So Mum left the room again while Dad carried on with his paper. But I know what the problem is; we're very poor, you see. Dad tries really hard, but what with debts after debts and him losing his job in a couple of days because of cutbacks there's not much he can do.

Dad stood up; he's a balding man with a thick moustache and he is plumpish. I take after him apart from no tash and a full head of brown, straggly hair. He went passed, rubbed my head and banged the boiler to turn the hot water on. He then trudged upstairs. I stood up and went to the window to see what Beetroot was doing, but unlike most dogs who bury their bones, he was burying himself!

A little later, I was doing the pots after tea, which because we are tight for money was fish finger, chips and peas. And I say fish finger because we only had one each. Mum had gone in the bath and in twenty minutes it would be Dad's turn, then ten minutes after that it would finally be mine. Now, I don't like bath time because we can only afford to have one bath between us, and tonight it was my turn for the mucky bath water.

When it was my turn I dragged my feet upstairs, trying to delay the experience. I stood over the tub and peered in at the water. It looked more like tar than bath water and even my rubber duck Nigel had sunk to the bottom.

I lay in the bath for quite some time and pondered how I could make things better for our family.

*

The next day, after school, I was in the back garden trying to dig Beetroot out of his hole when Dad came in from work, waved and went into the kitchen. As soon as Beetroot saw him he started to dig deeper.

I went into the shed and started rooting through all the stuff in there. In the corner, on the floor, were Dad's shovels and garden forks, and on top of the shelves were lots of paint tins, including a big one that was labelled TNT (must be Dad's weed killer, or what Mum uses for baking or summat). There were a couple of Dad's old bikes, Granddad's old army helmet, which had straw and a couple of bird eggs in it. The stuffed fox looked like it wasn't happy, and all around were spiders as big as horses — well, rats or mice — they were big spiders anyway.

I took a peek through the window and saw some Jehovah's witnesses knock on the back door. Dad opened the door and for a couple of minutes he was shaking his head and constantly saying no, but it was to no avail as they still wouldn't leave. Then, out of nowhere, Dad cocked his bum quite high to the right and let out a noise which sounded like a train horn. One of the men screamed, threw up, screamed, threw up again then ran. The other man didn't run; he just jumped straight over Mr Nettles' (who is our neighbour, by the way) seven foot fence, clearing it by a good three feet. Dad nodded and shut the door.

Later on, in the bath, as I lay there playing with the floating lumps of coal, I had an idea. If it worked out we could have a *clean* bath each and have fish fingers, not fish finger, for tea.

I got my pyjamas on and because it was Friday night and there was no school in the morning I could put my idea into practice tomorrow. Someone knocked on the door again. Excited, I went downstairs hoping it was some more Jehovah's witnesses, but it was only Mr Giles, who was returning a reluctant Beetroot, whose head Mr Giles had seen sticking out of his back garden; which is six doors down.

*

In the morning, Dad and Mum had to go out, Mum said they were going shopping, but it don't take two to buy a tin of beans, a pack of fish fingers and milk. Also I think Dad had gone to see if there was any work as his last shift as a coal man was on Friday.

While they were gone I went into the shed and sorted out a lot of old glass bottles, some thick, some thin, some short, some tall; then I went and laid them around the house, in the bathroom, bedrooms, front room, on the beds, under the beds, in the beds, everywhere I could think of. I made my breakfast of porridge, without the milk, and then took Beetroot for a walk.

On returning, I saw Mum and Dad walking in, both looking glum; Mum was clutching her half a bag of shopping to her. Me and Beetroot ran into the shed and in an old box was a couple of Granddad's old gas masks. After five minutes of wrestling with Beetroot, fixing the gas mask on him, I put mine on and we sneaked into the house. Mum had nipped straight back out again so me and Beetroot scrambled behind the settee, struggling to see in our masks, and there we waited. Dad was laid on the settee with the TV blurring out as he was half asleep. It seemed like we waited there for hours and Beetroot now had his head trapped in the door, trying to pull off his mask. Suddenly, the wait was over. Dad cocked his left leg and

PPPPAAAARRRRP.

Within seconds the windows steamed up, the wallpaper (what was left of it) started to peel and Beetroot was now banging his head against the door. I could even smell it in the gas mask but I still jumped up and started to put the lids on the bottles.

All day Dad was trumping and I fixed the tops back on every bottle and labelled them. I was only briefly disturbed when some lorry driver brought back Beetroot who'd been running down the motorway (which is over ten miles away) with his gas mask still on. For two days I laid down bottles to capture Dad's trumps, they were all so horrible that Beetroot had been found lying in the middle of the road, barking at cars to run him over. By the end of it I was as green as a cucumber; I looked like a mini Incredible Hulk — but it was worth it.

*

A few months later, we are now living in a big house, all new furniture, new clothes; we even have fish fingers, not fish finger, for tea.

You see, our business was an overnight success; my idea was Bernie Broom's Bubblebum Bottles for all occasions. We have different strengths for different jobs. You can buy a bottle of top strength, open the top and within seconds all the wallpaper is completely stripped off. A bottle of mild strength will get rid of any door to door salesman and any unwanted callers. Farmers love the weaker bottle; they can put it in a field and no bird or animal (or even human for that matter) will go anywhere near the crops — it's saved them a fortune on scarecrows. A pretty bad version goes down well with the men who, when they know the mother-in-law is coming round, just pop the bottle on the side; resulting in mother-in-laws that don't stay very long. The police use different strengths to catch criminals. They squirt it at them and the criminals are jumping into the van without argument; apparently truncheon sales are down a third. At the moment, we are currently negotiating our super-duper strength version with the military. All of our bottles also come with free gas masks and gloves.

Everything is so different now; my Mum and Dad are so happy. Mum's even told me why Dad's bubblebum smells don't bother her. On their first date, Dad sneaked one out in the pictures, which cleared in seconds. Well, Mum's sense of smell just packed in, it's never worked since (she always gets an envious look from Beetroot when she says that bit), but the story has a happy ending as Mum always says; at least they got the pictures to themselves.

We have two cars, a brand new telly; we've even got clean bath water, all because of my idea. So bottoms up to the smell of success (ha, sorry, I couldn't help myself!). But for the better everything has changed; well, apart from one thing — Beetroot is still tunnelling.

I Can't Stand Nosey Buggers

The garden was well overdue a good mowing and that was my intention on such a lovely hot day — but the mower had other ideas. For the life of me I couldn't get it to start; I changed the fuse in the plug and had it on its back to see if there was anything jammed inside, but to no avail. I started to get angry with it. I wiped the sweat from my brow and in an attempt to make myself feel better I gave it a good boot — but it still wasn't having it. As I stood there with hands on hips, tongue sticking out, wracking my brain my neighbour and mate Pete popped his head over the fence.

"How's it going, Tom? Lovely day, ain't it? Looks like you're having fun."

"Hey up, Pete, yeah gorgeous. I don't know what's up with this thing; I'm ready for throwing it." I gave the worthless piece of junk a hard glare. "Anyway, how are you, mate?" I hadn't seen Pete for over two weeks as he had become quite antisocial since his wife Sally had walked out on him three weeks ago.

"Yeah I'm OK, mate, thanks. Sorry, I've been hiding away."

"No worries, what you doing later? Do you fancy going for a couple of pints?"

"Yeah sound. Lisa's gone away, ain't she?"

"Yeah the wife's gone to her sister's. Do you fancy a beer now? I got a few in the fridge."

"Yeah sound, but what about your garden?"

"It don't really need doing that much." We both laughed.

"I'll be round in a mo then, Tom; gonna get me shorts on."

*

Five minutes later we were sat on the bench in the back garden with a can of Fosters in hand. "Are you all right, Tom? You look a bit thoughtful."

"Erm, yes, mate. It's just that I've tried to ring Lisa a couple of times, but it keeps going to her voicemail. It's not like her; she usually has her phone glued to her."

"Ha, probably no signal; you know what it's like down the Meadows, especially where your Lisa's Gemma lives. Didn't she move to the cul-de-sac on Wood Close?"

"True, it is bad signal reception down there. Yeah, mate, they moved there a couple of months back." There was a pause as we each took a swig of beer. "So how are you coping then, Pete? Have you heard from Sally?"

"I'm okay, been keeping myself busy, you know? It's just people sticking their noses in what gets to me; I can't stand nosey buggers. And no, not heard from her. After all I've done for her as well."

I knew what Pete was getting at; Sally's leaving had been the talk of the town. Pete had worked all hours to provide a good life for her. Her thanks had been to take up with his so called workmate Steve Sandford while he was pulling overtime in night shifts.

After the nosey people remark I didn't know if I should ask the next question — but I did. "Do you think you will sort it? You know, get back together?"

"I won't be hearing from her again; she's gone for good." Pete had a little chuckle to himself. Pete's laughter puzzled me; he was devastated when Sally left. I was going to question him further when he jumped up to get a couple of beers.

"Here you are, get that down you. Did you watch the match the other night?"

"Yeah, mate; it was a cracker, wasn't it?"

Pete nodded but he had a glazed look in his eyes like his mind was elsewhere. We talked for a bit longer about football then Pete announced that he had to nip out. He practically leapt up from the bench, said he'd meet me at the local pub about eight and then rushed through the gate. I thought it was all very strange.

Putting Pete's weirdness aside I decided to have another go at doing the garden, but I was going to try and ring Lisa again first.

*

I was in the pub, halfway through my second pint and still waiting for Pete, when Ted, one of the locals, came in and said, "Have you heard the news? A local woman has been found murdered in the woods; her body was found earlier today." I turned, confused, and my mind started to race. I still hadn't heard from Lisa, and Pete had been acting quite strangely.

I was about to ring Lisa for the seventh time that day when in walked Pete; he looked dirty, sweaty and out of breath. "Are you okay, Pete? Where have you been?"

"Hey up, Tom, sorry, mate, I went to pick some bits up from the DIY shop and the bloody car broke down. Can I have a couple of pints, Mick, please?"

I didn't know whether to believe him or not. "Is it sorted? The car?"

"No, mate, had to leave it at the shops. Have you heard from Lisa yet?" I didn't like the way he grinned when he asked me that — or was I just being paranoid now?

"No, pal, I haven't; I'm getting worried."

"I wouldn't worry. It's like I said, it's a bad signal; probably that or something daft."

"Hopefully. Hey, have you heard? A local woman has been murdered." I watched his face with curiosity.

He took a good gulp from his pint. "No, when was that?"

I was about to answer when I noticed what looked like blood on his hand; his jeans were ripped too. That could be from the car breaking down though; he could have ripped them trying to fix it. "I'm not sure when it was; Ted heard it."

Pete gave Ted a nasty glare. "Take no notice of that idiot; he gossips more than a woman." I had never seen Pete get angry. I thought it best to change the subject and we resumed our chat about football.

But a bit later into the evening it was no longer just gossip; it was all over the news. The victim was Joan Cartwright, a local and popular woman who worked at the DIY shop — the same one Pete had been to that day.

When the news broke Pete's face contorted with anger and he made a hasty retreat to the men's room. That had been ten minutes ago now and he was yet to re-emerge. "Mick, have you seen Pete?" I asked the landlord.

"He left, Tom, about ten minutes ago. It's bad business about Joan, ain't it? How's your Lisa by the way? Ain't seen her for a bit."

I trembled slightly at the mention of Lisa; I was growing more and more concerned. "Erm, yeah terrible, and, err, yes she's OK, thanks." At that I downed my drink, said bye to Mick and some others, and shot out.

My mind was working overtime as I started to run home. I hadn't gone far though when my run descended into a jog, then a brisk walk — it just shows how unfit you can get. As I got home I couldn't stop staring at Pete's drive. There, stood proudly upon it, was his car. I was so confused; Pete said it had broken down and had to be left at the shops. I slowly walked around the car to Pete's front door. It didn't look like he was in as it was all in darkness and the curtains were wide open. I knocked and then tried the handle but it was locked.

I went into my house and poured a whiskey. I took a deep swig and got my phone out to ring Lisa. I wondered what I would do if there was still no answer — should I ring the police or just go round to her sister's in a taxi? These worries stopped though when, for the first time, it didn't go straight to answer phone. It was ringing and I waited anxiously on the other end until —

"Hello."

"Lisa, i-is that you?"

"Hello, Tom, darling, I was panicking because I hadn't heard from you."

My heart danced with joy. "*You've* been panicking? You're not on your own there. Where have you been? I have tried to ring loads of times; God knows why Gemma don't get a land line sorted."

"You're right, she should really what with the signal down here, it *is* rubbish. Why, what is the matter, darling? Are you all right?"

"I am now, but, well, I think my imagination has been on turbo. Have you heard about Joan from the DIY shop being murdered?" Muffled noises caught my attention. It sounded like someone was dragging something heavy across the floor and it seemed to be coming from Pete's. There were also several bangs against the wall.

"Yes I have, the gossips are on overtime down here. It's horrible; such a lovely woman, but have you heard the other bit?"

My heart stopped dancing. "No, what?"

"Another woman, Judy Gillingham, she worked there too, the skinny one with blonde hair — you know, Tom, a nice woman, but always sticking her nose in where it wasn't wanted. She rubbed Pete up the wrong way gossiping about him and Sally once. Anyway, she's also gone missing."

"You're joking, my God, what is going on?"

"I know; it's not safe to go out on your own."

"Well, make sure you don't go out on your own, darling."

"Don't worry, Tom. Anyway, it's getting late; I'll ring you tomorrow, okay? Love you."

"Okay, darling, love you too." As I hung up I was sure I could hear Pete laughing next door. I poured myself another drink. I stood there for a moment thinking about the day's events before downing my whiskey in one. I put the glass in the sink and crept upstairs, listening intently with my ear pressed against the wall, but it all seemed to be silent. I went up to bed where I was so exhausted from worrying that I dropped off to sleep fully clothed.

*

I jumped up, startled. I looked over at my clock; it was 2.10 a.m. I could hear that same dragging noise from earlier accompanied by some heavy breathing, but this time it was coming from the back gardens. I sneaked over to the window and my heart felt like it was being squeezed; for there was Pete dragging a skinny blonde body into his shed.

I was trying to think of what to do when Pete looked up. I shot behind the curtains. Had he definitely seen me? I wasn't sure if he had. I stood frozen in fear for a good few minutes; my mind numb. Then, with a surge of adrenaline, I ran downstairs and went for the phone.

As I reached the kitchen I froze. There, in the middle of the laminate floor, were the malevolent eyes of Pete burning into me. He had a hammer in his hand. I was about to say something to him when he raised the hammer high above his head and leapt towards me. The blow made me writhe in excruciating pain. I couldn't make my body function; I tried to say something, tried to force my mouth to say 'why?', but nothing would come out. Blood started to drip down off my eyelids and I dropped to my knees. I tried to move my hands to block his attack but when Pete brought the hammer down, smashing my skull, I fell flat on my face. Blood was pooling all around me. I looked up at Pete who was stood over me, hammer at the ready. The last words I heard were, "I can't stand nosey buggers."

The Beautiful Snow

It was like being in heaven, or what I imagined heaven to look like, watching the snow fall down. The pureness of it was wonderful and peaceful; it made the world look so virginal and unspoilt. My town had been covered in a pure white blanket that looked cosy enough to snuggle up in. Children were already outside revelling in it, sledging and making snowmen. It made you wish it was Christmas, which was now a good two months ago.

I would have loved to go out and join all the folk in the fun, but I was getting ready for work. I got out my police uniform and after rebuttoning my shirt twice (as I was more interested in watching Melissa and her brother Ben from across the street finish building their snowman with the crooked carrot nose) I got ready and left for my night shift. Well, I say left; it took me thirty minutes to get the car off the drive.

Even though I admired the snow's beauty while I struggled to the station, I soon realized the danger and catastrophe that was beginning to happen around me. Already on the police radio there had been a report of a plane crash-landing at the nearby airport and as I turned a corner my faithful old Ford started to skid, pulling me towards a couple of parked cars. I was lucky and managed to regain control, averting any damage, but I knew that many drivers would not be so lucky out on the road today.

As I made my way, a bit more cautiously, to the station it came over on the radio that a man who had taken his dog for a walk at ten thirty this morning had not been seen since. It soon dawned on me that this wasn't going to be a quiet shift.

At the station it was chaos; calls were coming from everywhere and with more and more men being drafted in for the plane crash we were quickly losing manpower.

The sergeant shouted me. "PC Mark Welsh."

"Yes, Sir."

"Welsh, take PC Jacob Field, take the jeep and go and search for the missing man. His name's Stanley Meadows and he was last seen going towards Three Point Woods. Here's his picture." Before I could answer, the sergeant was off giving out more orders.

Jacob and I struggled in the jeep as the snow kept on coming. I was getting irritable as the journey that would normally have taken ten minutes had now taken well over twenty. As we neared the woods there was a car that had tipped over onto its roof at the side of the road. I parked up alongside and we jumped out. My heart was in my mouth because even though I have seen numerous accidents before you just never know what you're going to come across. The silver Ford Mondeo was badly crushed at the front from where it had hit a tree. There was an unconscious girl of about ten in the back suspended by her seatbelt. In the front was a half conscious woman, who I presumed was her mother.

Jacob ran to the jeep to radio for the emergency services. I bent down at the side of the woman, checking her over. "Hello, I'm PC Mark Welsh, you have been involved in an accident; what is your name?"

The woman was slowly looking up and from side to side, trying to understand what had happened. She then fixed her eyes on me. "Erm…my name is Sarah — Sarah Beeston."

"Okay, Sarah, just try and relax, help is on its way. What is the little girl's name? Is she your daughter?"

"Yes, Chloe — her name's Chloe; i-is she okay?" Sarah had been quite calm until that point but she then started fidgeting; she was trying to turn to look for her daughter. I was about to answer when she became hysterical. "Oh my God, Chloe — Chloe!" Sarah tried to reach her daughter.

"It's okay, Sarah, Chloe will be fine; the ambulance is already on its way."

"Are you sure?…you're lying." Sarah tried to reach Chloe again.

"No I am not lying, trust me, it will all be fine." I gave her a reassuring smile, but truthfully I wasn't sure what the outcome would be; I just knew it was my duty and, more importantly, the compassionate thing to do, to reassure her. Thankfully, this seemed to calm her slightly and she sat still while I moved round to check on Chloe.

She was covered in cuts and bruises. I listened to Chloe's chest to check her breathing and found a pulse upon pressing her wrist. My touch caused her to stir and she started to come around, a slow stir at first, but then she tried to move.

"M-mum?"

"It's okay, darling, I am here; the policemen are here to help, sweetheart."

She was obviously scared so I smiled warmly at her. "Hello, Chloe, it's all right, my name's Mark and that is Jacob; we are going to help you and your mum, okay?" Chloe apprehensively nodded. Both Sarah and Chloe were shivering with the cold so we brought blankets from the jeep to drape over them.

"Right, Chloe, we are going to get you out and put you into our warm jeep, okay, sweetheart?" Chloe started to weep with the pain and shock of it all.

"It will be all right, Chloe," said Sarah. After a few minutes of wrestling with the seat belt and clearing away debris Jacob and I managed to free her.

Jacob took her to the jeep, kept her warm and calm; her right leg was really bruised and cut, I wasn't sure if she had broken it or not. I went back to the Mondeo, and with it not being as difficult as freeing her daughter, I managed to get Sarah out and reunite her with Chloe in the jeep. It seemed like ages but the fire brigade and ambulance finally arrived; our job here was done. We were radioed from the station telling us to leave the scene and to go and look for the missing man.

We had been searching for half an hour on foot, neither of us was thinking the snow was beautiful at that moment; my vision of heaven was fast turning into hell. It was so bitterly cold it was cutting through me; it felt like my body was slowing down. It was like a punishment being made to battle through this atrocity. The snow was falling really fast and thick making it hard to see. Jacob was trying to stop his teeth from chattering and I couldn't feel my feet; they felt so heavy trying to plough through the cold snow it was like I had lead boots on.

We were about to turn back and give up any hope of finding the man when we heard a dog barking. We walked in the direction of the sound and we soon came across a springer spaniel, which was black with white spots. He was barking more frequently now, he was obviously pleased to see us and the feeling was mutual. He stood guarding his owner, who was only just visible amongst the snow. He was slumped with his back up against a tree, his light blue coat almost obscured by snow and his face partially covered by a thick woolly green scarf; in his right hand was a red handled dog lead.

We fought through the snow to get to him and I knelt beside him, detecting a pulse. I was no expert in such matters but my guess was that he had suffered a heart attack; his hand was clutching his chest and his breathing was very irregular. Jacob radioed in the situation on his hand held walkie-talkie and gave directions to get the ambulance as close to the scene as possible.

I kept Mr Meadows (who I had identified from his photograph) warm by wrapping him up in my long coat; I kept myself warm by throwing a stick for the dog, Jesse, whose name and address dangled down from his collar. It seemed like we had been there for days when I heard Jacob and the paramedics battling through the elements towards us. We put Mr Meadows on the stretcher and wrapped him up warm while the paramedics did their stuff.

After they had made sure Mr Meadows was safe for movement we all set off together through the deep, cold snow with Jesse leading the way. We took it in turns carrying the stretcher, only stopping twice, once for a breather and once to help Jacob up, who had fallen after getting his foot stuck in some hole. We were concerned for Mr Meadows who was still breathing funny and was still out cold. It felt such a relief when after all our struggles we got to the ambulance, and as we did Mr Meadows slowly woke up; he looked at me with curiosity.

"Hello, Mr Meadows, I am PC Mark Welsh, Sir; we are going to take you to hospital."

He looked at me confused before mumbling, "Where's Jesse?"

"Jesse's fine, Sir."

Mr Meadows slowly nodded and after years of doing this job people never cease to amaze me as Mr Meadows, who was close to death's door, then smiled and said, "Isn't the snow beautiful?"

We soon got Mr Meadows settled and after the paramedics (who confirmed it was a heart attack) had given him some treatment we bid them farewell. Me and Jacob were planning to go get a coffee to warm ourselves up, but after a brief conversation with our sergeant we realized that wasn't going to happen as now a lorry had lost control and smashed into a 24 hour supermarket. At this moment in time we were the only available officers as the plane crash had taken up most of the manpower.

We got to the supermarket to see that the lorry had gone straight through the window. The driver was in the cab, a couple of the staff was outside cut and shaken, but there was a third member of staff, Ian Noble, who was unaccounted for. Jacob comforted the two staff members and tried to find out how long the fire brigade and ambulance (who were pushed to their limits) would be. I climbed in through the lorry's passenger door. The driver had bad cuts to his arms and face and he was covered in shattered glass from the smashed windscreen. I took a pulse — there was none. I laid down the seat as far back as it would go and cleared off the glass and other debris. I checked his airway and then put the heel of my right hand on his chest, in-between his nipples, then, clasping my left hand on top of the right one, I started to give chest compressions. I gave him thirty then mouth to mouth. I checked his pulse again and detected a faint one. I gave a sigh of relief and couldn't help the feeling of pride that swept through me at having just brought someone back to life.

I kept him warm and with my personal first aid kit patched up his cut head as best I could. At that moment Jacob poked his head through the door. "Mark, the one that's missing; they think he's under the lorry."

"Have a look, Jacob, and be careful."

I got one of the staff to climb in and keep an eye on the driver and keep him warm while I went to help Jacob, who had located the man; he was covered in debris under the lorry. I managed to crawl under and clear away the glass, splintered wood and various pieces of fruit and veg. I checked his airways and pulse; he was breathing but knocked out and his arm was badly damaged; bone was protruding from the skin. I wrapped it up in a temporary sling. There were no more visible injuries so Jacob crawled to me and I got the man's head end while Jacob got his feet and we slowly shunted him from side to side, stopping to check he was still breathing. I banged my head on the diesel tank as we struggled out and as we got to the side of the lorry one of the staff helped us out with the man.

We didn't know how long it would take for the emergency services to arrive, but that wasn't our only concern at that moment as we had members of the public queuing up for a look. There was also a very annoying nosey reporter hanging around who was only interested in getting a gruesome report for the local paper.

A good hour passed and me and Jacob were exhausted after looking after the injured people and dealing with the public and the reporter when an ambulance finally arrived.

For the rest of our shift we rescued a cat that was stuck in a tree (Jacob wasn't amused as he ripped his trousers climbing up after it) and we also helped a tramp that had gotten snowed in inside an abandoned house. Jacob had heard him shouting when he was up the tree with the cat. The tramp had taken shelter in the boarded up property yesterday, but with the snow coming down so heavily it had blocked off all exit routes. We had to dig him out with our trusty shovel that we kept in the jeep. Normally, we would have taken him to the station and booked him for breaking and entering, but after a quick telling off we decided to let him go as the terrified look on his face told me he wouldn't be doing it again in a hurry.

We got back to the station to be praised from all quarters. The sergeant said everyone we had rescued was doing well and as miracles go there were also no fatalities at the plane crash. I had to laugh at him moaning, 'the ruddy snow; horrible stuff'.

It seemed to take me ages to get home and the first coffee of the night tasted divine, it certainly hit the spot. I slumped down in my armchair, turning on the box. Reports of the plane crash were on followed by further accidents caused by the snow; watching it all made the chaos of nature really hit home. I flicked through the channels, then, after a good yawn, I turned everything off and made my way upstairs.

After a couple of minutes wrestling with my shirt buttons I undressed and got into bed; I slowly cuddled up behind my wife and kissed her on the back of her head. She was out for the count so I just held her for a few minutes. There had been moments that night when I had wondered if I would ever arrive home to be safe and warm beside her. I gave her another kiss then turned over to get some well-earned sleep.

Later, I awoke to the noise of children who were sledging and snowball fighting. It did look beautiful out there. Me and my wife went out to join in the fun, we sledged down the hills and had two snowball fights (which I lost).

My mind drifted to the previous night's events. I couldn't stop thinking of the danger that I had witnessed: the people in the supermarket, Sarah and Chloe, Mr Meadows and Jesse all going about their daily routines when they had all nearly lost their lives because of nature — because of the snow. I shuddered to think of my and Jacob's pain as we struggled through the achingly cold snow, how we thought we would never feel our fingers and toes again. I was thinking of how close we all could have been to death when I was snapped out of my reverie by a snowball to the face.

My wife laughed as she ran; I made a snowball and ran after her, my throw just missing. I caught up to her and held her in my arms and kissed her. We tumbled, laughing, to the ground, which is where we then lay, making snow angels in the beautiful snow.

Champagne and Lemonade

It was the start of another day at the Dumpton hospital. The hospital was built in the '50s — 1954 to be exact — apart from an old building that was built in the Victorian times, and was used in the wars — it's still got the original paint on the walls.

The part that was built in the '50s apparently took six years to build. I don't know how; it looks like it was just thrown up. Some of the members of staff think it needs a lick of paint, while others think it wants knocking down and rebuilding. It has ten floors and each block has different colours on the walls so you can identify where you are going. So, for example, white represents north, while brown is south, yellow is west, and red is the east block. Once, one poor chap was wandering around for two days — he was colour blind.

The grounds are vast, car parks taking up the majority of the land; charging a fiver for an hour. The machines give you no change so when you leave your car to go and get some you normally come back to find it wheel clamped with an eighty pound fine stuffed so tightly behind your windscreen wiper that, when you do force it free, it normally costs another few quid for a new wiper.

At the front of the hospital is a large driveway for ambulances, but they can never get in there for all the taxis and pushbikes. So, most of the time, it's like a round of *Total Wipe Out* when trying to get the patients in. And for those patients who had only planned on a brief day clinic visit their ambulance bay experience usually leaves the poor muckers so traumatized that they end up having to stay in for days. I have known a couple of the ambulance drivers to be admitted 'an all.

It is a very scruffy and dirty area with chewing gum on the floor and rubbish all over; I don't think it has been cleaned since the day it was built. It was that bad even the rats wouldn't dare venture there. Patients with chest drains, catheters, feed pumps and every other piece of medical apparatus there is attached to whatever hole was available would come and sit out here in their pyjamas and onesies, breathing in diesel fumes. On their last legs some of them, but they were still determined to make it out at all costs to have a fag. So, if, like me, you're a non-smoker, you'll soon find yourself in need of a hospital bed after battling your way through the mounds of cigarette butts and thick smoke to enter the building.

Straight ahead of you as you walk through the hospital's front doors is the reception desk where you'll find Ethel and Margaret (one seventy-five, the other seventy-five and a half years old, both slightly deaf), two volunteers, both with Alzheimer's disease. It is their job to help people with directions and if you ask me you'd be better off asking Stevie Wonder to direct you. Once, they even managed to send some people to a totally different hospital; they're worse than some of the patients in the hospital.

To the right is the cafe where you can relax with a sandwich and a cup of coffee for £9.99, excluding VAT (£11.99 excluding VAT if you want a filling in the sandwich). Coffee shops are all over the hospital; I swear there are more of them than wards, and if your hospital stay amounts to more than a week, tell your family and friends who visit these shops that they'd be better off setting up a direct debit. Across from the reception desk is the security office where folk of different sexes, backgrounds and sizes are there for your safety and protection. Personally, I wouldn't trust them to look after my dead pet goldfish. We also have a small bank, which never has any money, with staff that are as polite as a German who has been ordered to take his towel off a sun lounger at the hotel pool; but still, we have one. When the bank is closed there is an out of hours cash machine which takes ages to get to as it is situated in the hospital grounds, in the middle of nowhere, and ten times out of nine is broken anyway. There's a little clothes shop, a gift shop resembling Oxfam and a hairdresser's too. It always tickles me to see women with monitors, catheters and other medical equipment attached to them, and stuffed up every hole the doctors could find, sitting there having their hair done at £55 a pop — oh excluding VAT of course.

Now, to get to some of the wards you have to use the lifts. Well, you could use the stairs but you would more than likely need to be treated for a heart attack by the end of them. Mind you, using the lifts is always a gamble too; I have scrapped better steel.

I do beg your pardon. My name is James Higgins, Higgo, and this is the place where I spend my working days. I stay here mainly for the laughs and the wellbeing of the patients, which at least takes your mind off the poor pay — I think the volunteers earn more!

I work as a hospital porter. 'What is one of those?' I hear you ask Well, we move patients from ward to ward on beds, chairs and tugs, which are like golf buggies. Mind you, half of our equipment is knackered; we'd be better off throwing the patients over our shoulders and carrying 'em.

We take patients to various clinics, take medical gases like oxygen to the wards and change them for the empty ones, and take medical equipment like syringe pumps, monitors, beds, mattresses and much more to the wards. We also have to take the deceased patients to the mortuary. Urgh you say, well someone has gotta do it and it might as well be us. Plus they have more life in them than some of the staff and you can have a better conversation with them, 'an all.

Anyway, we, and a lot of other members of staff, consider us porters to be a big part of the operation; pardon the pun — operation, hospital — please yourselves. But others, especially management, think that us and the logistics porters are lower than a snake's belly, bottom of the food chain; or, as Jim Kelsey (who is about four foot six, very round and fat, balding; with a great bushy beard and is as annoying as stepping in dog poo), the boss, once said, lemonade.

I have worked at the Dump hospital for a few months now and I have never known it so bad: cuts, no communication; the bosses, managers and workers a world apart, especially from us porters. I suppose it didn't help matters when the top dog, Jim Kelsey, said in a meeting that the management was like champagne while the rest of the staff, especially the porters, were like lemonade. My reaction when I first heard this was, 'Yeah, champagne — urine in colour and full of bubbles.' And, what with Kelsey agreeing to privatization, to say he is an unpopular figure with the staff at the moment would be an understatement. The general consensus was that he was selling us all down the river.

Now, you could join the union for twenty quid a month. I don't know why you would though really; all you get for ya money is 'we're sorting it' and a pen — a working one if ya lucky. Yes, seems to me that they're as much use as a thoroughbred racehorse with three legs.

I was on days today, which are from six in the morning till two in the afternoon. So, after the usual wrestling with my alarm blaring out at 4.40 a.m., I blearily got up. I must have splashed more than enough water on my face to try and wake myself up but I still made my way downstairs with both eyes shut. Then, after taking my t-shirt off twice because I had put it on inside out, I finally got ready. I had my usual bowl of porridge and cup of coffee, locked up (then went back twice to make sure I really had locked up), then, still with one eye shut, I made my way to the bus stop in zombie mode and trudged in to work.

Our department is located in an old bit of the hospital; the floors have got so many holes and craters in them that it's like walking on the moon, or what I imagine walking on the moon would be like anyway. We are situated not far from an entrance on the east corridor and on the front desk sits a computer screen which lists our jobs for the day. Near there is our communal space, which consists of a small sitting area with a few seats and a TV, and a small kitchen where our lockers and mashing facilities are. There were four of us on today, which is a lot really what with the cuts 'an all. There was the team leader, Jack Roberts, who was mashing the tea, Pete Watkiss and Barry Minchin.

Jack is into all the fitness stuff. He is a good lad and will always do what he can to help, but he is a practical joker, especially when he's together with Pete. Many of the porters have been signed up to grabagranny.com, which is a website that has mature, willing women offering let's just say *services* for men. So, in the past, a few of the porters have had an earful from their wives, partners, etc. when they have received texts and emails from these eager older women. Pete is a good bloke, apart from being a Liverpool supporter, but he is on the opposite scale to Jack — the only physical exercise he does is lifting his pint to his lips.

I got my uniform top on and nipped to the toilet. As I kicked the door open a water bucket dropped down from where it had been left perched on the door frame, just missing me. I smirked as I heard the giggles coming from the sitting room. We were always playing tricks on each other. You had to have a sense of humour in this job.

I went and sat in the sitting room with the lads. Now, I'm a Man Utd fan whereas a couple of the lads are Liverpool and Chelsea supporters, so, as you can imagine, because of Utd's poor form at the moment they were loving it. As I sat down I noticed, on the wall, that newspaper clippings and pictures of Utd's latest thrashing had been pinned up. Pete was sat there whistling *Ferry Cross the Mersey*, trying to act like he had nothing to do with it.

"Morning, ladies," I said, interrupting Pete as he now attempted to whistle *You'll Never Walk Alone*.

"All right, Higgo," they all replied.

"How did United go on?" smirked Pete.

I threw a bit of soggy tissue at him. "We were robbed. Not like jammy Liverpool — ya not win nowt, shag," I said.

Pete's answer was the same as it always was. He just sat in silence holding five fingers up, indicating the five European cups Liverpool had won in the past. Barry and Jack laughed.

I flicked Barry on the ear as I walked past where he was sitting reading the paper at the main desk and he tried to flick me back. We were always messing about. Barry is a laugh, though. Recently, he went to fetch a patient from a ward, but the patient was being argumentative. He picked his suitcase up and threw it at Barry. Now, sometimes these things can happen and we're supposed to keep calm and deal with the situation. Not Barry; he picked up the case and threw it back at him.

My first job of the day was to take some blood samples up to the labs so I picked up the container to put them in and set off to the ward. Now, it's normally quiet at this time in the morning, 6.25 a.m., but it was chaos on the corridors because the hospital had had a tip off, you see. The word was that on this particular day the CQC was dropping in on us for an emergency inspection. Now, 'what are the CQC?' I hear you say. Well, what they are are Care Quality Commission inspectors and what they do is drop in on organizations such as hospitals, like us, to check on health and safety and quality. And it was our turn today.

There were doctors and nurses rushing everywhere, maintenance men trying to make the place look tip top — a bomb would be my suggestion. The cleaners were dusting, polishing and scrubbing every nook and cranny they came across. Two cleaners decided to clean behind a coffee machine, which to their knowledge had never been done before. I wouldn't be surprised if they found a dead patient behind there.

I got to the Critical Care Ward; they care for all different things on here, and I popped the samples into my container. Working here sure makes you realize just how lucky you are when you look at the poor muckers lying there with tubes and wires and whatever else sticking out of them. A couple of patients lay looking at the ceiling, not wanting to look at the stump where their legs used to be.

"Morning, James, are you well, ma duck?" said Barbara, the ward receptionist.

"Morning, Barbara, not bad thanks, how's ya self, darling?"

"I'm fine, apart from running around because the CQC are coming. Thanks for that, duck," she said, pointing at the samples.

"No probs, see ya later." And off I went, making my way up to the labs.

A minute later, Dr Isaac Wilkutitov went running past. Now, I have heard about this geezer; a tough character, he was a bareknuckle champion apparently. He is from Ukraine, Poland or Russia, somewhere like that, well he ain't English anyway. He would have no problem being in the mafia (if he already wasn't). He was thickset, tall, with a skinhead and a scar to match. I heard last week that a couple of months ago he was supposed to have taken some dude's appendix out, but last week the chap collapsed. When he was examined one of his kidneys was missing, but his appendix was still there; still no one knows where his kidney has gone.

Dr Wilkutitov met another doctor, Dr Verity Sweat; they were needed in theatres to sort out a woman who had had a heart attack. She had been to the hospital shop and ordered four coffees, six sandwiches and a newspaper — it cost a quarter of her wages.

I swiped into the blood labs using the card that hangs around my neck. The card is plastic, has my name and photo on it, and it allows me access to most places in the Dump. All of the staff have these. I placed the specimen samples into the correct baskets, which are in a little room staffed by middle aged, lovely, polite ladies. The blood cultures go into a box. After I put everything in the correct places I bid the ladies farewell and made my way out.

As I was walking back a voice came from behind me. "Good morning; how the devil are ya, chiefy?" said the unmistakeable voice of Macko.

"Morning, Higgo, man; how's tricks?"

"Sound, Tez; how are you? How's Macko? Are you well, shag?" I said.

Now, what can I say about these two? Macko and Tez Phillips: rule breakers. They collect rubbish, dirty linen, take out stores, etc.

Macko nodded his head as he threw some rubbish into a cage, causing some liquid to seep from one of the bags and cover the wall. "Oh dear, look at that, guv; who's done that?" laughed Macko.

Laughing, I walked away with a 'See yas later' making my way back to base when my phone bleeped, informing me that there was a deceased patient. I accepted the job. When someone wants a job doing they put it in on a computer system, it then comes through to our devices and if you are free you accept the job. For example, it will say patient on a bed, chair or whatever, their name, what ward or wherever they are and where they are going to. Plus any other info like if they need oxygen etc. This particular job said: deceased patient then said location — Cherry Ward, name of patient — Seth Doodle, going to mortuary.

Now, God knows how many deceased patients I have taken down to the mortuary since I have been doing this job; hundreds I would guess. And people always ask whether it bothers me to which I say, "It's like owt else; you get used to it." A couple of my work chums, however, still don't like it when they can see a body part showing.

I can remember doing my first one when I was training. They say death is a part of life and here I was in a position where death was definitely a part of my life. I was on my way to do my first deceased patient, or Mickey Griff as the lads say. It didn't really bother me having to take a deceased patient as I knew it was a part of my job description and I would have to do it at some point. I did panic a bit though when I thought, *I hope he really is dead and the doc hasn't made a mistake.* I didn't want to be pushing him in the fridge and have him jump up and try to get out. Now something like that would make you want to drink a bottle of whiskey — and I can't stand the stuff.

Anyway, I wasn't scared, I was quite intrigued and just hoped I did it right and with dignity. I was with Andy Buckland, Bucko we call him, and he took me to, well, the best way to describe it would be an old closet (where the cleaners had certainly never ventured). It was from here that we picked up the trolley; the deceased's limousine.

I watched the looks on people's faces as we made our way onto the Apple Ward; one woman couldn't look. People generally know what's in this type of trolley or, in this case, what will soon be in it. On the ward, after asking the nurses where the deceased patient was, who was named Bert, we drew the curtains so that the public and other patients couldn't see.

I was excited and nervous at the same time as I looked at my first dead patient. He was wrapped up like a mummy in bed sheets. We removed the cover on the trolley and dropped its sides. Bucko took some papers off Bert's chest which had his details for the mortuary printed on them; he was ninety to which we both commented that he had had a good innings and that we would both be happy with that. I got a hold of the sheet at his head end and accidentally touched his arm; it just felt like he was asleep. On the count of three we slid Bert onto our trolley, draped the cover over and left the ward.

I felt the whole world was watching me as I pushed the trolley, my attention only temporarily diverted from the task in hand by Macko pushing a bin into a couple of unsuspecting visitors.

Bucko opened the mortuary door with the key and we turned on the lights. Bucko told me to lock the door behind me. The room was just full of old, white numbered doors. I had wondered if the room was going to be cold but it just felt normal really. Bucko had shown me how to fill the form in; you put the number fridge you've used on top of the form then at the bottom you simply put your initials and sign it. On each door there was a top tray, a middle one and a bottom one in which to place the patients. In our case, 12 was the top tray, 13 the middle and Bert was going to go into number 14, the bottom tray, which was empty.

Bucko got the motorized trolley while I put the 'in use' label on number 14 and then opened the door. There were bodies stacked up; some of them had their feet and the top of their heads showing, which didn't bother me. What did bother me though was the fact that they reminded me of a lot of unused sausages in a fridge. I remember thinking, *so that's how we all end up; no matter what we have achieved.*

We pulled out the silver metal tray using the controls on the machine, slid Bert onto it and put poor Bert into number 14, shutting the door on him. We then washed our hands and locked up.

And there you have it, that was my first deceased patient, even though later on that day I did go back to the mortuary for training on the motorized trolley. That was when I saw a patient whose face was exposed and when asked if it bothered me I said, "No, it's like a waxwork dummy."

I was on the way back to base and I have to admit I was very impressed with the cleaners today —they had even mopped. I got back and met Jack Roberts. We got the key and the trolley and set off to collect the poor, unfortunate soul. On the way, me and Jack couldn't stop grinning at the chaos unfolding, I never knew we had so many cleaners, they were dusting, polishing, sweeping. They even cleaned the trolley on the way past.

As we were walking back from taking the deceased (who was quite a large one to be honest; she nearly came off the trolley) Jack told me that at a hospital he had worked at before a couple of lads he knew had taken a deceased patient and to save time they had gone outside. As they had rushed to get the poor mucker to the mortuary the trolley had hit a stone and the body flew out, ending up in the stream that ran alongside the hospital.

I went to have a sit down, but couldn't get to the chair for the cleaners. My device bleeped again and I accepted the job, which was two D size oxygen cylinders to Orange Ward. I got the cylinders from a cupboard in our base where we store some. If there happens to be none there, or we want bigger sizes, then there is a big shed outside that we have to fetch them from; it is just about falling down and is about as safe as England's back four.

I made my way to the ward and, as I did so, I passed Dr Wilkutitov, who nodded — I'm sure he was looking at my kidney area.

I got to the ward and asked where the cylinders were that wanted changing. Now, on the top of these cylinders is a flow meter that has a dial on it, telling you how much gas is in it. One was empty, which I changed. I said to the nurse, pointing to the other one, "Is that one full?"

She looked at me and said, "How can you tell?"

At first, I just stood there waiting for the pun, but with the blank look she was giving me I realized she wasn't joking. I pointed at the dial to show her — and these are the guys that are on Band 4 and 5 while I'm a measly Band 2.

After the oxygen incident I was making my up the west corridor when Jim Kelsey and the managers appeared in front of me. They were making their way to their daily meeting at one of the meeting rooms in the hospital. I always look down when I go past Kelsey and avoid his gaze — to me he always looks like he wants to chop my head off or summat.

There were loads of them on their way to this meeting. There was Arthur Grantham, who is the logistics and escort porters' manager (my manager); he nodded at me as I got alongside him. Then there was John Titly (and to be honest I haven't got a clue what he does), Miranda Bung is the HR person who didn't care about anyone but herself. Arthur was flirting with Miranda; well, I say flirting, it was near on sexual assault but she didn't seem to mind. Then there was Granville Day, who I believe has something to do with the maintenance side of things, and just behind them was a young lad, Joshua Stokes, who had recently been promoted to under manager. In other words, there were more managers in the Dump than in the Premier League.

A reliable source had told me that today's meeting was to briefly cover the CQC's visit and then move on to talking about the working of the hospital; in other words, cuts and squeezing more out of the overworked staff. The same source told me the other day that Kelsey had sacked two nurses to fund a golf trip.

I caught Kelsey's glare as I went around the corner heading towards the Plum Ward; he made you feel about as comfortable as a zebra that had wandered into the lions' enclosure at the zoo.

Jim Kelsey is sixty-two years of age; he used to be in the SAS, so he says. He wouldn't put a plaster on your cut finger unless there was something in it for him.

I looked back to see them get to their meeting room, where they were met by Selina, the nursing manager, who was once a confident woman but Kelsey had reduced her to a wreck.

They all got to their seats to begin the meeting.

*

I was down by the main entrance after having just visited the bank. Usually I avoid going in there because they're about as helpful as a bloke with no tongue and arms trying to give you directions, but I needed to see if a bill had gone out. After three failed attempts at getting into my account and the cashier talking to her colleague about her hair and nails the whole time I stormed out with a parting shot of, "You want to sack ya hairdresser; it looks like badly made candy floss."

I was now trying to help a member of the public who had asked me for some information about what ward their relative might be on. I pointed towards the desk that Ethel and Margaret occupied and told the woman that they were the ones who could help her.

What happened next could only happen at the Dump. As I started to walk off towards A&E, passing the CQC, who had not long since arrived, a right disturbance kicked off. Ian Brickhouse and Grant Bull, two of the security guards, came rushing to the ruckus. Well, Bull did, it took a few seconds longer for the overweight, out of breath Brickhouse to get there.

They finally arrived at the scene to see a nurse shouting and trying to separate two women fighting and rolling around the floor. Ian went to pick one of the women up and, after a struggle to get her to her feet, she swung her handbag into his face, knocking him into Grant.

"Ladies, please calm down, let's have some order," yelped Ian as his face caught another blow from the five foot, large, greasy haired, blonde woman who was in a grey tracksuit two sizes too small.

"What is this all about?" enquired a mad looking Grant.

It was the nurse who answered, "Well, I told the lady in the blue that she was next, but the person in the grey insisted she was, and all hell broke loose."

The woman in grey gave the nurse a nasty look then roared, "I was before that cow." And it all kicked up again.

Doctor Shala Sharmalar had welcomed the CQC members, Bev, Neil and Greg, and was pointing down the corridor, trying to divert the CQC's attention from the large lady in the grey tracksuit, swinging her bag at the security guards as they tried to eject her. This tactic proved unsuccessful, however, as one of the CQC, looking at the incident, said "Errm" and scribbled some notes. The doctor and the rest of the welcoming party hurriedly led the CQC off to continue their inspection of the hospital.

It made my day looking at the horrified expressions of the staff as they witnessed the two women rolling about on the floor like a couple of hippos rolling about in mud. The faces of the CQC were a treat; they looked like they had found a fifty pound note only for the owner to come along and claim it right back again. Doctor Sharmalar was worried that the ever growing public was drawing the CQC's attention as they were swamping around the ruckus. One young lad shouted, "This is better than going to WWE wrestling."

My phone beeped; a woman needed to go to radiography on a trolley. Not long afterwards it also rang. I answered and spoke to Pete, who was coming along on the job with me and wanted to know where I was. "I'm on my way back now," I told him and set off, smiling to myself as the woman in grey had just kicked Brickhouse hard in the shins.

As I made my way to Pete I bumped into my *source*. Yes, I have a source or information getter, tickle tackler; call them what you please. But anyway, I get all the gossip on the happenings of the Dump. 'Who is it?' you ask. Well…I'm not going to tell you that, am I? Everyone has their secrets and we porters are no different. So what I normally say to nosey parkers that keep digging is 'keep ya nose out before it gets bitten off'. Anyway, we had a hurried conversation in hushed tones; I told them all about the CQC's arrival and they gave me a blow by blow account of what occurred in that morning's managers' meeting. From what I gather it went something like this:

Kelsey kicked things off with his usual bellowing tone, "Right, what is happening with the nursing staff, Selina? I mean, why isn't there just one staff member looking after twenty patients? It can't be hard. And another thing, have we done a check on that Doctor Wilkutitov yet? He is up to something, I can sense it."

Selina gulped before answering, "Well, erm, Sir, they can only go as fast they can; it's very busy and the patients' care comes first."

Kelsey's look could have burned through steel. "Who says the patients come first? You are not cracking the whip hard enough and I can soon find someone who will."

"Right, Arthur, John, what is happening with that shower? Porters, they're a bad lot; why are we getting complaint after complaint about rubbish being left everywhere?"

Arthur took his hand from Miranda's leg. "Well, Sir, since we dropped them down to twenty-five porters from the original forty and gave them more jobs, for some reason, they said they are struggling. I don't know why."

"They don't want work, that's why. Get rid of a couple more to set an example," Kelsey replied.

"That is wrong, Sir, surely?" interrupted Joshua, to the annoyance of Kelsey, who glared at Joshua's name tag.

"Cuts, Stokes, times are hard," replied Kelsey, looking at his three grand watch. Before Joshua could speak, Kelsey did. "What needs to happen is all the team leaders need to muck in more, and tell them to do a ten hour shift, and we will pay them for eight," Kelsey shouted.

Joshua, looking a little uncomfortable, spoke, "Sir, it seems to me that the staff is being cut more times than my hair. Surely, if we are to help them, and the hospital, then we should look at ourselves and start cutting at the top."

Selina smiled, Miranda started crying and gave her reasons why she shouldn't have her wages cut, which ranged from sunbeds, meals to hair and nail treatments. Arthur sat shaking his head at Joshua and said, "Are you mad? How could I take four holidays a year?"

Joshua looked at Kelsey, whose face was as red as a baboon's bottom. "Yes, you are right, Arthur. I mean, how can I buy a new Ferrari and a kitchen and another holiday home? No, with talk like that you will not last long here, Stokes." (He was fired straight after the meeting.) Jim Kelsey looked at the time. "Right, it'll not be long before them nosey — I mean the CQC — will arrive so we will have to conclude another time; off you all go."

What my source told me didn't surprise me at all. Kelsey and his bum lickers couldn't care less about patients and the public, and as for the staff we were just a number. I said 'thanks' and 'toodle pip' to my source and then had to steady myself as I had nearly slid down the corridor because the floor had been mopped that many times by every cleaner on shift. I checked that no one had seen my attempt at *Come Dancing* before going on my way to meet Pete.

I met Pete and we went to fetch the trolley. On this trolley is a blue airbed and what we call a hoover ('cos it looks like a Henry Hoover), which is a blower. And what you do is blow the blue airbed up with the patient on and slide them from their bed to the trolley.

Now, you're probably wondering why it takes two of us to take a patient on a trolley or a bed and to fetch a Mickey Griff (deceased). Well, everything is health and safety mad these days. You have to have one of us pulling and guiding from the front while the other pushes to avoid back injuries and such. Also it's for the safety of the patient; if they have a funny turn, and I don't mean telling a few jokes on a night out, then one of us can go and get help while the other stays with the patient.

We had just passed the shop when we saw a member of the public: a man; I would say in his sixties, he was wearing a bright red coat. He wiped his sweaty brow as he shook his head from side to side. He approached Pete and myself.

"Are you okay, shag? You look lost, pal," I said.

"Hey up, lads. Lost is not the word; I've been here ages. I have had more directions than a Sat Nav, and I still ain't found what I'm looking for."

Me and Pete laughed then Pete said, "Where are you looking for, mate?"

The old, red coated man wiped his head, wheezed, then spluttered, "The Peach Ward."

"Well, what you do, Pop — you see the bottom of the corridor? Go to the end, turn right and you will get to some lifts. Go up three floors, follow it round and you will come to the Peach Ward."

The old, red coated man looked confused so after Pete had explained another two times we bid him good day and left.

As we set off again for the patient I said, "Hang on, shag, you've sent him the wrong way."

"Oh ahh, crap. Oh well, he'll find it."

*

Well, what a job that was, the woman who was going to radiography was a rather big woman (the correct term is bariatric patient). Anyway, we had to take her to radiography for her treatment. It took us ten minutes to get her on the trolley because with every twist and turn she was moaning, saying it hurt her. The pain wasn't enough, however, to stop her from, more than once, jumping up and grabbing a bag of crisps, cheese and onion at that, and a sausage, bean and potato pasty from her bedside table.

As me and Pete pushed her along the bumpy corridors, dodging cleaners, she whinged about every bump we went over. In fact, the only time she didn't moan was when she was stuffing her mouth with crisps. Then, after having another go at us about the bumps, Pete, in friendly terms, told her that we had to get her there. I was trying my best not to laugh as she carried on moaning and saying 'ooh' and 'ahh' most of the way.

When she saw one of the dinner ladies she commanded us to stop as if we had been assigned to her and her only. She jumped up and said, "I want fish and chips for my dinner, Sandra; I will not be long." And then we set off on our way again with her moaning and 'ooh'ing and 'ahh'ing.

After doing that, we were making our way back to base when two of the cleaners, Doris and Don, went running past us. Both of them are as nice as a stripper in a lap dancing club, but not very bright. For example, not long ago, I was walking to fetch a patient in a wheelchair, who had the whole hospital looking for his insulin (which happened to be hidden in his slipper, but that's another story). Anyway, I was behind Doris and Don, who were talking about Stoneboom Bitter coming back, which was a popular beer a few years back. They were both excited by this and Don said, "Yeah, it'll be good if it comes back, I can't wait. Mind you, I hope it tastes better than last time."

We had just got back to the base to a nice cuppa that Jack had made — it was nice 'an all to say he hardly mashes. I told the lads about the fight between the two women as I grabbed a sandwich that I brought from home — tuna, cheese and pickle — and we all laughed.

Barry too had a story to share and said, "Well, me and Jack were coming back from taking a patient to chemo day care when there was a commotion by the shop near the main entrance. There were people all around, two doctors trying to resuscitate a man, while Dr Wilkutitov was enquiring about his lungs and kidneys — wa'n't he, Jack?"

"Ya joking, he's nuts he is. Who was the bloke?" asked Pete.

"It was some old man in a bright red coat, apparently he said he hadn't done this much walking when he did his three peaks challenge for charity, then he keeled over," said Jack. Me and Pete looked at each other.

About ten minutes later I had just taken an oxygen cylinder to Critical Care when I bumped into Don the cleaner again; this time he was alone and without Doris in tow. "Hey up, Higgo, ma duck, how are ya?"

"Hey up, Don; not bad, marra. Your lot are going for it today, ain't ya? I didn't know ya had two gears."

"Cheeky git, yeah we're busy, mate. Anyway, what happened to United the other day?" said Don, grinning.

"They got hammered, pal, that's what happened. You come across the CQC yet? I bet that idiot Kelsey is fobbing 'em off with his usual rubbish."

Don was that busy that he was wiping everywhere he could wipe: on top of the heating pipes that ran up the corridors, around the pipes, in the pipes, under the pipes. Why? I don't know, you couldn't even see under them pipes. "No, mate, I ain't seen the CQC, but hey, listen to this," Don said, still wiping the pipes while at the same time having a quick look around for prying eyes.

You see, Don always made out he could keep a secret when the truth was he told more gossip and spread more rumours than — well, someone who spreads a lot of rumours.

"I was cleaning Kelsey's office area earlier and was outside his door when Arthur Grantham turned up and knocked on it."

"Oh, him, he's another waste of skin; he's supposed to run our department but he couldn't run a bath," I sniped.

"Yeah, ya right there, duck. Now, ya know me, Higgo, I don't gossip or eavesdrop, as you know, but I accidentally overheard them talking."

I had to smile at the fact that Don's ear was still tellingly red from where he had no doubt had it pressed up hard against the door to hear what followed.

"Why? What was said, Don?" I said, at the same time thinking that I had never seen cleaner looking heating pipes.

"Well, Grantham walks on in and says, 'Sorry Sir, but the CQC is here and Doctor Sharmalar is wondering where you are'."

"What? Kelsey hadn't even met them? What a joke."

"I know, how he got the job I'll never know."

"It would have been some dodgy deal, pal, I tell ya that for free."

Don was cleaning frantically as he told the story — even I nearly got the once over with his duster. "Yeah, ya right, duck; he is a dodgy git. Anyway, Kelsey made up some excuse about being caught up in something important and he said to Grantham, 'Go down and carry the flag for me, I'll be there when I get there'."

"What and he sat on his ring while Grantham did his dirty work?" I said.

"Dirty work's right, Higgo, listen to this. I went into his office to empty the bin and I accidentally caught a glimpse of Kelsey's computer screen. You'll never guess what the important job was."

"What?" I replied as I watched Don fill with glee; he knew that I couldn't help but want to know.

"Ordering a set of three grand golf clubs," beamed Don.

"You're joking; three grand on some clubs? We can't even get new wheelchairs out of him."

"I know, Higgo, mind ya, they were good 'uns," said Don, wiping over the pipes again.

"It's a joke, but nowt surprises me with him; he'd sell his own mum for a profit. Right, I had better crack on, Don, see ya later."

"Yeah, I'd better get these pipes done. Oh, and, Higgo, don't say owt; you're the only one I've told."

"No worries, shag, see ya later, 'tator," I said as I made my made my way to collect a patient named Trevor. On the way I bumped into a cleaner, a logistics guy and a nurse who all mentioned Don's golf club story to me.

Apparently, a few minutes after Kelsey had ordered his golf clubs, he was seen making his way down a corridor and as he did so he tripped over some rubbish bags that were on the floor. He kicked a bag at the wall just as Macko and Tez had come around the corner.

Kelsey went red and foamed at the mouth as he yelled, pointing at the rubbish, "Hoh, you, what the hell is this?"

"Looks like black rubbish bags to me, guvnor," Macko had replied.

"Well, get them moved — now," was Kelsey's order.

"It's break time, man; we will sort it later, won't we, Macko'?

"If we get time, mucker; come on, I'm ruddy Hank Marvin, me ode." And they had started to walk off.

Kelsey had jumped up and down yelling, "Do you know who I am?"

Macko had turned to Tez, "We got an idiot here who don't know who he is, chief; the filthy creature. Come on, Tez." And they had gone off for their dinner.

Kelsey then booted another bag of rubbish, knocking a member of the public to the ground as he did so.

Kelsey had then joined up with the CQC on the tour of the hospital, but he was more concerned about Dr Isaac Wilkutitov, who was just staring at Bev's kidney area. Kelsey, looking at his watch, met briefly with the CQC then made some excuse that he had been called away and would leave them in the capable hands of Dr Sharmalar.

*

Since I have been in this job the things you see and hear make you realize how lucky you are and how precious life is. I constantly remind my Mrs and family when we bicker and moan about daft things like having too much milk in ya tea or bumping ya car (it's only metal after all) of how much worse things could be.

And today was no different. I fetched a patient, a Mr Trevor Ropewalk, he was a nice chap, in his late forties. I got him in the wheelchair and we set off for his chemotherapy treatment after me asking him where he was from, which always breaks the ice.

Trev told me he was a bricklayer. Up until recently he had been fit and well and up to date with his finances. And now, just a couple of months after the cancer had been detected, things are different: his health is up and down and his finances are permanently down as he can't work. He had a smile on his face the whole time I was with him, even though he wasn't very happy that day because the nurses hadn't given him his pain relief — again, and they hadn't even told me I was coming. Dodging around the cleaners I asked, "How are you coping with it all?"

Trev spat in his sick bowl. "Well, James (we introduce ourselves to the patients when we pick them up and it's displayed prominently on a nametag anyway), the chemo is very draining and tiring, but the general care, apart from no tablets on the ward, has been good. And I know that if I didn't have the treatment I wouldn't stand a chance; so it is all for my own good."

I nearly lost control of the chair as the sun beamed through one of the windows. "Ya joking, no tablets? And ya right, Trevor, it's the old cliché but you are in the right place, I suppose." I admired how he took it on the chin and got on with it. He was thankful for what he had got. I admired his jolly spirit and it made me think about the petty things we all take for granted every day.

I got him to his destination, gave him a friendly pat, and said, "I might see you later, all the best to you."

"Thanks ever so much, James, I hope to see you later."

As I left him I could sense that he was putting a brave face on a horrible situation. I wished I could have stayed with him, but a patient on a bed needed to go from Critical Care to theatres. Now, normally on dayshifts the theatre porters do this and we do it on the nightshifts, but it was that busy today with the CQC visit that we helped out. So I met up with Jack and we made our way to Critical Care.

On the corridors there was a commotion as Doris, the cleaner, was yelling at a logistics porter who had nearly wiped half of the cleaners out with his tug, which is like a dodgem car that pulls cages and bins etc. Now, the driver of this particular tug was a right crackpot; he had defiantly been some experiment somewhere along the way. Why they let him drive around on these things is anyone's guess. Last week he ploughed into a bed, patient, nurses and all, and two weeks ago he took the door off the Ear, Nose and Throat Department. Then, a few days ago, he knocked a doctor twenty foot up in the air and the doctor landed head first on the floor while the porter just drove on. Dr Wilkutitov happened to be passing and helped the doctor, taking him away on a trolley. Last I heard that doctor hadn't been seen again since.

Me and Jack held back and made sure the porter (who was known as Barmy Bob) had gone before we carried on. We got to critical care and took the chap to theatres. His name was Fred and he was having his shoulder operated on.

The CQC were in the theatres too, inspecting everything — even us, watching how we manoeuvred the bed and everything. They stood silently, not saying a word, apart from one chap who scribbled some notes and said, "Errm". As soon as they turned their backs to look at some equipment and other stuff a cleaner jumped out of a cupboard and quickly cleaned under the patient's bed.

After me and Jack left the theatres we went back to base. The CQC weren't far behind us and their next point of call was to visit the labs. The labs are situated near the plaster clinic on the corridors and they are huge. They did everything down there: testing blood and urine samples for illnesses and working on new treatments. When you go in there to collect blood for transfusions there is always someone doing tests and experiments on seemingly every illness there is. We take blood and other samples there, and when I was a logistics porter I used to empty the rubbish bins. There are loads of the top brains down there, all draped in their long, white coats, and the stench of dead, rotting things bombards your nostrils as you walk in.

At the base we had a quick cuppa and I told the lads about the golf club story. Then our phones beeped; it was Trevor Ropewalk waiting to go back so I accepted the job as I wanted to see how he was after his treatment.

Upon arriving I made my way to him and clicked off the brakes on the wheelchair. I took him back, but the difference in him drained me. He now looked forlorn, pale and he hardly spoke.

"That didn't take long, Trevor. How are ya, pal?" I said, very concerned.

"Okay, but it's tired me out." His drive and earlier confidence had diminished.

"You don't look as chipper as ya did on the way here, mate. I'll get ya back and settled as quickly as I can, pal." Trevor could only manage a very weak nod of his head. He was very quiet on the way back to his ward, apart from the odd gurgled spit into his phlegm splattered bowl.

I got him back and settled and he forced a smile. "Thanks, James, sorry I was quiet; I feel terrible," he muttered.

"No problem, Trevor, get some rest. All the best to you, pal," I replied and then left as the nurse came to attend to him, which gave me some comfort.

I was quite taken aback by the change in him; I wished it would all work out for him. It also made me think of what I have got, and how you should enjoy every minute of every day.

On the way back, still reeling from the shock of seeing the difference in Trevor, I bumped into a young girl named Kelly, who worked in the labs, she was talking to a female cleaner and the story she told us was already doing the rounds — Don had got a hold of it. There is a guy who works in the labs, he's a nice guy but a right nut job; we all think he escaped from the mental wards. Sidney Squeak is his name. Apparently the visit went something like this.

The CQC were all introduced to Professor Nigel Lowbottom and he showed them around a blood testing facility. In the room was Sidney Squeak clad in comical goggles that enhanced his shining bald head (except for a clump of hair on the front), wearing yellow rubber gloves and draped in a white lab coat three times too big.

"Aaaahh, at long last," an eager Squeak had exclaimed as he clasped Bev's hand and covered it in kisses. Before the horrified Bev could speak Sidney had done so instead. "Allow me to show you what I have been working on."

Nigel Lowbottom, shaking his head, had looked for support from another assistant to try and stop him, but the assistant just returned the baffled look. Squeak pulled down his goggles, dissected a frog and started mixing various powders and pouring liquids into a bowl.

"Stand back and be prepared to be amazed; I give you the cure to the common cold or, its Latin name, *shiverous onyourbikeus.*"

Bang.

The explosion set off the water sprinklers. Staff went running and screaming. The Professor, under a dirty lab coat, hushed out Neil, Bev and Greg, who had all looked like drowned rats.

"I do apologize to you all. Mr Squeak is a little eccentric; but what do you do with him?" said Lowbottom.

Bev and Neil shook their heads, while Greg coughed, mumbled "Errm" and scribbled some notes.

Most of them then left the labs except for a couple of assistants, and Sidney, who had been looking at his experiment for some time, rubbing his chin. "Well, what happened there then? I can't have put too much TNT in it, surely?" He had then bent over and stuck his tongue into a bowl of powder; before shooting straight back up. "Yep, too much TNT in it."

Well, me and the cleaner were laughing that much at the fiasco that I had tears running down my face and the cleaner had to promptly mop them all up off the floor.

I made my way back to base with mixed emotions, still chuckling from the Sidney Squeak story and thinking about Trevor. Suddenly, all four of the Dump's on duty security staff went running past me followed by three nurses; they all looked to be heading for Grape Ward.

I shouted to Selina, the nurse manager who I knew, to ask her what was happening. She beckoned me to keep up with her as she told me what all the commotion was about. Apparently, some male patient had lost the plot and wanted to jump off the hospital roof — I reckon he had probably tried the hospital food.

As I walked along with Selina she said, "I've just come from Kelsey and he's ordered us to not let Wilkutitov anywhere near the scene and to make sure that the CQC don't get wind of it — as if we don't have enough on our plate already. I mean, how are we supposed to prevent that?"

"Knowing Kelsey he'd probably rather you just pushed the poor sod off there as quickly as possible," I said

"Ha, funnily enough he did say something to that effect," was Selina's reply.

A security guard then shouted over to Selina and informed her that the patient now had a student nurse by knifepoint and was threatening to jump off the roof with her. The order from the personnel on the roof was to grab something soft in case we needed to break their fall.

Selina went white. "Oh my God, I have to go, James," she said, shaking.

"Is there anything I can do?" We were now in a jog as we talked.

"Erm, could you help get some mattresses round to where they need to be?"

I patted her on her arm. "I'm on it," I said as I went one way and Selina continued up to the roof.

I went to get some mattresses and spotted Jack coming towards me on his way back from the shop. I told him what was going on and we hurried off.

We got to where the equipment is kept, which is in an old, unused ward. This is where beds, mattresses and that sort of stuff is kept along with a room for medical equipment that houses such things as monitors, feed pumps, syringe pumps and lots more.

Tez and Macko luckily happened to be nearby; they were clearly supposed to be working but were instead laughing themselves silly over Sidney Squeak's escapade. I quickly filled them in and we dragged some mattresses around. We hauled one up each, grabbing them by the handles on the side. Macko and Tez asked if this would be on overtime rate.

A nurse who met us outside was organizing the mattresses in the hope of cushioning the man's fall. She spoke to someone on the roof via some sort of walkie-talkie thing and said, "Okay, I'm on my way." She then asked me and Jack for assistance. We grabbed a trolley armed with oxygen for the young nurse who was a bit worse for wear and we made our way to the roof.

When we got there the police, nurses and security were still trying to reason with the male patient. Ian Brickhouse's eyes lit up when he saw the oxygen as he was still out of breath from running up the stairs. Kelsey and the CQC were on the roof now and me and Jack shook our heads at the sight of Kelsey impatiently checking his watch. One of the CQC still just stood there, scribbling notes and mumbling "Errm".

Suddenly, out of nowhere, the man started crying and loosened his grip on the nurse, enabling her to run to safety. She broke down in the arms of her matron. I felt for the young nurse and wondered what she must be thinking. I mean, you don't expect to come to work and get attacked with a knife and do a bungee jump without the bungee, do you? I thought about how it was unfair; why couldn't it have been Kelsey at knifepoint waiting to be thrown off the roof? I doubt there'd be a shortage of volunteers for *that* job. As for the event itself, it didn't bother me. There is always summat happening at the Dump; it's better than watching telly.

We got the young nurse on the trolley so that a doctor could take a look at her. He suggested that she be taken home; Kelsey suggested a twelve hour shift for her instead.

The patient shouted "Goodbye" and went to jump. Security and police jumped for him, grabbing his legs. He swung over and hit his head on the edge. It took a handful of people to drag him up to safety; he was cut up and knocked out so they now had to take him to be checked out. Barry and Pete came up to fetch him.

Me and Jack made our way back with the trolley that we brought up for the nurse that was no longer needed. Kelsey too was leaving, walking ahead with the CQC, on the way to his office for a chat with them on the day's findings. We had just overtaken them as they turned to go into Kelsey's office when Barmy Bob ploughed into them on his tug (well, into the CQC, Kelsey got out of the way).

*

Well, what a day, I was shattered, but with it being nearly home time this would be my last job. I was on the way to pick up a patient from his ward to take him to his radiography treatment. I was thinking about the day's events. I was still taken back by Trevor Ropewalk's bravery and I chuckled about Sidney Squeak. But the drama on the roof had been on another level; I couldn't wait to tell the Mrs about it all.

I got to the ward and entered the patient's room; he was waiting and smiled. I, on the other hand, was gobsmacked as he only had one eye, and where the other one ought to have been was exposed to show a big, scabby hole. I tried not to look, but you know what it's like, you can't help it, can ya?

I introduced myself and got him in his wheelchair; I then picked up his notes from the nurses' station and set off. Frank was a nice chap, he told me he was a writer and working on a book about his life story. I told him that I liked writing and that I was doing a story about the hospital. He told me about him getting cancer — that's how he lost his eye. The only time we stopped talking was to dodge the cleaners.

Frank was telling me about him going to live in Jamaica when a noise rattled the corridor. I looked at the chair, thinking something was caught in the wheels, when Frank informed me he had trumped, just as two nurses walked by. "No," he said, "it wasn't the wheels, it's me, and I know those nurses weren't impressed. But I'm not bothered," he said, "When ya gotta go, ya gotta blow." He said, "I did it once and pushed a bit too hard, and there was a ball of poo in the bed. I felt embarrassed, but what can you do?"

"Shit happens, Frank," I said.

I got him to his treatment room, booked him in and made my way back to my base.

*

Well, that's it for another shift for me. Another quiet day at the Dump. I'm gonna have a steady walk home today, fish and chips for me tea; battered haddock, which means fried in batter, not battered to death.

The two ladies who were fighting have been charged; the one in the blue with disturbing the peace, the one in grey with ABH (actual bodily harm). Apparently, she gave one of the police officers a crack round the head. The man on the roof has woken up and, apart from cuts, bruises and a very sore head, he his OK. But instead of thanking the staff for saving him, he is now suing the hospital. The CQC didn't look too pleased about the visit, but then again apart from 'errm' not one of them has said anything. And, in case you are wondering, the old man in the red coat is fine, but for some reason, he said he is going private.

Harry and...
The Pirates of Rock Bay

It was a typical summer's day and Harry was at home, staring out of his bedroom window, wondering when the rain was going to stop. He jumped on his bed and carried on reading his pirate book: *The Pirates of Rock Bay*.

There were two main pirate gangs in Rock Bay: Captain Shannagan and his ship, the White Wind, and the bad Captain Greed and his smelly, big, black ship, the Devil's Bottle.

One really hot day, the Devil's Bottle was in hot pursuit of the White Wind. "Faster, you dogs, faster," bellowed Captain Greed, who was dressed in a long black coat, a scruffy ripped red shirt and big black boots. He also wore a bandana round his head and an eye patch over his right eye. He had recently grown a beard to cover up the scar on his chin that Captain Shannagan had given him some years back. In his hand he held his faithful sword, which had beaten many a pirate.

"More speed, Mr Mcgruff, I demand it," Greed shouted.

"Aye, Captain," shouted Mr Mcgruff, Captain Greed's right-hand man.

"We're gaining on them, Captain," yelled one of Captain Greed's men.

"Good, but I demand more speed; we will catch the White Wind and that dog Captain Shannagan at Turtle's Cove."

On the White Wind, Captain Shannagan was looking at the gaining Devil's Bottle through his telescope. "They're gaining on us, Captain," shouted Billy Jones, Captain Shannagan's second in command.

"Keep speed and keep on course, Mr Jones, to Crab Claw Pass. We can set up an ambush there." Captain Shannagan knew they couldn't afford to be pushed into Turtle's Cove.

Bang bang. The Devil's Bottle fired her canons. The shots missed the White Wind by inches, but they were enough to start forcing her off course; to Captain Greed's delight.

"Fire, Mr Mcgruff," screamed Captain Greed.

Bang.

"*Arrrgghh,*" screamed the White Wind's Captain and crew as the cannonball hit the back end of the ship and pushed her into Turtle's Cove.

"Hoorah," shouted Captain Greed and his crew.

"We have the dogs where I want them. Even if they leave their ship, they can't get out of Turtle's Cove. Prepare to engage in battle, Mr Mcgruff."

"Aye aye, Captain Greed."

Back on the White Wind that's exactly what Captain Shannagan and his crew were doing — abandoning their ship to take cover in Turtle's Cove's caves and hills.

Not long after, the Devil's Bottle arrived at the cove and Captain Greed and his crew made their way on land.

"Come out, Shannagan, you yellow dog, and give me that treasure map or I'll come and take it from your dead body," yelled Captain Greed.

Captain Shannagan and his crew, which was a lot smaller than Captain Greed's, were hiding in the caves with pistols, ready to defend themselves.

"Get ready to fire, Mr Jones."

"Aye, Captain," said Mr Jones as he wiped his sweaty brow.

"Attack," yelled Captain Greed.

Bang bang.

Captain Greed's crew charged at the White Wind's crew...

"Harry, everyone is here, are you coming down?"

"Yes, Mummy," replied a startled Harry, who shut the book, laid it on his bed, and reluctantly ran downstairs to see his daddy sorting the barbecue.

Harry went round and gave all his family and friends a cuddle; there were all of his grandparents, his uncles and aunties, his cousins and some friends. After all the cuddles were over, Harry couldn't stop thinking about what was happening to Captain Shannagan and his crew; so he, cousins Daisy and Holly all went back upstairs to his room.

Daisy and Holly started to draw pictures while Harry jumped straight back onto his bed and picked up the book; quickly finding the page where he had left it.

*

"We nearly have them, men," roared Captain Greed.

Mr Jones looked at Captain Shannagan. "What now, Captain?"

"We need help, Jones, we need a saviour, but who will come?" said a tired looking Captain Shannagan.

Harry touched the book and said, "I'll come and help you, Captain Shannagan."

The next minute, Harry and his crew were making their way to Turtle's Cove on his beautiful, fast pirate ship, the Mum and Dad. Harry was at the wheel in his white pirate shirt with black and white striped trousers that were tucked into his pirate boots. On his head was the best pirate hat around and his sword and pistol were in his belt.

"Steady as she goes, Miss Daisy," Harry yelled. He looked round at his crew; his grandparents, uncles, aunties, friends and of course his mum and dad were all in their pirate clothes

"Get ready to attack; remember I want Captain Greed taken alive. Load the cannons, Miss Holly," Harry roared.

"Aye aye, Captain," yelled his crew.

It was looking helpless for Captain Shannagan and his crew by now. They had engaged in a sword fight with Captain Greed's crew and most of Captain Shannagan's men had been captured.

Captain Greed was now in a ferocious battle with Captain Shannagan. "Surrender, you yellow sea rat," shouted Captain Greed.

"Never," shouted Captain Shannagan, just managing to get out of the way of Captain Greed's sword.

"Then die, you rotting dog," replied Captain Greed. He was about to thrust his sword into the belly of Captain Shannagan when...

Bang bang bang.

Captain Harry's ship and crew fired on Captain Greed's ship. The crews of Shannagan and Greed stopped fighting.

"Who on earth is that, Mr Mcgruff?" asked Captain Greed.

"Why that's Captain Harry Sparr, the bravest pirate there is by far," Mr Mcgruff said to the angry looking Captain Greed.

"Fire again, Miss Holly," ordered Captain Harry.

"Aye, Captain, fire," Miss Holly yelled.

Bang bang.

And with these final two shots the Devil's Bottle turned on her side. Captain Greed's face went as red as beetroot with anger and he swung his sword at Captain Shannagan. Captain Shannagan and Captain Greed engaged in battle again and so did both their crews.

"Prepare to land and prepare yourself for battle, crew. Land as close as you can, Miss Daisy," said Captain Harry, loading his pistol.

On Turtle's Cove's beach the fighting was intense. Captain Shannagan and Captain Greed were matching each other blow for blow, until Captain Shannagan fell over a rock and landed on his back. He found himself looking up at the squinty eyes, red face and gritted teeth of the angry looking Captain Greed.

"Where's that map, Shannagan?" Captain Greed bellowed.

"I'll never tell you, Greed, you'll have to kill me first," replied Captain Shannagan.

"Your wish is my pleasure, you yellow rat," said Captain Greed with a smirk. He lifted his sword above his head and brought it swinging down.

Clink.

Captain Shannagan looked up to see Captain Harry's sword together with Captain Greed's, right above his head. Captain Shannagan watched Harry push Captain Greed away from him;

Greed stumbled but regained his balance and slashed his sword at Harry.

"You sea urchin, who are you?" yelled Captain Greed.

"Captain Harry Sparr, at your service," was Harry's answer as he cut Greed's face.

"Prepare to meet your end, dog," screamed Captain Greed.

"Don't think so, dude," was Harry's quirky reply and at that, Harry who was much faster, stronger and braver than Captain Greed, started to get the better of him. Harry tripped him over and stood above Captain Greed with his sword at his neck. Captain Greed looked up at Captain Harry Sparr and threw away his sword. At that same moment, Miss Daisy and Miss Holly had beaten Mr Mcgruff, who was on his knees.

"Stay still, Mcgruff, or I'll run you through," Miss Holly shouted.

They'd done it; Captain Harry's crew along with Captain Shannagan's had beaten Captain Greed's crew. "Hoorah," they all yelled.

Captain Shannagan smiled at Captain Harry while shaking his hand. "How can I ever thank you, Captain Harry?"

"Not a problem, matey." Harry grinned.

"What we gonna do with this lot, Captain?" asked Mr Jones, pointing at Captain Greed and his crew.

"Yes, what do you suggest, Captain Shannagan?" asked Captain Harry.

Captain Shannagan paced around looking at the angry Captain Greed. "We will tie them up in the coves where the mermaids, sharks and sea monsters can fight over them," he said.

"Cool." Harry nodded approvingly,

"You yellow dog rats, you'll pay for this. I'll get my revenge on you Captain Shannagan, and you Captain Harry Sparr," screamed Captain Greed.

"Silence. Take them away and tie them up," ordered Captain Shannagan. To which the crews of the White Wind and the Mum and Dad, under the orders of Mr Jones, did just that.

"Well, Captain Harry, I thank you again. Would you like to join us aboard the White Wind for a feast?"

"Thank you, Captain Shannagan, but I must say no, as I have a big family feast waiting for me," Harry politely said.

"Well, till the next time then," Captain Shannagan said, shaking Captain Harry's hand.

"Thank you, and goodbye," said Harry as he and his crew set sail on the Mum and Dad.

*

A little later, Harry, Holly and Daisy ran downstairs. "There you are, Harry, what have you been doing?" asked his mum.

"We have been to Rock Bay to help Captain Shannagan and his pirates, Mum," Harry replied, smiling.

"Oh, I hope it was good?" asked Mum, putting his food on his plate.

"Yes, it was, Mummy," was Harry's reply as he sat there quietly eating his food and thinking about his next adventure.

The Cleaner

The alarm clock was making that same ruddy noise at the same ruddy horrible time again — 4 a.m. to be precise — and, just like every other Monday morning, Fred's wife Doris slid out of bed with her eyes still shut. Fred broke wind as he blew her a kiss and rolled back over.

Bleary-eyed, Doris slipped into her fluffy, pink slippers and then wrestled with the wardrobe door handle, trying to free her snagged nightie that was exposing her big, pink pants.

Downstairs, Doris was now dressed in her cleaner's uniform; she's a cleaner, you see, at a big supermarket called Pesdas. Her husband always says she must be mad doing the same boring thing every day especially when they didn't even need the money; but Doris says nothing and just smiles back at him. She finished her coffee and morning fag and toddled off for the bus.

"Morning, Arthur."

"Morning, Doris," chirped the bus driver.

Doris jumped on and sat in her usual seat: the window one, fourth back on the left. She applied more of her blood red lipstick, which, when Arthur turned the corner, ended up all over her mouth; she looked like she had been smacked in it.

After she had gotten off the bus, Doris gave Arthur a little wave as he pulled away. She lit up a cigarette, had five puffs, put it out, and went into Pesdas.

She sat in the staffroom with a nice big cup of coffee and chatted to Valerie, another cleaner. After a ten minute chat, which consisted of grandchildren, lady's problems and Tuesday night at bingo, Doris got her cleaning gear.

"Here we go again," grimaced Valerie.

"Another boring day," said Doris with a grin.

"I know what you mean, Doris. Why do you do this though? You told me before you don't need the money. What does Fred say about it all?"

Doris smiled. "Oh him, he can't get his head around it; he's always moaning about me going. He says I must be mad with it being the same, boring day."

Valerie was about to pry a bit more when Doris exclaimed, "Look at the time, Val. Oh well, better make a start; see ya in a bit, love." With that Doris toddled off. She made her way by the home entertainment section, having a quick look at a couple of the on offer CDs, before making her way up to start the offices.

About an hour later, Doris was cleaning away when she was sure she heard a scream. She stopped and listened, but couldn't hear anything more. She came to the conclusion that it must be the two young cleaners messing about, so she carried on regardless and plugged in the hoover. She was about to turn it on when she heard a commotion outside. Abandoning her post, she sneaked to the door and peaked out. Outside stood two men with guns; they were leading Graham, the manager, to his office.

Doris crept back into the room. Now, ordinary people like you and I would ring the police right about now; not Doris though. She tightened up her pinny, tied a headband round her head (she looked like Rambo gone wrong) and then grabbed hold of her sweeping brush, clasping it in pink Marigold covered hands.

She left the room and slowly crept down the corridor to Graham's office, she was on her tiptoes, swinging her brush around and looked a bit like a drunken trapeze artist. She then commando crawled to her target, jumped up and put her left ear to the door.

"Here, Biffo, hurry and tie the boss man up. I'll help you empty the safe then I will go and see what else is about while you go and help Billy with the hostages down in the staffroom."

"Righto, Frank."

Doris ran down the stairs and in no time at all she was creeping up to the staffroom where Billy had got the staff, including Valerie, tied up.

Doris went over to the display of Easter eggs and, after eating some chocolate for a quick sugar rush, she steadied her nerves and pushed over the display. There was an almighty crash as Wispa eggs, Crunchie eggs and Snickers eggs all came toppling down on top of each other. Doris could feel her adrenaline pumping as she ran and hid behind the shelves of the pet food aisle. She crouched down and waited in anticipation for what was about to come.

The noise had attracted the other robber and Billy came out of the staffroom holding his gun. "Is that you, Biffo?"

Doris started making tapping noises with her broom handle on the floor to draw him in her direction. Billy slowly crept round the boxes of cereal (he had never seen so much porridge) to where the noise was coming from.

When he reached the pet food aisle there, standing halfway down the aisle, was Doris leaning on her broom, looking very mean for a pensioner. Billy had started to raise his gun when Doris bent over and tried to pull a moonie, but with her big, pink pants and Marigold gloves it was too big a problem so she gave Billy the finger instead and went round the corner.

"Hoh, cleaning woman, come here or I'll shoot," roared Billy as he gave chase. As he flew round the corner he went bottom over head, slipping on the dog biscuits that Doris had scattered on the floor, and went flying into a display of half price Pot Noodles. He struggled to his feet, looking for his gun, which was now in Doris' possession.

Billy turned and looked at Doris who was stood in a karate style stance holding her broom like a weapon; Billy rubbed his head and grinned. "Give me my gun back, granny, I don't wanna hurt you." He smirked as he rummaged for his flick-knife.

Doris threw her broom forward in the air and cartwheeled towards the shocked looking Billy. She landed on her feet, caught the broom and swung it around before bringing it down on Billy's head. He staggered backwards. Doris flung forward whacking Billy in the stomach then karate chopped him to his neck, knocking him to the floor. She quickly tied him up with cling film and

Sellotape and threw him in one of the freezers in between Häagen Dazs and Ben & Jerry's.

Biffo came downstairs and went into the staffroom; a minute later he came back out. "Billy, where are ya?" he yelled as he helped himself to his second Mars Bar. Doris went over to Pesdas' customer restaurant and let off some champagne bottles that were on offer on a nearby display. *Pop pop pop.* "Billy, what are you doing?" Biffo made his way to the noise and as he arrived at the hissing champagne bottles he saw the restaurant door swing shut. Doris had run off to hide behind a big fridge in the restaurant kitchen. Biffo followed and kicked the door open.

"Billy, what the hell are you doing? What the…who are you?" muttered Biffo as a tough-looking Doris jumped up from behind the fridge and stood in front of him. She knocked the gun out of his hand with her trusty broom. Biffo snarled, knocked his fists together and went for Doris; she ducked his punch then unloaded two punches into his stomach, followed by a swift kick where it hurts. Biffo screamed like a girl; Doris then gave him a left, a right, another left and two rights around his head, then pushed his head into the open microwave and pressed start.

Pppiiiinnnnggg.

"Muvver," yelped Biffo and fell to the ground where Doris then grabbed him and tied him up. Doris wiped her brow then clasped her hands together and said to herself, *Right two down, one to go*, and made her way to Graham's office. She went into the room and put the Hoover on.

"Biffo, Billy, you ain't got time to hoover up," Frank shouted as he came out with a big duffel bag full of money in his left hand and his sawn-off shotgun in his right.

"Biffo, Billy, for God's sake." As Frank got to the door the hoover stopped; then, from Doris' mobile phone which she had put on the table, came Carl Douglas' song *Kung Fu Fighting*.

"What the —" Frank opened the door and crept into the dark room.

Wallop.

Doris and her trusty broom had knocked Frank's sawn-off shotgun to the floor and Doris kicked it under the table. Frank turned on the lights and there, stood in front of him, was Doris in a Kung Fu stance. Frank's face was a picture; he thought it was a setup. He soon realized that it wasn't, however, when Doris skipped across the room and gave him such a clout to the stomach that Frank staggered back. He took a moment to regain his composure then he lunged at Doris, smacking her full on, his fist lodging between her hazel brown eyes and button nose. As she stumbled over Frank thought he had killed her, but fortunately (or unfortunately for him) he had only succeeded in making Doris mad. She jumped back up, Kung Fu kicked him then gave him a one two. Frank went to hit back but Doris blocked him, chopped him to the neck then jumped up holding Frank's arms and head-butted him into the wall. Frank was out cold.

Doris quickly tied him up then left. She ran into another office and, in a gruff, put on voice, dialled the police and told them there was a robbery in progress. She then went into a stockroom full of microwave meals, various pop bottles, a couple of TVs and various other household boxes and tied herself up. Now, please don't get all technical, reader, and ask how Doris tied herself up, she just did all right? She is quite clever, after all.

Later, Frank, Billy and Biffo were in the police van, waffling on about a superhero, Kung Fu granny, which just gave the police a good laugh. The staff had been released and it was a mystery as to what had happened. Valerie had asked Doris about it but she had just smiled and said "God knows, I was tied up".

Back on the bus, on her way home, Doris smiled. You see, Fred and her family and friends all think that she works all week and then just comes home to be a housewife. When the reality is that on Tuesday afternoons she attends karate classes, while on Wednesdays she goes rock climbing and on Thursdays it's paragliding — but not this Thursday as she is doing a bungee jump for charity.

You see, reader, when Doris was a young girl while other girls wanted to be nurses, actresses, housewives etc. Doris wanted to be a superhero so she could use her powers to help people like you and me. Superman and Supergirl were her favourites; she still remembers first reading about Supergirl in 1959 on her ninth birthday. As she grew up she soon realized that she didn't have superhero powers, but that didn't mean that she still couldn't help people. She took up karate and boxing in her younger years, and unbeknownst to her family she had fended off a fair few muggers and violent youths in her time. She doesn't tell anyone about her extracurricular activities and incredible feats though because just like any good superhero she wants to remain inconspicuous.

She got off the bus, went to have a cigarette but then looked at the packet and threw them all in the bin. She'd been meaning to quit and now seemed like the best time seeing as she was going to do a spot of cave climbing next week; she didn't want her cough hindering that adventure now, did she? She gave a stern nod at the bin and went into her house.

She was soon in her slippers and comfy pyjamas with a nice mug of coffee in hand. Fred came in and gave her a peck on the cheek.

"Hello, love, how was your day?" he asked.

Doris sipped her coffee, looked at Fred and grinned. "Oh, you know, darling, just another boring old day at Pesdas; I am only a cleaner, after all."

Nothing That Money Can't Buy

Tim Green was sat in a room which he would describe as being fit for a king. It was a good mixture of modern and antique and it was obvious that no expense had been spared. The curtains alone looked like they had cost more than Tim's car.

He had been sat with his notepad and Dictaphone for a good twenty minutes and was becoming more and more impatient. He started to chew his pen, followed by checking his watch, then looking over at the expensive looking, antique clock. After clicking his Dictaphone on and off a few times he blew out his cheeks and stood up to admire some of the art hanging on the walls of the massive living room in this amazing house.

Tim, who was an up and coming biographer, started to drum his fingers on the table as he slumped back into his chair and continued waiting for the owner of this wonder of architectural triumph — Larry Breen. Larry Breen was one of the richest men in the world and Tim had been commissioned to write his biography.

When Larry finally did arrive he walked in as slowly and casually as his stocky, six foot frame would allow. He had short, brown hair flecked with white and a thin, greying goatee. He was wearing a grey, shiny three-piece suit, which must have cost at least two grand. He smiled at Tim as he went over to the drinks cabinet in the corner of the room and poured himself a scotch, simultaneously throwing down his Ferrari keys on its surface.

"Morning, Tim, how are you?"

"Fine, Mr Breen," he replied shaking his hand.

"Call me Larry," he said, sitting down.

"Okay, Larry, shall we make a start?" asked Tim as he pressed record on his Dictaphone. Larry nodded. "Well, Larry, you are one of the most successful businessmen of our age and have revolutionized the mobile phone with your company Wantafone. As we all know, your company has enabled even those of us who are not so well off to own a top phone, such as the Green 6ZJ541, for example, at affordable rates tailored towards the individual. Now, you were once quoted as saying that 'life is all about success and money', would you care to expand on that?"

"Well, Tim, the funniest thing I ever heard was a chap saying that money isn't everything and I beg to differ. You see, ever since I could toddle I was intrigued with notes and coins. At first it was just the image of them that mesmerized me and I used to find them in the house and collect them. I used to get shouted at by the old man from time to time, I can tell you. But as I grew bigger I realized the power of money and how it ruled and ran the world. As I got older and wiser all I wanted was money and success, and I have achieved all that but I still find myself wanting more. I believe there's nothing that money can't buy."

Tim pressed the pause button on his Dictaphone and scribbled down some notes. "How did you start out, Larry?"

"I was thirteen; I got a job helping on a market stall where I quickly learned all the basic principles of buying and selling. Then, at nineteen, I had saved and borrowed enough to start my own stall selling handbags, and from there I went into mobile phones. By the time I was twenty-five I was a millionaire with my company Wantafone."

"You got married and have family, don't you?"

"Yes, I have been going out with my lovely wife Suzanne since I was twenty-five. We met in a night club; she didn't fancy me at first till she got to know who I was. Then, after a couple of dates, she wanted to marry me so we married when I was twenty-six, and when I was twenty-seven our first son Mark was born, at twenty-eight James was born and I was thirty when my daughter Melissa came along."

"Wow, you were busy then," Tim laughed.

"Yeah, and I can't even use the 'we had no telly' gag as we had six of them. I also have a lovely Grandson, Olli — our Mark's."

"Lovely." Tim stopped his Dictaphone and briefly scanned his scribbled notes. "So why do you believe that there's nothing that money can't buy?"

"Well, Tim, I have everything: cars, houses all over the world, yachts, this watch on my wrist is worth more than you make a year — and that's by no way meaning to be rude — I have seen all the world and so has my family, if I wanted to I could buy prostitutes — the good ones — go to the top chefs' restaurants — which we do — get the best doctors; even my daughter is a result of IVF — everything. Now, I wouldn't have had any of that without money. No, Tim, my life will be forever happy because of my money."

Tim sat making some notes and Larry had just got himself another scotch when his phone rang. "Hello, Mark, son, how are you? How's the new Ferrari?"

"Hey, Dad, err, yeah, good thanks. Dad, listen, I have something to tell you."

"What is it, mate? Have you seen another motorbike you want?"

"No, Dad, it's serious."

Larry started pacing around. "Mark, what's up? And who's that crying?" It was Sarah, Mark's wife, that he could hear crying in the background.

"I have just had a call from Dr Ippliss and he has had those tests back — the ones I had a couple of weeks ago…" Mark took a deep breath. "I have stomach cancer, Dad."

Larry nearly stopped breathing. "A-are you sure? No, Ippliss has got it wrong. I'll send you to this other one I know in America, he's not cheap, but that's not a problem."

"Dad, it's incurable."

Horsing Around

The constant birdsong, the rasping of grasshoppers and the buzzing of bees could all be clearly heard on this warm summer's morning. Flowers were in full, glorious bloom, trees were filled with delicious fruits and the field overflowed with glorious, red, majestic poppies. These were all things which Farmer Tankard had always admired and he found himself doing so as he led Duke — an ex-guardsman horse once belonging to Her Majesty the Queen — up to one of his fields on Tankard Meadow. Duke, fine looking, grey, tall, strong and proud, had no idea that he had been retired. He believed he was going for a well-earned rest and a relaxing groom. So, with no reluctance at all, he marched, head held high, to his destination.

At the gate, Farmer Tankard watched Duke for a little while as the fine animal trod very carefully towards the other three horses in the field.

Champ, an ex-racehorse, was a beautiful, light brown animal who was charging around the field jumping various obstacles; his mind on his last race. He was neck and neck with Rolylad, his old rival, they both pushed for the winning post and, by a neck,

Champ had clinched his 4th Grand National win. Happy memories of days that were sadly long gone.

In the corner was Nelly, a tall, heavy Shire; black with a white neck. She was nibbling away at the grass but she did so long for a tasty carrot, just like she would receive on her old rag and bone rounds.

Just beyond Nelly was Lightning, a gorgeous, white, ex-dancing horse. She was walking on her hind legs doing a trick that she used to perform in her circus days.

Duke elegantly tiptoed up to the three of them, who paused in their activities to look at him. Champ muttered to Nelly, "Hello, who have we here? Lord Snooty?"

Nelly smirked then went up to Duke. "Hello, mush, nice to meet you, I'm Nelly."

Duke's eyes widened. "Mush — mush? How dare you? I am Duke, her Majesty the Queen's finest; and don't you forget it, Madam," he yelled. Duke's attitude did not bother Nelly one bit.

Champ pushed past the others. "Nice to meet you, mate, I'm Champ, the best racehorse that ever graced any racetrack — especially that at Aintree. You know, the Grand National," he blurted out happily. He was just contemplating taking part in another imaginary race when Duke shot up to him.

"Aintree? That is positively untrue, you cad. Have you not heard of Red Rum? Three times winner, my dear, eccentric steed."

Champ blew a ball of mist out of his snout. He smirked and in a sarcastic tone said, "Old Red, my first cousin, three times winner? Yes, I have heard of him, but winning the National four times like I did slightly beats it, don't it, stuck up?" Champ pushed Duke out of the way and carried on with his business. Duke gave him a nasty glare and then Lightning strode up to him.

"Hello, my name is Lightning, please do excuse Champ he is a bit into himself, but he really is quite harmless."

Duke couldn't take his eyes off the beautiful creature in front of him; she was mesmerizing. She had a coat of pure white and her eyes sparkled like the stars above at night. She moved with such elegance as she slowly flicked her long, white mane from side to side. To him, she was nothing short of perfect. Duke repeatedly dragged his right front hoof along the ground, tracing lines in the grass as he smiled at her. "I am Duke and it is an honour to meet you, Madam; and your friend, dear lady, is excused; but please, four Grand Nationals? It is a bit of a farfetched imagination one would say, wouldn't one?"

"Yes, I suppose one would, but if only his hind legs hadn't given way with a furlong to go it would have been five wins, but you can't have everything, can you?" replied Lightning.

Duke gulped and, shaking his head, he muttered, "N-no, my dear, you cannot."

Nelly came up to them, munching on some grass. She swallowed and hiccupped. "Oh gawd, my heartburn; it ain't half giving me grief, it's really annoying. Mind you, it will be all right when it comes out the other end, hey, Dukey old boy?" she said, giving a guffaw which soon turned into a racking cough.

Duke glared at her; he found Nelly to be as common as muck and didn't think her toilet habits were something that should be discussed during polite conversation. He was very confused by her behaviour as he had never encountered such a thing, and he was disappointed to see Lightning was laughing too.

"Riff raff, totally uncalled for, what. Anyway, if you would be good enough to let me know what time the groom normally gets here then that would be most helpful, because I really should be getting back to the palace; the Queen will be missing me, you know," Duke said with a smile.

Nelly and Lightning looked at each other, both very confused. At that moment, Champ, who had overheard Duke's conversation, shot straight up to him and faced him, snout to snout. With a sly, sarcastic grin he said, "Excuse me, Sir Duke, mate, but did I, ha-ha, did I hear you mention being groomed and going back to the palace?"

Duke took a few paces back, looking awkwardly at him, "Yes, I did indeed, my fellow, and it is about time the Sir came into it."

Champ looked relieved. "Thank God for that, I thought my old ears had let me down."

Laughing, Champ looked at Nelly, who had now sorted out her toilet business due to her laughing so much. It was the biggest pile of horse dung Nelly had ever parted with; it must have been four foot high and the steam that was coming off it looked like it was from a steam engine. Duke was somewhat shocked at Nelly's behaviour and he looked to Lightning for support; but Lightning was having a little chuckle to herself as Nelly's antics always made her laugh. He couldn't believe their rudeness and with him always being right (or so he thought) he happily blurted out, "Ha-ha, I get it, a joke, yes, ha-ha. Well, you can't fool, Sir Duke, oh no, good try though, spiffing good try." And with that, he elegantly strode off.

Nelly and Champ rolled about in a heap along with the Rabbit and Hedgehog families (who lived in the hedge bottoms of their field), laughing so hard that they couldn't stop. Duke, with his nose in the air, strode off, oblivious to the truth, while Lightning, feeling very sad, stood shaking her head. She liked Duke. He was elegant, robust and looked very strong. His manners were endearing and he seemed to be very caring. She thought he was the most handsome horse she had ever encountered (but she would never tell him that). Lightning loved the warm, tingling feeling that overpowered her when Duke looked and smiled at her. However, she also found herself feeling sorry for him as she remembered how scared she was when she was first retired to the field. Lightning had loved to do her dancing tricks; they had made her feel alive. She remembered her denial that she had been retired and her belief that she had merely been sent for a rest or a holiday or something. So she knew what Duke was going through; but also knew words would not comfort him, and as it was with herself, it would be down to time to heal.

*

Two weeks later, with the sun beating down on Tankard Meadow, Nelly, Lightning and Champ were drinking out of the water trough in an attempt to cool themselves down from the scorching sun when up strode Duke.

"Okay, so you are right, there is no groom, but retired? That surely is a joke, isn't it?"

Champ laughed, Duke glared at him and Nelly, shaking her head, went up to Duke. "I think someone's pulled a fast one on ya, Dukey. Ya like us, here to stay — dog meat, ha-ha," she joked. Nelly started to cough; it was just a little hiccup at first, but then as she constantly banged herself in the chest with her front left, rusty shoed hoof her cough soon turned into what sounded like a lorry chugging up the road. "My gawd — wheeze — cough — I feel like I have been smoking them Park Drives cigarettes that Tankard — cough — used to smoke," she wheezed.

"Nelly, go and eat something," yelled Lightning in an attempt to get her away from Duke, who was looking distraught at the events.

Duke felt so low; he thought this was the end. *But how could this happen to the Queen's number one*, he thought. After all he had done for her Majesty and country. Why had they retired him? Because he certainly hadn't wanted to go. He wondered if he had done something wrong, but he soon discounted that from his mind as he had always been prompt, thorough and proper. So, with it all remaining a mystery to him, it made him feel even lower, plus he hated this place. He hated being in unfamiliar territory with rude inhabitants and no nice warm barracks to lay his weary head. At that moment in time, Duke hated everything about Tankard Meadow — apart from Lightning.

"Listen, Duke, it's not that bad being retired. I mean, we've got each other and our freedom," said Lightning, not very convincingly.

"Each other?" he stormed, casting his steely eyes at Champ, who was a few yards from Duke, wriggling his rear end in the air and grinding his hooves in the dirt at the starting line of his race. "A-are you sure about all this, Madam?" Duke stuttered. Lightning softly nodded. Their tender moment was disturbed, however, by a huge commotion over at the far end of the paddock. Champ had tried to jump the hedge in a rerun of his very own Grand National, but his hind leg had clipped the top and it sent him head first into the Rabbits' house.

Champ was dazed but he was getting a piece of Mrs Rabbit's mind, nevertheless. Champ was oblivious to this, however. He had been convinced that he was going to win as he was a good furlong in front on the second lap. That was until Rolylad had clipped his hind leg, sending him flying. He wanted Rolylad disqualified for unsporting behaviour as Champ was sure that Rolylad had purposely nudged his hind legs because Champ was about to win another race. Champ was going to complain to the race officials.

"You moron, look at our house, what do you think you're playing at? And you lot can stop laughing, it isn't funny," stormed Mrs Rabbit, waving her stubby index finger at her youngsters.

"C'mon, Champ, me ode spider, talk to me," chortled Nelly.

Champ looked up, his eyes rolling around in his head. "Ah, Nell, me old Nell; I caught me leg on Becher's Brook, Nell," he yelled.

Mrs Rabbit jumped up and down ranting. "You and that race, you're retired, you all are, you're all in the kna—" Mrs Rabbit caught sight of one of her youngsters looking up at her. "Erm, I mean, you're all in the place where clapped out horses go. You know, like you are." These words really hurt a proud horse such as Duke, but the others just shrugged it off. "And God knows what Mr Rabbit's gonna say when he gets home."

"Where is Mr Rabbit?" asked Lightning, trying to dampen Mrs Rabbit's rage and avert it away from Champ.

Mrs Rabbit was still looking disgusted with Champ. "What him? Oh, he's over at the Tankards' borrowing some grub for dinner," she blurted.

"Is someone gonna give me a hand with old Champ or what?" raged Nelly, kicking the ground.

Mrs Rabbit was still angry. She was stood with her arms crossed, tapping her feet, when Duke strode up. "Whatever seems to be the trouble, Madam? I'll tell you what the trouble is, there is no organization that is the trouble, what," said Duke very sternly.

Mrs Rabbit quickly intervened. "Well, well, if it isn't 'better than the rest of us'. We don't need you, go and get groomed, ha-ha-ha," she quipped.

"Now, now, Mrs Rabbit, there's no need for that; Duke didn't cause this catastrophe," said Lightning.

"No, I know he didn't, old Champion the blunder horse did, and I still haven't had an apology," she yelled.

Champ, still dazed, looked at Mrs Rabbit and, with a silly grin, he muttered, "Erm, sorry, Mrs R."

Duke intervened. "Yes, anyway, my delirious rabbit, I am over the grooming and retiring episode; I am very happy here." He grinned. Lightning looked at Duke and gave him a warm smile.

At that moment, Mr Rabbit, looking quite flustered and scared, came towards his family and the horses at top speed. He stopped in front of them all, shaking. His stomach was going up and down very fast as he tried to control his heavy breathing. He was flapping his arms and pointing them in various directions.

"What is it, man? Speak up. We would not have had this in the guards, you know, quite improper, what," said Duke, slowly pacing around Champ who was still half dazed. Duke blew a couple of balls of mist out of his snout as he took charge of the situation.

Mrs Rabbit ran up to her other half and patted his back with tremendous force. "Yes, what's up, my lovely?" she smiled, patting his back even harder, which brought on a bout of coughing.

Champ was now on his feet again due to the organizational skills of Duke, who had managed to wedge his head under Champ's neck, and with Nelly and Lightning taking charge of the rear end they had managed to work Champ up in a seesaw motion.

Mr Rabbit had now got his breath back, "Ooh dear, have you gone mad or what? My poor back," he shouted.

Mrs Rabbit stared angrily at her husband and yelled, "Don't you start on me, where have you been? And any —"

"Now, now, enough of that it's not good for the children, you know, and anyway, my good man, what on earth is wrong?" interrupted Duke and earned himself a nasty look from Mrs Rabbit for doing so.

Mr Rabbit started flapping and waving his arms around again making himself look like a chicken with distemper. "Meat," he yelled as he finally cleared his throat.

"Meat? We've already eaten, love," said Nelly with a grin.

"And anyway we're strict veggies," murmured a dazed Champ.

"Yeah, grass, ya know what I mean, man?" chortled Nelly.

"Don't be a dope," joked Champ.

Mr Rabbit was getting really annoyed, especially with Nelly, Champ and his youngsters all giggling. "No, listen, they're coming in the morning and —"

Mr Rabbit was rudely interrupted by Nelly, "Who's coming? The aliens? Santa and his reindeer? Who?"

Mr Rabbit was jumping up and down with rage. "I'm trying to tell you," he yelled, pulling hard on his ears.

"Do calm down, Mr Rabbit, you'll hurt yourself," said Lightning.

"I'll hurt someone in a minute," yelled Mr Rabbit as he started off on another fit of jumping up and down.

Mrs Rabbit rushed to her husband's aid. "Please calm down, dear, or you'll start off your asthma. Right, everyone, please listen or we'll be here all night. Go on, dear," she said.

Mr Rabbit gave his wife a look, he didn't know whether to thank her or go mad. He rubbed his eyes and carried on with what he had been trying to say. "I was at the Tankards' and I heard them say that...well...in...well..."

"Well, go on, man, out with it; nothing can shock me, what," interrupted Duke with the others nodding their approval.

"Well, all right; in two days' time the farmer and his son are... well..."

"Well, go on," yelled an impatient Nelly.

Mr Rabbit glared at Nelly; he took a deep breath and yelled, "The Tankards are gonna butcher ya for meat — there done it," he sighed and fell into a tired heap.

Nelly and Lightning gulped, Champ went on another Grand National to distract himself, the Hedgehogs and the Rabbits gave each other horrified looks, while Duke stood there shaking, trying desperately to keep his pride intact, and was just about to join Champ in his race, but the sight of Mrs Rabbit tapping her stubby foot on the floor and hitting a rolling pin against the open palm of her stubby left hand stopped him. Duke flicked his mane from his eyes and got himself together.

The Rabbits were confused over the matter. "What does it all mean?" asked one of the twenty-three youngsters.

"It means we'll be the property of some fast food place — or Findus," muttered Nelly.

"Oh that's horrible," groaned Lightning, who then decided to go and talk to Duke. "It is okay to be scared, Duke, I am too, but I know a brave horse like you will figure something out," she said with a kind smile.

Duke smiled back. "Thank you, Madam; it just sits a bit uneasy with one. After what I have done for my country to end up in a stew...but I agree, we have to think of something."

At that moment Nelly trotted up to Duke and Lightning, flicking her head to try to get off the flies. "Well, me ode 'tators, why don't we do something and stop Champ racing about again; he's scared an' all."

Duke bravely stepped out in front of Champ and stood on his hind legs, loudly neighing and flicking his two front legs at Champ to stop him, which is exactly what it did. Champ came to a halt.

Nelly brushed up to Champ. "I know ya scared, me ode pal, I am too, but it will be fine I'm sure." She looked to Duke for reassurance.

"I didn't think you were scared, Nell. I like to run; you can forget your troubles that way," said Champ.

"'Course I get scared from time to time, mucker; especially about being butchered! I would imagine that would hurt," replied Nelly.

The four horses were now close together again. "It will be fine, my dears," chirped Duke, with a fine, authoritative glow. And for the moment they were content.

Mr Rabbit, who was now completely calm and no longer tired, jumped up. "Well that's life, at least we're all right; what's for tea?" Mr Rabbit froze; he started pulling his ears and jumping up and down yelling, "Aaahh, my house, what's happened to my house?" But no one was listening.

*

That night, the four horses were lying down, all very quiet and feeling sorry for themselves. Lightning lifted her head and in a soft, scared voice murmured, "C-come o-on, we must be able to do something, hey, Duke?"

For once, Duke didn't have an answer, but Champ did. "Yeah run, and run far," he blurted.

"But where we gonna run to, Champ?" asked Nelly.

"Well, I don't know, there must be somewhere, hey, Lightning?" Champ replied.

"Yes I suppose, but if we do run we will eventually be caught and then what?" she replied.

Duke lifted his head. "My dear comrades, running is not the answer," he said.

"Then what is, your lordship?" asked Champ sarcastically.

"Look, Champ, he is one of us now; he is in the same boat. You should apologize for that comment," snapped an angry Lightning, taking a swipe at Champ.

"You mean he is in the same field, not boat," joked Champ.

"Champ, can we stop the jokes and focus on the task ahead? Duke is trying to help," said Lightning.

Duke shook his head. He looked at Champ then Lightning and said, "Don't worry, my dear, I'm —"

"I'm sorry, Duke," interrupted Champ, sounding like he genuinely meant it.

Duke smiled at him and then they all smiled at each other, and for a moment they had forgotten all about their dilemma.

A few minutes later a jubilant Duke yelled, "I've got it."

"Well you didn't get it off me," joked Nelly.

Duke stood up, feeling very pleased with himself. Lightning stood up too and gave Duke a warm smile, and along with Nelly and Champ she waited to hear Duke's idea.

The noble steed paced about for a couple of minutes before clearing his throat and turning to his now impatient friends. "As I see it, the only option we have got left is to help the Tankards."

Nelly screwed up her face in confusion as she yelled, "What do you mean help them? Help them do what?"

"Simple, Madam, we help them by doing a good deed for them; prove our worth. It's easy when one puts their mind to it, what," Duke chirped, quite happy with himself.

Lightning was very pleased. "What a brilliant idea. You are quite cool, do you know that?" she said.

"Why, thank you, Madam; it just comes naturally." Duke smiled.

Nelly was still confused. Champ jumped up. "It sounds fine, but do *what* exactly? What good deed?"

Lightning's happy expression dropped and Duke shook his head. "Someone always has to spoil it," he moaned.

Lightning was now becoming less convinced about Duke's plan. "You're right, they do, but it is a good question though, Duke."

Nelly swallowed some hay and mumbled, "Aye, and, chomp-chomp-chomp, where's the answer, Dukey ode boy?"

Duke looked at his puzzled friends. "Well, it is up to us to think of something; and, Madam, do you have to eat like that? It is positively common one would say; chew, girl, chew. Goodnight," Duke snapped, fed up of Nelly's rudeness and negativity. He then went to settle himself down to sleep.

The others bedded down for the night, thinking of a plan, and all was still on this quiet night. In fact, the only noise that could be heard was Mr Rabbit's moaning and groaning and the continuous banging as he repaired his roof.

*

When the morning arrived, Duke and Lightning woke up both thinking of a plan. Their thoughts were quickly disturbed, however, by Nelly and Champ, who were already putting their help the Tankards plan (or as Nelly called it: 'stop us becoming dog food plan') into action. Duke and Lightning trotted over to the bewildered Rabbit and Hedgehog families who were glued to the spot watching the morning's activities.

"No, no, Nelly, that piece over there!" shouted Champ.

"Sorry, me ode mucker, here ya are," Nelly replied as she pushed the wood to Champ using her front hooves; Champ then knocked it into place with a good, hard blow of his powerful hind legs. Together they had started building a pile of wood into a shed.

Lightning looked at Mrs Rabbit, who just shrugged her shoulders. "Morning, Mr Rabbit, what on earth are those two rascals up to?" asked Lightning.

"Beats me; it's a pity Champ wasn't feeling this handy yesterday," Mr Rabbit groaned, still mad from having his house rearranged.

The rabbits and the hedgehogs laughed. Duke and Lightning looked at each other in confusion before Duke trotted up to the would-be carpenters. "I say, what on earth are you doing? Are you going mad?" he snapped.

Nelly spun round. "At least we're doing summat, hey, Champ?" she snapped back.

"Aye, all your bright ideas and it's me and Nell doing all the work," Champ replied.

"But, my dears, you don't understand," said Duke.

"Oh, we understand all right, you're bone idle," stormed Nelly.

Lightning strode up to try to give Duke some backup; plus, the constant laughing and barracking of the rabbits and hedgehogs was driving her mad. "Nelly, Champ, will you please listen to what Duke is trying to say?" snapped Lightning.

"Oh, we might have known you'd take your precious Dukey Wukey's side; why don't you just get married?" heckled Champ in his sarcastic tone.

Duke and Lightning's eyes met and they exchanged warm smiles. At that moment in time, Duke felt like he wouldn't want to be anywhere else in the universe apart from stood with

Lightning. If he had a choice of becoming the Queen's lead horse again or to be stood in a field with Lightning; the latter would win hands down. Unbeknownst to Duke, Lightning's thoughts echoed his as she stared at him, wishing she would never be apart from him.

Duke coughed and, straightening his shoulders, he snapped out of his daydream of him and Lightning cuddled up in their cosy barn for two. He caught sight of everyone coldly staring at him for his response and said, "Enough of that. Now listen, you can't build that because —"

"Because of what, my dear Duke?" interrupted Champ rudely.

Duke was about to speak again when Mr Rabbit went past on his way to the Tankards'. "I don't know why you two are bothering with that," he said, giggling.

"Why's that, Mr Rabbit? Have you got some better wood?" asked Champ.

"No…Farmer Tankard knocked it down last week; it's gonna be firewood, toodle-loo." Laughing to himself, Mr Rabbit set off on his merry way.

Duke was relieved. "Thank you, Mr Rabbit, stifling good show," he yelled after him.

Nelly and Champ were seething. Champ was just about to take part in another Grand National, to deal with his disappointment, when he caught the dead eye from Mrs Rabbit. She watched him scrape his left hoof along the ground, his bushy tail going like windscreen wipers, and he blew a mist of air from his snout. All traits of Champ's racing technique, familiar to Mrs Rabbit.

"Thanks for telling us! And any road where were me and Champ when he knocked it down?" stormed Nelly.

"Don't come that, what do you think we were trying to do? And I think you were in the barn with the vets," replied Lightning.

Feeling very low, the four horses walked slowly to the water trough, desperately thinking of a plan B. As they were drinking Champ snapped out of his low ebb. "Hang on a minute, we've already done him a good deed, but he soon forgot about that," yelled an excited Champ.

Duke rushed up to Champ, "When? I cannot remember."

"Oh, it was before you came here; remember, Nell?" Champ chirped.

Nelly and Lightning stood thinking. "Ah yeah, I remember, ode Mr Lastpenny, ha-ha, it was a good laugh that was," said Nelly with a grin and Lightning chortled.

"Mr Lastpenny, what are you going on about, man?" asked a confused Duke.

"Well, what it was, Farmer Tankard had fallen behind on his taxes so Mr Lastpenny (the taxman) came out to put the squeeze on him. Farmer Tankard then led him up to our field and ran away shouting that he'd treat us if we ate the taxman, ha-ha," laughed Champ.

Duke, who was totally astonished, murmured, "Y-you did-didn't eat him d-did you?"

"No, he wouldn't let us; people are miserable like that, ain't they? Mind ya, he shot out of here like his rear end were on fire, ha-ha," bellowed Nelly.

"Aye, he'd have made a good horse; he cleared two hedges without even touching the ground," snorted Champ with Nelly and Lightning laughing alongside him.

"Mind ya, it was the rabbit and hedgehog youngsters that I felt sorry for; they was upset," said Nelly.

"Why was that?" asked Duke. "Did they think the taxman was going to close down Tankard Meadow?"

"Hey? No. They was really looking forward to seein' Mr Last-penny get eaten," said Nelly with a grin.

Duke opened his mouth, gulped and shook his head. "So did Farmer Tankard treat you for getting rid of the cad?"

"No, did he 'eck as like," snarled Nelly.

"Yeah, that's what we mean, we're wasting our time," intervened Champ, feeling gutted again.

A couple of hours later, after taking it in turns trudging up to the fly-ridden water trough for a sip of water, Nelly and Champ were still feeling sorry for themselves, but Duke was determined not to give up so he and Lightning had started putting together a plan B. As he thought hard, Duke stood as still as a concrete block, the only movement was his tail swishing from side to side as he stared at the empty field next to them, which also belonged to Farmer Tankard. All of a sudden, his ears pricked up and he smiled to himself as he noticed all of the scrap wood and a couple of scrap cars in the corner of their own field. He remembered that he once heard the farmer saying to his son that they would have to clear the rubbish onto another field. Duke grinned because he believed that he had finally cracked plan B.

"Come on, my dear Lightning; I, Duke, have saved us, what. Get Nelly and Champ," he ordered, unable to stop grinning.

"What's the plan then, Duke?" asked Champ, slowly walking towards them after having another sip of water from the dirty trough.

"Simple, my dear fellow, we move all the rubbish onto the unused field; it would save the Tankards from doing it. That bounder, Mr Rabbit, said he heard the Tankards saying they needed it for some other use," he replied.

Smiling, they all went to work, dragging all the rubbish onto the next field through the two missing panels of fencing (another job waiting to be done by Farmer Tankard). Mrs Rabbit and Mrs Hedgehog were dumbfounded, but their youngsters were getting in on the act and giving the horses a hand.

Mrs Hedgehog and Mrs Rabbit stood next to each other and watched Plan B in action. "Lovely day; how are you, Mrs Rabbit — Spike Junior, watch what you are doing with that hammer — sorry, love."

"It's all right, love; kids, eh? I'm okay thanks, ooh sorry — Felicity Rabbit put down that saw this instant."

Mrs Hedgehog put her spiky head in her hands as Spike Junior and Champ attempted to pull some wood apart. "What are those donkeys doing anyway, Mrs Rabbit?"

Mrs Rabbit was standing, cross faced, with hands on hips as all of her twenty-three youngsters were banging and pulling at the scrap to help the horses move it all. "Well, Lord Snooty — Duke — thinks if they clear up the field they'll not end up, well, chopped up so to speak."

"Oh, they do get some ideas — I'm gonna throttle our Spike if he don't put down that ruddy hammer."

Mrs Rabbit nodded her head in agreement. "Like I say, kids. Anyway, how are you coping these days, Mrs Hedgehog?"

"Oh, not bad, Mrs Rabbit, and you?"

"All right, thanks," she replied. "Mind you, I bet you're still a bit lonely without Mr Hedgehog aren't you?"

"Yes I am a bit, you know for the kids' sakes as well; but how many times did I tell him not to mess around in the road?" Mrs Hedgehog replied.

"What did happen exactly?" Mrs Rabbit asked.

"He was in the middle of the road chasing a bug when he got one of them four by fours stuck up him," was Mrs Hedgehog's reply.

"Ooh, I bet that hurt; I am sorry, love."

"Oh, don't be, he was a pain anyway. Ah, talking of husbands, here comes yours," chortled Mrs Hedgehog; and sure enough Mr Rabbit was coming over the hill, constantly looking at the activities being caused by Duke and company.

He approached his wife and Mrs Hedgehog. "What are those lot up to?" he asked, pointing at the horses and the children.

Mrs Rabbit gave him a blank look. "Oh, hello, dear, how's your day been? I love you too," she snapped sarcastically.

"Are you going barmy, woman? What are they up to?" snapped Mr Rabbit.

"Oh, they think by moving the rubbish to the next field they'll be in Farmer Tankard's good books and they won't end up in a beef burger," replied a cross looking Mrs Rabbit.

"Oh, do they now?" he said, shaking his head as he set off towards them.

"Ah, good afternoon, my dear Mr Rabbit; a bit of brain power, that is all it takes, what? Duke greeted him with a broad grin.

"Is that so?" replied Mr Rabbit, smirking and scratching his right ear.

Champ stopped pushing one of the old cars to take a breather, "How's life at the farm, Mr Rabbit?"

"Oh, it seems all right; they are going out drinking tonight."

They all looked at each other astounded. "Ya joking? That boring lot going out drinking and partying? That'll be a good night," joked Nelly.

"Aye, they must be flush. What have they done? Won the lottery?" asked a grinning Champ, just as he was about to start pushing the car again.

"No, they've sold this field to Farmer Giles to grow crops in," Mr Rabbit answered in a loud tone, grinning.

"What?" screamed Lightning.

Duke slumped on the ground, looked at the others and mumbled, "Well, as some grumpy humans would say: I don't believe it."

*

Later on, once all the rubbish had been put back again, the horses were stood grazing behind a very tall hedge at the top of the field when Farmer Tankard and his son went strolling by. "But, Dad, are you sure that's the only option left?"

"I'm afraid so, son; I'm getting rid of all the fields."

"Well, just hire a field to put them in then, Dad."

"Don't be daft, what a waste of money. They're old, son — no, I'm sorry, they'll be slaughtered for meat." And the farmer and his son carried on up the path, leaving the horses standing there absolutely speechless.

Later that night, the moon had started to replace the sun and the Tankards had gone out looking quite smart. Duke, Champ and Lightning could be found lying down on some dirty, smelly hay; Nelly had just come back from a slow canter around the field and was now stood over her comrades.

"Well, that's that then. I told you — gratitude," moaned Champ.

"Oh, it's horrible," said Lightning.

"Will it be quick? Ya know, the chop?" asked Nelly, looking for reassurance.

"Do not think like that, Madam, I'm sure things will work out just fine," murmured an unsure Duke.

All their minds drifted as they found themselves reminiscing about their pasts. Champ thought about how he would love to be gracing Aintree again; he pictured himself in the winner's enclosure with the flashing of the cameras, everyone cheering his name and his owner constantly patting him in praise. Nelly imagined the treats she would get from pulling her heavy cart full of scrap — carrots and potatoes and at least twice a week her favourite — chocolate. Lightning pictured the happy faces of the children as they watched her performing her tricks. The one she had loved to do best was standing on her hind legs while she swung a hula hoop around her neck; the kids had loved it. Finally, Duke could see the Queen in her carriage with himself proudly at the forefront, his chest sticking out with pride, as the public looked on in awe.

Their happy thoughts were once again smashed though as Mr Rabbit came tearing up to them. "Quick, come on," he yelled.

"What on earth is the matter, man?" asked Duke.

Mr Rabbit was bent over trying to get his breath back. "Ooh — gasp — bur-burglars at the Tankards' — come on," he shouted.

Duke, Nelly and Lightning all jumped up, but Champ didn't budge. "Come on, my dear fellow," yelled Duke looking across at Champ.

"Are you mad? Have you got sieves for brains? We're gonna be turned into the kebab house menu and you wanna help 'em?" snapped Champ.

"Enough of that; get in line," ordered Duke.

"I will not — never," replied Champ.

"Very well, come on troops, keep it tight at the rear," yelled Duke as he gave Champ a hardened stare; he was not used to his fellow horses back at Buckingham palace disobeying his orders. He thought Champ should be court-martialled or even beheaded.

"Ya joking, have ya seen my rear?" chortled Nelly.

"That'll do; silence in the ranks," Duke ordered and with Nelly and Lightning and Mr Rabbit in tow he made his way to the Tankards'.

It took the horses a good five minutes before they arrived at the Tankards' and sure enough there were burglars: one in a van parked outside the front gate and another two who were just entering the house.

"Have we got a plan then, Duke?" asked Mr Rabbit.

Nelly was getting nervous. "What's that smell?" asked Lightning, sniffing the air. Nelly smirked. "Nelly, really?"

"Sorry, I'm scared."

It was at this point that Duke came into his element and demonstrated why he was once one of the palace's finest. "Steady, let's have some discipline. Right, here is the plan."

*

Meanwhile, in the Tankard house, the burglars were ransacking the place, looking for whatever they could get their hands on.

"Come on, George, get a move on; it's not a picnic, ya know."

"That's a shame, Bert; I'm starving."

It was at that moment that they stumbled upon the Tankards' safe. Bert's eyes lit up and a sly grin spread all over his thin, weasely face. "Hah, hah, bingo, hey, George, my boy?"

"No, I don't fancy bingo tonight, Bert."

"Shut up, ya buffoon; here, hold this," Bert raged as he passed George the crowbar.

Back outside, Harry the driver, who was supposed to be keeping watch, had put down his paper after rereading the same articles several times; he was getting bored of waiting. Slowly, he reached for his double barrel shotgun and he rubbed his rumbling belly as he took careful aim at his supper, which just so happened to be in the form of Mr Rabbit. Harry was just about to pull the trigger when Mr Rabbit toddled off. Silently, Harry followed him around the corner, annoyed that he had to get out of the warm van, but his hunger was stronger than his annoyance and he slowly crept after Mr Rabbit, forgetting all about his role as the getaway driver.

As soon as they got him out of the way, Duke fastened the van to Nelly. It was a small, battered, old, Renault van, which was no problem for Nelly; it bought back happy memories of her dragging around her old cart on her rag and bone rounds. So, excited, she set off and soon pulled it out of sight.

Around the corner, Harry was quietly easing up his gun. He was about twenty feet away from Mr Rabbit, whom he now had firmly in his sights. He was rubbing his index finger over the trigger when he felt a puff of air on the side of his face. He turned to see a grinning Lightning. "Hello, gorgeous."

"Aaaaaaaaaah," yelled Harry as he chucked his gun in the air; his instincts told him to run, which he did; stopping dead as he knocked himself out cold, thanks to the stone wall.

A couple of minutes later, after the horses had pushed the van out of sight, Bert and George came out of the house with a bag of goodies. They stopped, looking dumbstruck.

"What the —? Where's the van?" groaned a puzzled Bert.

"Has Harry gone to the bingo, Bert?" asked George with a grin.

Bert, who was getting annoyed with the whole situation, swung the crowbar around in the air before bringing it down on George's head, flooring him in seconds.

"George, ya ain't got time to lounge about; you go that way and I'll go down here," growled Bert, sticking his size eight boots into George's ribcage.

Bert set off; a few minutes later George remembered who and where he was and set off on his route.

"Harry, for God's sake, stop horsing around," yelled Bert at Harry who was still out cold, slumped against the wall.

At that moment, Lightning appeared in front of George, balancing on an old, tin barrel to get his attention. Bert turned and saw her too. With both men watching Lightning it enabled the others to try to catch the burglars. "You know the plan — charge!" Duke yelled.

George smiled and fainted; Bert tried to run but Nelly walked out in front of him. "Boo," she yelled.

"Aaaaahh — help," screamed Bert as he dodged around her and headed down a pathway in-between the Tankards' house and one of the barns, which was too narrow for the horses.

"Quick, the cad's getting away," shouted Duke.

Bert turned, blowing raspberries at the horses, but as he did so he watched Champ appear from nowhere, jumping one of the biggest walls he had ever seen. Champ was ecstatic as it took him back to the time he cleared Becher's Brook and won the National in record time. "Aaaaah, help me," yelled Bert as Champ knocked him flying into the pigpen.

Bert, half dazed, looked up. "Here, do you mind? You're in my supper, mucker," blurted one of the pigs, Bert smiled and fainted.

"Hooray," they all shouted.

"Well done, my dear comrades, we showed them. What a jolly good show," shouted a triumphant Duke.

*

Later, the police arrested the would-be burglars and the Tankards and the police congratulated the horses for playing their part in catching the crooks; they all received a friendly pat from Farmer Tankard. Our heroes watched and smirked as the police shoved the burglars into the van.

"I'm telling ya, Constable, them horses can talk," screamed Bert, pointing at the horses.

The constable shook his head at Bert. "And I suppose the next thing you'll be telling me is that the pigs can talk too," snapped the constable looking over at the pigs.

Bert, shaking his head, looked at him, astonished. "You don't believe me, do you?" Bert said.

The constable looked Bert up and down and replied, "Whatever gave you that idea? Get in, you buffoon," yelled the constable as he shoved Bert in the van.

Farmer Tankard shook hands with the officer in charge as Farmer Tankard's son began to lead the horses back to the field. "Thank you, officer."

"It's not me you should be thanking, Sir, it's your horses; I don't know how they did it, but they sure did. Talking horses — ha, that's a good one — goodnight, Sir." The police left and Farmer Tankard went to check that the farm was secure.

*

A good hour after the attempted burglary, the horses were back in the field, cuddled up together and feeling very pleased with themselves.

"Well, that should do it. I'm so tired, but I just can't sleep; I'm much too excited," said Lightning, smiling. The others laughed

"I must say, Champ, when you jumped that wall...spiffing good show, what."

Champ smiled at Duke. "We couldn't have done it without you leading us, Duke, and I bet that felt good, Nell, pulling the van. Was it heavy?"

Nelly blew a big ball of mist out as her cough started again. "Wheeze — ooh dear — no I have pulled a lot harder; like the one I had to drag up Primrose Hill once. I had to have new horse shoes put on, me ode 'tator."

The horses laughed and continued talking about their adventure long into the night.

*

Morning soon came and the horses were up and about, still excited from the previous night's events.

"Morning, Mrs Rabbit, where is Mr Rabbit? I didn't see him coming back last night."

"Morning, Champ; after he helped you lot with the burglars he went back to see what food he could scrounge from the Tankards and ran smack bang into Shep their dog. I've never seen him run so fast, ha ha," Mrs Rabbit chortled.

"Oh dear, he's all right, isn't he, Mrs Rabbit?" asked a concerned Lightning.

Mrs Rabbit dusted down her carpet, which was now looking a bit worse for wear; Mr Rabbit had got it from the Tankards' outside toilet as a present for her a few months back. "What? Oh him, yes dear, he's in bed, getting his strength back," she replied. Lightning smiled and trotted off.

Duke was standing behind the top hedge of the field when Farmer Tankard and his son were making their way back from their morning rounds.

"There they are, Dad, our heroes, eh?" said Farmer Tankards' son, batting a fly off his neck.

"Aye, the only talking horses in the world, hey?" Farmer Tankard and his son laughed.

Duke turned and winked at the others who had trotted up to join him.

Farmer Tankard and his son straightened themselves up and smiled at the horses. "Yes, well done you rascals, you certainly saved the day," Farmer Tankard said with a smile.

"Yes, well done; right, what were you saying on the way down, Dad?" They started to slowly walk away.

"What? Oh, I said we'll take them to be slaughtered in the morning." And they disappeared around the corner.

Nelly and Lightning gazed at each other and started to cry. Champ kicked the hedge, bringing down a branch that just missed Lightning and showering the others with leaves. Duke just stared into thin air, while Nelly licked her chops and started to eat the leaves. Champ yelled, "I told you, that's the reward you get." Duke very slowly trotted off with his head bowed low.

*

After a sleepless night, which was not helped by Mr Rabbit's constant ribbing about them becoming the next batch of cat meat, the sun started to rise.

The horses, who had nothing to say to each other, were drinking water when their aching minds were disturbed by Mr Rabbit jumping up and down on the fence yelling, "They're coming, they're coming."

The horses were plucking up the courage to say their goodbyes when Farmer Tankard leaned over the gate. "Morning, my burglar alarms, ha ha. Come on, son," he shouted and they left for the next field, leaving the horses feeling confused.

"What is going on? There's nothing like keeping you in suspense," moaned Champ.

Duke gave him a stern look because even though he was shocked, he always tried to maintain discipline. "Silence in the ranks."

A few minutes later Farmer Tankard and his son made their way back toward the farm with their stock of old cows. "It's a shame to have to slaughter them, Dad."

"Aye, but I'm afraid that's life; come on, mush," Farmer Tankard replied.

Two of the cows, Jenny and Daisy, who were at the back, looked at each other. "Well, it looks like goodnight Vienna for us, hey Daisy?"

"Aye, mind ya, I am glad, Jenny, me rheumatism's killing me."

"Oh, I don't know, Daisy, them slaughterhouses are no houses of fun, you know."

"Ya what? Ya joking, ain't ya? I've been told some of them butchers are right darlings," replied Daisy.

"What? Well what are we waiting for? Make way for a couple of big 'uns," chortled Jenny and off they trudged.

Nelly and Lightning shared a tender moment as they brushed their heads together while Champ ran jubilantly around the field, happier than he had felt for a long while, but Duke looked over at the smirking Mr Rabbit. "You bounder, you knew all along! That was a bit below the saddle that was, what," he moaned.

Mrs Rabbit came marching over, swinging her rolling pin around. Even though she loved her husband she never liked it when he wound up the horses. "You coward, you will run, come here," she yelled as she took a swing at Mr Rabbit, who had the good sense to run.

Later on, Farmer Tankard and his son entered the field with some treats for the horses; there were carrots, other vegetables and some chocolate. "Here you are, my lovelies," said the son as he took a bite out of some of the chocolate, for which he received a dirty look from Nelly.

"Aye, and if this is not enough, tomorrow afternoon you're all going to a new destination; and don't worry, you're all being kept together," said Farmer Tankard as he patted Duke on the back.

*

Another day soon arrived and after a good breakfast the happy horses went to say their goodbyes. The Rabbit and Hedgehog youngsters kissed and waved at them, while Mrs Rabbit and Mrs Hedgehog were trying to hold back the tears.

"Goo-goodbye, my dears, we'll miss you," snivelled Mrs Rabbit. This started Nelly off crying.

Champ had all of the youngsters on his back, stroking his mane and patting him, apart from Spike Junior, who was sat on his neck, revving Champ's ears, pretending he was on one of those motorbike things that had nearly ran him over once.

"Oh please don't cry; we will miss you too," sniffed Lightning.

"Yes, goodbye, ladies," said Duke, smiling.

Mr Rabbit cautiously approached Duke. "Goodbye, Duke, I'm sorry about yesterday; I hope I'm forgiven?" he said with his sad eyes flickering at Duke.

"Goodbye, Mr Rabbit — of course you are forgiven, man. Oh, and by the way, someone wants to see you."

Mr Rabbit gulped and slowly turned around, rubbing his ears nervously, to see Shep standing glaring at him. Shep's white, sharp teeth were shining and saliva was oozing out of his growling mouth. "Aaaaaahhh — you rotter," yelled Mr Rabbit at the chuckling Duke as he set off with Shep in tow. It was the funniest thing the youngsters had ever seen.

"Here, ain't you going to help him, Mrs Rabbit?" asked a concerned Mrs Hedgehog.

"What him? No, I'm not; I'm going to have some peace and quiet." And they both joined in with the laughter of the horses and their youngsters.

Not long after the laughter died down, Farmer Tankard and his son came for the horses and, with tears in their eyes, they left. As the horses slowly trotted off they all turned to look at the field that had been their home, which helped dry their tears as some good memories came flooding back to them.

*

A couple of weeks later, Farmer Tankard and his family arrived at the town's gala and settled themselves into their seats. They had arrived just in time to see the beautiful Lightning performing her greatest tricks, while elsewhere at the gala you could ride on Champ on the pretend Aintree race track for fifty pence. Around the corner was Nelly, who was taking families on cart rides, getting the odd carrot as a reward; and there, leading the parade, was

Duke, making sure everything was running smoothly and casting the occasional glance at Lightning, his new girlfriend.

However, the town's people weren't the only ones who were enjoying the show, because hidden safely in the hedge bottoms were the rabbits and the hedgehogs. Mrs Hedgehog had just finished lecturing her new man, Needles, about the dangers of the road, and beside him was Mr Rabbit who was covered in plasters and on crutches looking very cross.

All of the animals and the Tankards smiled at the horses, who were all feeling proud and very happy, but more importantly together as one family.

Stand Together

We were now on our fifteenth day of being stuck on top of this goddam hill in North Korea. I'm Benny Dukes and I am a member of different regiments known as scatterings, which is what our lieutenant has named us. Brigade would probably be the more correct term as we have French, English, Dutch and a host of others from Europe all representing the United Nations in this conflict. Yes, I never thought I would become close to a French man, but we were all together as one now; we no longer belonged to our proper regiments. My unit got ambushed a couple of weeks back. Yes, Sir, all split up from our own units owed to this blasted war.

We have taken siege of this hill and held it against all the odds. It is important for the outcome of the war, apparently; we must keep it from the Japs. I say Japs — which probably isn't the right name as they're technically Korean — but we call them Japs because they all look the same to us, and it's easier to say. We are supposed to hold the hill until the Yanks come, which was supposed to be today, but then again, that is what we were told yesterday.

"Here they come again, Lieutenant," yelled a soldier. A chorus of sighs and moans went around as we wearily geared ourselves up for yet another battle. The sun had barely started to come up.

"Right, take positions and hold till I say," was the lieutenant's reply.

We all rushed to our positions, soldiers everywhere; fear in our tired eyes.

The Japs were once again coming up in their hundreds; most with sticks, knives, and a rifle between every ten, and you could guarantee that they'd fight to their last man.

Shots were fired. "Hold your fire; hold your fire," the lieutenant screamed.

I looked over my left shoulder to see the sweaty, white face of Fuzzy, who had turned twenty this very morning. I winked and gave him a reassuring smile.

"Attack, attack," followed by, "Fire, fire," was yelled.

The battle seemed to last for ages. Gun shots, blood curdling yells and agonizing deaths could be heard all around, but all my sore, bloodshot eyes could see were dead bodies and tired, frightened faces. From what I could tell, just like the previous fourteen days, we were managing to hold the hill. Then, from within this tense, bloodthirsty battle, I heard a scream and I looked round to see the lieutenant on the floor. His leg had been wounded; shot in the right thigh. I rushed towards him and a Jap charged at me; with one thrust of my bayonet he fell to the ground.

Explosions, gunfire and screams filled the misty air. I shot a Jap; he fell to the ground with half his head gone.

I got to the lieutenant, he looked up at me. "L-leave me, man."

"Quiet, Sir." I flung him over my shoulder and made my way back up the hill, dropping two more of the enemy.

At the base, the medic, Aart Houben — Dutch — took care of the lieutenant and I went back to my position at the front of the trench. My legs were getting really heavy as I tried to manoeuvre in the thick, slippy mud with the added weight of my backpack and equipment. My uniform felt as heavy as a coat of metal with all the sweat and mud that clung to it. I pulled myself together and turned around and looked out over the chaos of the battlefield: overturned tanks, dead soldiers of all nationalities, craters in the ground from bombs dropped, the whole area covered in a thick smoke from all the fire power.

As I looked a few feet in front of me there was a young soldier who had met his gruesome death. But, as my eyes fixed firmly on this unfortunate soul, my heart skipped a beat for there, on his back, was Fuzzy with a rusty blade stuck firm in his throat. I was overpowered with anger. "Fuzzy — no." I charged at two Japs; I shot the first and then ran out of ammo so I brought my heavy bayonet blade down on the other, splitting his head like a melon.

It seemed to me that the Japs were slowly retreating, and on that fifteenth day, the hill would be ours.

All of a sudden, the hill was overwhelmed by a deafening noise; helicopters, jeeps and plenty of Yanks (twice our number) appeared as if from nowhere. I rushed down to their corporal. "About time, where have you lot been?" I shouted.

"It's Corporal Zimmer to you, and relax, England, the best are here now so go home; we don't need you."

I was furious; the arrogance of these guys. It was as if the long hours, blood, sweat and deaths of our comrades in trying to keep this hill had all meant nothing. I just wanted to go home and let them have this goddam hill and all the pain that came with it.

My anger kept on building up inside of me, but at that moment our lieutenant limped up to us, he was heavily patched up, but he otherwise looked OK. "Good, 'cos I wouldn't help you if you were the last Yank of all time, which wouldn't necessarily be a bad thing," I shouted. We squared up to each other but a couple of soldiers pulled us apart. Zimmer was about six foot three and quite thick set, whereas I was five foot seven and possessed a smaller frame than him. But that didn't deter me; I still wanted to tear him in two.

"Right, men, in position; march," yelled the patched up lieutenant, supported on a crutch made from a tree branch.

"Yeah, leave it to the experts," shouted a grinning American soldier; Matthews his name, according to the badge on his uniform.

We couldn't believe the Yanks' arrogance; they arrived in all the top gear and we had to march off on foot. And march we did, stopping only to have five minute breaks, which were very welcome after first marching through thick mud and then sharp, hard, rocky ground. Our trek was made harder still by the heavy burden of helping the wounded: men that were on crutches or had their eyes and faces bandaged up. And now, with the falling rain beating down on us, we wished they were hour breaks instead.

As I marched I was thinking about Fuzzy; how it was his birthday today and how he was looking forward to seeing his wife and kid. I thought about myself and how at one point I wouldn't hurt a flea. I can remember being so shy and saying to myself that I would probably hide at every opportunity instead of fight. Then I saw my best friend get chopped in half by these monsters and with the anger that overwhelmed me I killed my first, shooting him straight between the eyes. After that I had wanted more, wanted to kill every last damn one of 'em. And here I am now, having done more courageous acts than I can count; like the time when I attacked about twenty Japs on my own to rescue an officer who was a POW. How glad I now was to let them Yanks have that hill and hopefully to be going home. I have done my bit for my country and seen far too much needless death. I couldn't wait to hold my wife and son again.

We were all very tired; we must have marched close to ten miles when we were ordered to stop because someone was trying to get through on the radio.

"This is Bluebird Five Zero, repeat again, Yankee Ten, repeat again," said Ginny, our radio operator. There were cackling noises and faint screams coming from the radio.

"Try again, keep trying; rest, men," ordered the lieutenant.

"I repeat, this is Bluebird Five Zero, state your situation, over." The radio crackled and fizzed, then...

"Come in, Bluebird Five Zero; come in, Bluebird Five Zero."

"This is Bluebird Five Zero here; what's your situation? Over."

"Bluebird Five Zero, this is command; Yankee Ten have lost the hill. I repeat, Yankee Ten have lost the hill. You must return and take back the hill; we'll get help to you as soon as we can, over and out."

I slumped to the ground, the lieutenant shook his bloodstained head and the look of horror on the men's faces was something I would never forget.

"Right, men, about turn, quick march," the lieutenant ordered wearily.

*

The next morning we reached the hill. We sneaked through the smoke filled woodland to see that they were still fighting but the Japs were in control.

"Good luck, men, get me that hill. Charge," yelled the lieutenant and in we went.

The fighting, as normal, was intense. Grenades and gunfire echoed around the hill, bodies littered the landscape. A Yank was buried deep in the undergrowth, lodged in like a tick on an animal; he was picking Japs off one by one with his rifle. He shot one in the head, another in the back and was just about to shoot another when a grenade landed on him, decorating the trees and landscape with his body parts.

A good hour had passed and we were getting closer to the top of the hill. We had made good time considering it was steep and caked with mud. I charged and with my bayonet, gun, gun butt and bare hands I killed what seemed like hundreds, and then, in front of me, I heard a moan. "H-help, Eng- England, help me." There, badly wounded with a blade in his right leg and fingers missing from his right hand, was the Yank, Corporal Zimmer. My first instinct was to leave him, but it hit me that, no matter what I thought of him personally, just like Fuzzy he could have a wife and kid and they didn't deserve to be without him. So I picked him up and made my way to a medic.

"Medic, medic, sort him out," I shouted to Aart.

Zimmer's eyes met mine. "Thanks, Eng-ahh, England." I nodded and made my way to find the lieutenant.

The noise of the battle was deafening with the cries of pain and screams as men met their untimely deaths; the sound of grenades and mortar shells filled the air and bullets cracked out of all sorts of guns. My focus came back to me as one Jap tried to jump me, but he met his death on the end of my bayonet. Then I heard the lieutenant's voice, "Aaah, Benny, help." I ran, but it was too late, a Jap had stuck his knife into the lieutenant's chest. I ran, pressing my trigger, to find I was out of bullets. The Jap charged at me with a sly smile on his face, which I had the pleasure of wiping off as I clubbed him to death with the butt of my rifle.

"Lieutenant, Lieutenant."

"Listen, Ben-Benny, you must take the hill." The lieutenant's eyes rolled and he drew his last breath as I felt his body flop in my arms. Those were to be his last words. This hill, that I hated so much, had become my destiny; I loaded my gun and, with some of the scatterings, charged up the hill.

Nothing was going to stop me from taking back the hill; I'd do it for the lieutenant and my country. I knew how important the hill was and how important we were to command; plus, help was on its way.

I was helpless (our numbers were dwindling fast) as I watched another scattering meet his gruesome death. He was at the side of me and was shot in the head, some of his blood splattering my face. I charged at three of the enemy, slaying them all in seconds. I had the urge to take control because all of our leaders had either fallen or were nowhere to be seen, and I wanted so badly to take this damn hill.

"Come on, men, we're nearly there," I yelled.

Near the top of the hill I saw a medic. I went to him and I tapped him on his back; he fell back, his eyes wide open, with a machete firmly lodged in his skull.

"Eng-England." I looked down. There was the arrogant Yank soldier Matthews. Surely I couldn't take this injured soldier with me, I hated those guys, but I also knew I couldn't leave him. I draped him over my shoulder and dragged him with me, still managing to fight; I dropped the Yank near the top of the hill, hiding him behind a thick tree.

With one last surge, I jumped over the barricade, followed by some of the men. I clubbed a Jap of about sixteen to his death, with no sorrow. Then their leader attacked me, burying his blade in my arm. "Aaah, you'll not take me," I screamed. With my uninjured arm I punched him, but I fell back and he jumped above me with an empty gun which had a bayonet fixed to it. I was doomed.

A shot was fired; the Jap fell to the ground with blood pouring out of his head. I looked up to see the arrogant Yank Matthews on his knees with a gun in his hand. He fell to the ground but soon showed signs of life when he tried to crawl to safety.

A chorus of 'Hoorah' echoed around the woods; we had taken back the hill, we knew command would send help and soon we'd be gone.

Corporal Zimmer, who was seemingly OK, limped his way towards me. "Thanks, England, a job well done," he said with his uninjured hand held out, which I shook with my left hand as my injured right arm was still oozing blood. I nodded my head. Just then the radio fizzed and cackled.

"This is Bluebird Five Zero, over."

"Bluebird Five Zero, this is command. At this point in time we are unable to get help to you as we no longer need the hill. Our priorities have changed; we are going to give you some new coordinates, you will make your way there and take the target. Your coordinates are —"

Bang.

"Aah, what are you doing, man?" yelled the radio controller as I shot up the radio.

We all looked at each other wondering what to do. I turned to see a young, tired lad, name of Jacob Wiggins, pointing; his arm was shaking and his lip trembled.

He shook his head and yelled, "Japs, more Japs."

Look Mum I Can See

It had been an uneventful day in Blindasabatsville, which was very unusual for a private investigator such as meself. Bob Cheesecake's the name. Let me tell you how I got into this biz. I was out doing my hobby — trainspotting — and I was walking across the train tracks when a bolt of lightning hit me smack on the head. Ooh it did make me hop! I was running around in circles for ages. Before the accident I couldn't see very well at all (not even with me spectacles on) and now when I take them off and give me ears a little twiddle me eyes glow red and I have X-ray vision. I can also run fast and not just your everyday kind of fast — as fast as a train. I raced one the other day and beat it by a minute (it would have been two if I hadn't ran into that fence). I remember running round to me mother's shouting, "Look, Mum, I can see."

"That's nice, dear, but I'm your mum's neighbour Joyce."

It was at that moment that I said to meself I would use these skills in me quest to become a private investigator — that is if I ever got a case.

I was reading the local paper on a cold October day in 1946 when I found meself staring at the headline 'ANOTHER CORGI

STOLEN'. It made me wonder who would do such a thing and for what reason?

I leaned back in me chair and surveyed me tiny office. It was so small you couldn't swing a mouse around. I was just about to pick me nose when the phone rang. "Hello, Bob Cheesecake PI, how can I help you?"

"Listen, and listen good, my life's in danger; meet me at the lake at 10 p.m."

"Hello...hello?" Whoever it was had hung up. Work at last! Although I wasn't sure I liked the sound of it, but what with me curiosity driving me mad and with me being so skint I had no choice but to be there.

*

It was very cold and quite foggy at the lake so I took cover under the old oak tree. As it turned out I would later be glad of the fact that I had turned up early for this meeting at nine forty-five.

A tall man wearing a long tweed coat with the collar turned up and a trilby hat on his head slowly approached. He was constantly looking all around him. All of a sudden I noticed a drop in temperature and it became really cold. After a few moments I realized why — I'd forgotten to put on me trousers.

I was about to make me way towards him when I heard a noise in the bushes. I took off me spectacles, twiddled me ears and me eyes glowed at the bush. I couldn't believe what I saw sticking out of there; it was scarier than any woman I'd dated before and that was saying something. Someone's hairy behind was going up and down like a fiddler's elbow.

I couldn't get me eyes to stop glowing so I had to give meself a quick smack on me head before putting on me spectacles and making me way towards the man. *Whack. What a place to put a tree.* Me clumsiness startled the man in the tweed coat and he ran off. I cleared me head and *whoooshh* shot past him, stopping dead with the aid of a wall. "Ooh, Cheesecake, you idiot," I said.

"You're Cheesecake? Quick, come with me," said the man. He led me to his car: a 1942 two door Ford Coupé, black in colour with white tyres. It had a few visible bumps and scrapes, which was not surprising considering we had just come through the war. It took a couple of attempts to start the car and the man made sure to check all around him before getting in. He made no attempt to speak until we drove away.

"Why meet at the lake, Mr —?" I asked.

"I don't feel safe at my home at the moment," said the man.

"Why, what is happening, Mr —?"

"Sorry, it's Mr Iball, Ivan Iball, I'm a doctor — well an optician — and I've come up with a brilliant business plan but someone is trying to blackmail us...I-I mean me."

"For the business idea?"

"Yes, it is certain to succeed; I mean we all have eyes."

"Eyes, Sir?"

"Yes, the plan's for an eye clinic; like I said, we all have eyes."

"Yes, but mine are fine, Mr Iball."

"Well why are you talking to the dashboard then?"

"Yes, well...what is this secret then, Mr Iball? You know, the plan?"

"I beg your pardon, Mr Cheesecake, but it's a secret."

"Look, if you want me help I'm going to need your co-operation. Also where exactly are we going?"

"To my house; and the plan is *Two for the Price of One*." The plan didn't mean nothing to me.

I wish this guy would slow down; he must be pressing his foot through that floor board, I thought to meself as the car began veering from one side of the road to the other. I looked over at Mr Iball, who seemed very calm apart from the crazy smile etched across his face. I, on the other hand, hadn't sweated this much since I got married (mind ya, the divorce was a good knees up a few months later).

We arrived at his house (well mansion would be a better description; but with me living in a poky flat I would consider an air raid shelter to be a mansion by comparison). It had a long driveway which led up to a heavy wooden door, oak I would have said, and it had ivy running all the way up the side of the building. In the hallway there were paintings covering the green coloured walls; the most prominent of these being a painting of Winston Churchill which looked down on you as you walked in. I didn't fancy even making a guess at how many bedrooms it had.

Mr Iball showed me into the lounge while he went and made a pot of tea. Again this room was full of pictures and paintings, a large grandfather clock stood in the corner and there was a large wooden sideboard with a photograph of what I presumed to be Mr Iball's family perched on top of it. I started to have a look around and poked through a couple of drawers, but there was nothing of note. As I went over to a window, a big bay one at that, I had the urge to pick me nose — so I did so. Mr Iball chose that moment to come back into the room.

"Here you are, Cheesecake," he said, putting the tray on the table. While he wasn't looking I wiped me fingers on the most beautiful (and I bet most expensive) curtains I had ever seen.

"Thank you, Sir." I took a sip of me tea. "Ahhh, a lovely cup of tea. Now, who lives here Mr Iball?"

Mr Iball pointed towards the photograph, confirming that it was indeed his family. "Myself, my wife, Iris; my daughter, Betty; and m-my s-son, Matthew." *Interesting, why did he stutter when he mentioned his son?*

Soon afterwards he showed me some threatening letters that he had been receiving and I cast me eyes over them. They were all neatly written in blue ink and the sender was threatening to leak Mr Iball's business plan to his competitors if he didn't give the blackmailer everything he owned. I pondered and then pondered some more before realizing I didn't have a bloody clue.

"Mr Iball, Sir, you say you have been receiving these letters for how long?"

"Oh, about two months now, Cheesecake. They were just asking for money to begin with, but now they want everything I own or they will go to my competitors."

"Go to them with what, Sir?" Mr Iball paced around shaking his head. "Mr Iball, if you want me to help you have to tell me the lot.

"Okay, Cheesecake; as you know I am an optician and I have designed machines out of this world for eye testing. These persons or person have found out my ideas and are threatening to ruin me. These machines and treatments will be great for mankind and the plans must not get into the wrong hands. So will you help me; will you take the case, Cheesecake?"

I looked at the anxious Mr Iball. I was about to ram me finger up me nose but I thought better of it. "Okay, Mr Iball, I will take the case."

"That's great; so what happens now, Cheesecake?"

"I've got what I need for the time being so I'll be in touch." I was about to leave when his wife walked in; the look they gave each other told me that there was no love lost in this marriage. I was about to say hello but she avoided my gaze and ran up the stairs as if she was hiding something in her brown handbag.

I reached out to shake Mr Iball's hand. "Right, Sir, you'll be okay; I'll be here first thing in the morning."

"Thanks, but be sure to sort it quickly, won't you?"

I was on me way home (after having spent over half an hour wandering around outside Mr Iball's house looking for me car before realizing that I don't even own one) when I heard a scream. With a quick tweak of me ears me vision soon located where the screaming was coming from: a woman was outside her home crying and looked in shock. I shot past her and entered her living room and there on the wall was a splattered corgi dog; a note was pinned to it which read 'KEEP YOUR NOSE OUT'.

"Come and sit down, Mrs —?"

"Sorry, Miss Loveitt — Ida Loveitt."

"Has this happened before, Miss Loveitt? My name is Bob Cheesecake, I'm a PI."

"No, never."

"Is it your dog, Miss?"

"No, Mr Cheesecake, I have never seen it before."

"Okay, have you someone to comfort you, Miss Loveitt?"

"Well, sort of." *Hmm, what did she mean by sort of?* I stayed with her until the police arrived and then headed for home.

As I zoomed along looking at various things with me X-ray vision it made me realize that with the powers I possessed I could become a superhero. I just needed to learn how to stop — *ouch, what a place to park up a bus.*

I went back to Mr Iball's a day later, not first thing as I had promised though. Why, you ask? Because I forgot. As I arrived at the Iballs' home a girl came running out with Mr Iball running after her. The girl was sobbing as she ran past me down the drive. Mr Iball stopped at my feet, shaking his head. "Hello, Mr Iball, I —"

"Where have you been, man?"

"Sorry, Sir, what's going on; and who's that?"

"That's my daughter, Betty; she's going to her friend's. If you care to follow me I'll show you why she's screaming." We walked into the study and there on the wall was another splattered corgi.

There was a six-inch nail firmly embedded in it and I deduced that this was why it hadn't fallen off the wall. You don't get to be a private investigator just like that you know.

"Where are your wife and son, Sir? I mean, it's nearly half past ten at night." I made that deduction by looking at my watch.

"God only knows." From the tone of Mr Iball's voice I soon detected he hadn't a clue where they were. I looked out of the window pondering about his wife and his son, and then there was also the intriguing Ida Loveitt to think about. I had seen Ida and Mr Iball having a heated discussion outside the post office that morning and couldn't help wondering what it meant.

I had a quick look around the room, checking for signs of a break-in but I couldn't see any evidence of a forced entry. I then took a closer look at the corgi and after two minutes of examining it one thing I concluded was that it was definitely dead. "Ah, yes I thought as much," I exclaimed.

"What is it, a clue, Cheesecake? Have you solved it, man?"

"Hey no, Sir, this dog has fleas. Could I stay a while, Sir, to have a sniff around?"

"Yes, man, just sort it out, will you? It's driving me mad. Right, I'm off to bed; just watch where you're sniffing."

"Yes, Sir, thank you, Sir, and Sir —"

"What is it, Cheesecake?"

"Goodnight."

A while into the search of the house I tripped over a table, landed near the curtains and fell on top of a pen. I wondered, *have I found a clue or have I just found a pen?* Then, all of a sudden, the door flung open and in walked a young man who I recognized from the family photograph to be Matthew Iball. He was breathing heavily, his clothes were dirty and he was sweating. "Who-who are you?"

"Relax, Master Iball, Bob Cheesecake's the name. I'm a private investigator; your dad has asked me to look into the threatening letters he has been receiving. Can I ask you some questions? Where, for example, have you been tonight, Sir?"

"Out."

"Are you okay, Sir? You're sweating a lot; and where exactly is 'out', Sir?"

"James', my friend's house."

"And what have you been doing at James' house, Sir?"

"I beg your pardon but that's my business."

"Okay, Sir, calm down; you may go now, thank you." Matthew disappeared off to bed and after such a thorough investigation as that I decided to retire myself, so I made up a bed in the study.

*

I was awoken by the creak of a window opening. I looked at the big clock; it was 2.15 a.m. I sat very still and I heard someone whispering, it was a man's voice saying, "Come on, this way." I hid under a table and made a noise to startle them. I say 'them' as I could just about make out the silhouettes of two intruders; but the noise (which was an attempt at a cuckoo but sounded more like a strangled chicken) worked because they hurriedly left amongst panicked whispers. I stood up feeling quite pleased with meself and then it hit me, why didn't I see who it was and catch them? It was probably the letter writers. Well I am still learning this PI lark, you know.

I tweaked me ears as I made me way upstairs. I looked through the bedroom wall to see no Mr or Mrs Iball. I then left the house, stopping off at Miss Loveitt's. When I looked through her wall the whole thing started coming together. This super eyesight is a blessing — "Aaaahhh!" Fancy not putting the manhole cover back on.

In the morning, I made a quick diversion to Mary's, who was a breeder of corgi dogs. She was still upset as her favourite, Queenie (which I thought was a stupid name to associate with corgis), was still missing. I didn't have the heart to tell her Queenie was now a doormat. As I shot back out again I noticed a man bent over. I didn't recognize his face but there was something about him that I did recognize.

I stopped off for a drink at the *Goose And Fat* pub to gather me thoughts. I went to use their phone and rang Mr Iball at his work and told him to get all of his family together for seven o'clock that evening; I then made a couple more calls.

In the pub I was getting some attention from a lady who was on the large side and looked like her face had been whacked with a shovel, a heavy one at that. She started by smiling over at me and then she was blowing me kisses and repeatedly winking at me. I looked at me watch and I had a minute to spare so I took up the offer.

*

I arrived at the house at seven o'clock on the dot and knocked on the door. I waited a minute and then knocked again, a bit louder this time. After I still didn't get a response I realized I had gotten the wrong house.

When I finally got to the *right* house I went inside to find Mr Iball and his family waiting for me; they were all looking quite confused and nervous.

"What's going on? I have got better things to do than wait around for you," yelled a very anxious Mrs Iball.

"Yes, what's the matter, Cheesecake? Have you solved it?" asked Mr Iball.

"I think so, Sir, and it's not Cheesecake no more —" I threw off my trench coat and Betty screamed. I stood there in amber boots and tights, a pair of red goggles covered my eyes and I was wearing a green jumper which had a motif of a pair of spectacles and a train on it. "I'm Vision Express Man."

"Ha ha, stupid idiot man more like, ha."

"Quiet, Matthew, let him speak," said Mr Iball.

"Thank you, Sir, cheeky sod."

I walked over to Betty, looking intently at her. "You, my dear, are in the clear. All I can say about you is stop wearing that hideous flower patterned underwear." It's amazing this vision.

"Wh-what, how do you know?" muttered Betty.

"Yes, Cheesecake, how do you know? You were supposed to be looking for clues, not rifling through the knicker drawer."

"Nothing like that, Mr Iball, it's called being a great detective, which means sniffing about."

There was a knock on the door and I was very interested to see their reactions to who was about to walk in, especially Mr Iball's. I opened the door and in walked Miss Loveitt bang on time.

"What's going on?" asked Mr Iball, who was looking very flustered.

"Calm down, Mr Iball."

When the police then came in with a man the look on all their faces was a right giggle — well it made a change from everyone laughing at me; I was starting to feel like a right idiot now.

I rubbed my hands together and said, "Mr Iball and Miss Loveitt are lovers, and together they both have a brilliant business idea. They still haven't got a name for it yet but you can't pick your nose without getting your finger stuck every now and then —"

"Get on with it, you clown."

"Patience, Matthew. Anyway, as I was saying, Mrs Iball found out about them and their plan so she tried to steal the contract. She wasn't so bothered about her husband having an affair though as she's been having one for years."

"Mum, Dad, how could you? I ca—"

"Yes, all right, Betty, stop interrupting for God's sake, me brain's numb enough as it is trying to remember everything. As I was about to say, a few years ago you had an assistant, Mr Iball, that's him, Harry, over there with the police. Any road, I believe he stole from you and you sacked him; so as revenge he started an affair with your wife and together they schemed to steal the plan," I explained proudly.

"What about the corgis, Mr Cheesecake?"

"Well, Ida, my dear, Harry works at Mary's corgi grooming parlour. And see, well, he hates the dogs 'cos they gave him fleas; that's why they call him Harry the Fleabag and it's probably why Mrs Iball is scratching. He's a nasty piece of work, ain't ya, chum? I said, "You're a nasty git."

"Better than being a silly git," snarled Harry. I went to clip him behind his ear but missed and ended up clouting one of the policemen; he didn't look amused.

"So how did you catch them out, Mr Cheesecake?"

"Well, Betty, first I found a pen — it's the one they wrote the threatening letters with and it's got their fingerprints all over it. Then, the other night, they tried to steal the contract and I scared them off. On my visit to Mary's I heard Harry's voice, he was shouting at a corgi, and it matched the voice I heard outside that night. I also knew there was something about him that I had seen before. Lastly, the first night I met Mrs Iball I realized that I had already seen her handbag somewhere before. So, there you have it." Betty ran upstairs crying and Mr Iball gave Mrs Iball a disgusted look as the police put handcuffs on her and Harry.

"Brilliant, man, brilliant."

"Thank you, Mr Iball, Sir. Right, take them away...and stop laughing at me costume it ain't funny, it don't half itch."

There was a bit of moaning and groaning from Mrs Iball and Harry as the police led them away. As one of the policemen walked away I watched Matthew looking him up and down. This solved another piece of the puzzle. Matthew was gay and the other night I had caught him coming home from a secret tryst with his lover James.

What I really couldn't understand though was why no one had asked where I had seen Mrs Iball's bag before and what exactly it was that I had recognized about Harry. Well, let me tell you. Mrs Iball's bag had been hanging on a branch in the bush at the lake, the same bush where she had been getting friendly with Harry whose backside it was I recognized from this event. But should I tell them? No, what do they want for two bob an hour? I shot out the front door and came to a sudden stop thanks to a lamppost.

*

A couple of months later I was on a case: the case of the sheep, the apple pie and the slippers. I was running down the high street and there was Mr Iball and Miss Loveitt in their new shop. The sign proudly read:

'IBALL EXPRESS: TWO IS BETTER THAN ONE.'

Vampire of Apartment 133A Greenstone Street

Another girl missing on page four of the local paper; the front page dominated by a local man found dead in unusual circumstances. I dropped my digestive biscuit as I read on. The man's body had been found in a warehouse. He was thought to be in his forties though reports suggested he looked more like ninety. He was found on his back, his body twisted and deformed; his complexion as white as a pure cloud. His eyes had sunk deep into their sockets and his mouth was gaping open as if the life had been sucked out of him. There were two unusual puncture marks on his neck. His stomach had been ripped open and his heart torn out. Mangled intestines surrounded the body; the rats and insects had feasted on the rest. The coroner was blaming some sort of ferocious animal.

I stood up and looked out from my apartment window; a thick, scary fog engulfed Greenstone Street. Who or what was doing these murders? The police had no clue; but I had my own theory, it was a vampire who had been driven into town looking for fresh meat. This was Kelly's theory too. Kelly was my flatmate and had just walked into the room. "Your coffee is on the side, Kel." I had known Kelly for a couple of years now. We met at college where we were both studying for our medical degrees.

"Thanks, Jack. Look at it out there. The fog. It's horrible... scary."

"I know, it's been like that for a couple of days now."

Kelly sipped her coffee. "Are you okay? You look anxious." A noise came from across the landing and Kelly and I looked at each other.

"Have you seen the paper?" I asked, throwing it over to her. She caught it and started to flick through the pages. While Kelly was engrossed in the story I went to investigate the noise.

"My God, Jack, it's getting to the point where I don't even want to go out at ni...what are you doing? Why are you looking through the letter box?"

"I'm seeing if I can see what's making that noise. I'm sure someone is out there." I slowly unlocked the door to take a look outside, but just as I pushed it open the noise, which had begun to fade, suddenly sounded like someone beating a drum. I banged the door shut and locked it.

"You still think it's him, don't you?" asked Kelly. 'Him' being a guy called Mark Bernshaw who we haven't met yet. He moved in across from us into flat 133A about three weeks ago and since then the murders have gotten worse. Myself and Brian, a guy who lives in the flat below, have also seen him going out late at night looking suspicious. Brian found out Mark's name by accidentally falling over his mail and had once tried to speak to him but Mark just ignored him.

"Yeah I do; it seems strange. Can you hear a sort of tapping noise? It keeps getting louder like a drum; it sounds like someone is in the basement trying to escape or something."

"Don't say things like that, Jack," said Kelly looking worried.

I edged towards the door again and Kelly followed; she grabbed my hand and squeezed it harder and harder as we got closer. We reached it and I was pondering what to do when there was a loud bang on the door. We both jumped. I wondered whether Mark had realized we were on to him and had come to silence us. We stood very quietly and I was hoping that Mark would go away when another bang on the door put paid to that notion. Kelly was trembling. I was about to go and get some kind of weapon when a familiar voice shouted, "Come on, you two, let me in. What you doing? It's me, Brian."

Relief flowed through me as Kelly opened the door and hissed back, "Brian, my heart nearly stopped."

"Thanks, Kel, I didn't know you liked me that much. What's the matter with you two? You look like you've seen a ghost or something." I looked at Brian in disbelief, I don't know what I expected to come through our door but it was no ghost.

"We heard banging, and well, we thought..." Kelly uttered.

"You're not still going on about that new lad are you? I just bumped into him in the hallway; he was moaning that he couldn't have a shower as his plumbing has been playing up. The pipes were tapping and banging away all night apparently. I felt sorry for him so I took the liberty of inviting him for drinks later, hope you don't mind?" Kelly and I looked at each other and nodded apprehensively. "Good. What time are Stella and Megan coming, and what film are we watching?"

Still in shock at the idea of Mark coming over to my flat I replied, "Err, any film you want, and not sure about the girls. So what did he say then, Brian?"

"Who?"

I stared at him with anger and curiosity; Kelly had gone to change. "Mark about coming around for drinks?"

"Oh, sorry, apart from him moaning about the plumbing he didn't say much. He was dressed in black with a hood on and just said 'no thanks' as he pushed past me." I was now convinced he must be up to something, where would you be going in this fog and dressed all in black?

I sat down with Brian and grabbed a couple of beers. "Don't you think this Mark is being a bit strange?"

"In what way?"

"Well, since he's been here there have been the noises, he keeps going out late, he always avoids us and then there are the disappearances and murders of people in the town."

Brian looked at me oddly then laughed a little. "Wait a minute, you don't think he's the murderer do you? Just because he doesn't want to come and have a few drinks?" Brian laughed and I was lost for words. I just smiled and shrugged my shoulders. "You know your trouble, Jack, don't you?"

"Please enlighten me."

"You've been watching too much scary stuff on TV, mate."

"You're probably right."

"I know I am. I'll tell you what; shall we watch the new *Saw* film?" Before I could reply Kelly walked in. "How do you put up with him, Kelly? He thinks that new lad Mark is a killer or something."

Kelly was looking subdued but I couldn't take my eyes off her. She looked amazing from head to toe of her beautiful petite frame. She had on the tightest pair of jeans I have ever seen coupled with a low-cut blouse which just covered her amazing breasts. Her brunette hair was fastened up in a tidy bob; a pink shade of lipstick coated her lips, lips that you just wanted to kiss. Her skin looked smooth to the touch and her blue eyes glistened like the finest diamond.

"Well, I've got to say, Brian, I agree with Jack. Mark is behaving quite oddly, especially when you consider all the strange goings on that have been happening around here lately."

"I don't know, I think you two need a holiday or something. It's never the ones you suspect, trust me on that," Brian remarked. I was wondering what he meant by that comment when our conversation was interrupted by the doorbell. Stella and Megan, who lived in the building's basement flat, had arrived. I watched Brian lick his lips; he couldn't take his eyes off Stella as she walked into the room flicking her long, flowing, blonde hair over her shoulder. She smiled at Brian, leading him on as usual.

"Right, who wants what?"

"I'll have a glass of rosé, Kelly, please."

"Okay, Stella, what do you want, Megan?"

"Same, Kelly love, ta."

"Right oh. Jack, sort you and Brian out and sort the film out please."

I sorted the drinks, popped the DVD in and sat down. My friends started chatting and enjoying their evening but I found that my mind was focused on other matters. Why was Mark going out dressed all in black, what was he up to? What had those strange noises been? I was convinced that they weren't down to the plumbing. And how exactly do you expose a vampire? I sat trying to answer all these questions and couldn't concentrate on my friends' mindless gossip.

*

Morning came and I jumped up to the sound of my alarm. I didn't know which was worse: the ringing of the alarm or the ringing in my head. I must have drunk a bit too much last night. When I staggered out of my room Kelly was in the kitchen making breakfast. "Morning, Jack, ha you look rough."

"Morning, yeah I feel it, what were we drinking?"

"Anything and everything would be a good description; it was a good night though wasn't it?"

"Err, what I can remember of it. I don't even remember saying bye to Bri, Stella and Megs."

"Yeah, you had zonked, they left about one. I couldn't believe you last night though." I sat down on our very old, hand-me-down, two-seater sofa. The TV was blaring and I had a strong mug of coffee in hand as I tried to figure out what I could have said or done. The way Kelly was grinning and shaking her head told me that she knew I was struggling to remember. "You were filling all of our heads with theories of Mark being a vampire killer thingy. I thought it was good but a bit too much for the others, especially Brian, very weird really."

I was intrigued. "Weird in what way?"

"Well, he was just grinning and disagreeing with you, saying Mark isn't a killer. It wasn't Brian how we know him but then he did drink a lot. Anyway, come on, Jack, we're going to be late for uni." I jumped up, just grabbing my half mug of coffee before it fell. I put my mug along with my half eaten breakfast plate in the sink and grabbed my satchel and books. Kelly too picked up her books and phone while quickly finishing her drink. I was just about to follow Kelly out of the door when I remembered my wallet. I doubled back, grabbed it, locked up and left to catch our bus.

*

About an hour in to our lecture, in which I had gotten closer to being sober, the class was disturbed by lecturers running up and down corridors and police who were patrolling everywhere. I looked at Kelly and we both turned to where Brian should be sitting — just an empty chair. He normally caught the bus to university with us but after a couple of hard, unanswered knocks on his door we had to leave him and run for our bus.

I will never forget the look on people's faces that day when the news started to filter through. Mrs Jones, a lecturer who had been missing a couple of days (even though the word was she had gone away), had been murdered. Her white, twisted corpse with the neck ripped open had been found in an old warehouse around the corner. I watched Kelly glaring at Brian's empty chair with tears streaming down her face.

*

The town was in chaos as the news spread and it got much worse by the time we arrived home as two more decapitated corpses were discovered.

Kelly was shaking. I went to comfort her and she threw her arms around me. The embrace turned into a kiss which was long and warm. I held her so tightly, it was beautiful. After what seemed like an age we stopped and looked into each other's eyes. I stroked her face; she smiled and then hugged me hard. I felt so happy; I had wanted this for so long. Kelly looked happy too but there was a bit of awkwardness between us. She let go of me and slumped down in a chair. Returning to the matter in hand she said, "Oh, Jack, what the hell is going on and where was Brian today?"

"What are you saying? You don't think that Brian had something to do with these killings?"

"I don't know what to think. He wasn't there today, he's been acting weird and now I'm worried about Stella and Megan. Then there's this Mark and the police haven't a clue what's going on."

I knew it was no man, it had to be a vampire or a wolf creature or something. Kelly was right about Brian, he had been acting strange, but my suspect was still Mark. "We must do something, come on."

"What can we do, Jack? We have to leave."

"No, we will go and see Brian." I grabbed a carving knife and went to the door. I looked back at Kelly and she reluctantly followed me.

Once outside Brian's door I took a deep breath and with Kelly just about breaking my hand with squeezing it so hard I took an even deeper one. After I knocked it felt like an eternity waiting for a response. I could feel the sweat dripping off the knife handle as I clasped it tight. Finally, the door creaked open. "Jack, Kel, sorry I wasn't there this morning. My head, I have the worst hangover, come in."

I left the knife outside the door and followed an uneasy Kelly. "Brian, you look like crap."

"That's good because I feel like crap, Jack, I've been in bed all day. What the hell did we drink last night?"

"It was more how much you drank," said Kelly with a smirk, she was obviously feeling better.

"Never mind that, Brian, haven't you heard?" I watched Brian very closely.

"Heard what? I have been in bed all day, mate…Jesus, where did I put them tablets?"

"Mrs Jones, the lecturer, they found her body in a warehouse on Beck Street."

Brian slumped in his chair and looked genuinely shocked. "You're joking."

"No, and that's not all, they've found two more bodies, and Stella and Megan have gone missing as well, haven't they, Jack?" Kelly added. I nodded.

Brian stood up, shaking his head. "What do you mean Stella and Megan have gone missing?"

"They weren't at uni and Kelly checked earlier, with the spare key, their beds haven't been slept in."

Brian paced around. "I can't get me head around this; they can't have gone far surely? Who're the others that have been found?"

"Not sure, two blokes I think, but they have all been found in the same circumstances: white, drained, necks ripped out; I think it's a vampire or a wolf thingy."

Brian laughed. "For God's sake, Jack, they're a myth. Have a word with him, Kelly."

"Well, to be fair, something is going on, I'm not sure about Jack's theories but these creatures have been reported before."

Brian looked uneasy. "I think you two have gone mad, it'll be some nutter running about."

I rubbed my head and stood up. "Like that Mark?"

Brian looked at me. "Why do you think that, Jack? Tell me."

Kelly stood up. "I agreed with you before Brian when you said that it wasn't Mark. Now I'm not sure, it could be anyone. Jesus, Brian, I was even suspecting you." I was in awe of Kelly's honesty.

"Well thanks, Kel, sorry to disappoint you but I've been asleep all day."

"The murders happened a few days ago, Brian."

"Cheers, Jack, who needs enemies?"

It was getting to the point where I didn't know what to believe. "I'm sorry, my mind is everywhere. I, however, am convinced that Mark has got something to do with it."

Brian took some more tablets, looked at Kelly then glared at me. "Okay, Jack, what do you propose to do?"

"I'm going to follow him tonight; I will go alone if necessary."

Kelly put her hand on my shoulder. "I'll come with you." I smiled back at her.

"I don't know, you're both raving mad. I'll come, but I'm going back to bed for an hour first. Have you also tried ringing Stella and Meg's mates or anything?"

"No. Me and Jack will try while you go and get yourself sorted."

"Okay. Shall I bring a stake and some garlic, Jack?" Brian laughed.

"Very funny. Get ready to go and I'll see you later."

A couple of hours later, all wrapped up like ninjas, we peeked out of Brian's window. You could just about make out Mark leaving the building surrounded by the fog. We followed him very closely, he kept stopping and looking around and the fog was so murky and thick that Kelly wouldn't let go of my hand.

As we got to the river Mark's pace quickened and Brian was looking really anxious. We hid behind a wall as Mark stopped and looked around once more. Then, in the distance, we heard what sounded like a scream.

Kelly had tears in her eyes and was really hurting me with her grip. "Let's go back, Jack, please?"

"What's up?"

"I agree with Kelly, Jack."

"No, we must follow him, come on." We carried on our pursuit, the noises filling the murky air, and I realized that we were very close to the warehouses where the body of Mrs Jones had been found.

"Where is he, Jack? I can't see him."

"God knows, Brian."

"Jack, for Pete's sake, let's go back."

I looked at Kelly trembling. "God damn it, where has he gone?" I was angry that we had lost him but I could see how scared Kelly was, and Brian wasn't doing much better, so reluctantly we headed back home.

Later, we were all sat in our flat with a hot cup of coffee, Kelly had just come back into the room after trying to trace Stella and Megan. "Anything, Kel?" asked Brian.

"No, the family and friends I did manage to get in touch with haven't heard from them."

I slumped down in my battered old armchair and flicked on the television, a local news report came on. Kelly dropped her cup of coffee, spilling it everywhere, and me and Brian stared open-mouthed at the screen as the reporter said that another body had been found in a warehouse by the river about an hour ago.

"What is going on, Jack? I think we should go to the police," said Brian.

"With what, my vampire theory? They'll throw away the key. No, we have to prove it. That's why tomorrow I'm going to go into his room early in the morning because vampires don't like daylight." Brian stood looking at me in disbelief.

*

It was 5.30 a.m. Kelly was in bed; I was in the kitchen. I had shaved a stick into the shape of a stake and my heart pounded as I slowly crept downstairs with it in my hand. I knocked on Brian's door still in awe of how he had agreed to help me. Now he dealt me a double shock as he opened the door — Brian was up and dressed.

As I went into his flat I could smell something really bad, something dead and rotting. "Jesus what's that smell?"

"Don't look at me, Jack; I know it's horrible. What you got there?" he asked pointing towards the stake.

"A stake to kill that bloodsucking vampire Mark with."

"Jesus wept, Jack, you're convinced about that crap, you'll get yourself locked up carrying that around."

"So what the hell is that great carving knife doing in your belt, Bri?" I had to grin to myself.

"Protection. Have you seen the size of him? And where's Kelly?"

"I left her in bed asleep, all this vampire talk is taking its toll on her."

"Not just her. Well, come on, if we're going to go through with this madness."

I looked at Brian sheepishly because despite my great plan there was one little detail I had overlooked. "Well, we have got a problem to be honest."

"And what would that be? Dear me, it just gets better."

"How are we going to get into Mark's place?"

Brian looked at me, I wasn't sure if he was going to laugh or cry. "And you're supposed to be the clever one. It's a good job I know where he leaves a key."

The key was under a plant pot in the hall near Mark's door. We uncovered it and before I knew it we were slowly entering Mark's flat. I immediately noticed the horrible rotting smell, my heart was thumping like a train with fear and by the look of Brian he was faring no better. We got outside his bedroom and we both gulped, giving each other a not so reassuring nod of our heads. We busted into Mark's room. Brian, as planned, flicked on the light and flung open the curtains, letting the daylight pour in.

"Aaarrrggghh, what the —" Mark yelled as he threw his bed covers over his head. I got my stake out, expecting to see Mark bubble up and explode or something, and Brian was fumbling around trying to get his carving knife from out of his belt. Then Mark jumped out of his bed and, not bubbling at all (well, unless you count him seething at us), came towards us, his massive frame shaking the flat as he hit the floor. "What the hell are you two doing?" Mark raged. I was just about to offer some sort of explanation when his clenched fist flew towards me.

*

Twenty minutes later we were back in my flat. I was on my chair with an icepack and tissue trying to stop my nose bleeding from where Mark had smacked me in it. Kelly was making drinks, shaking her head. "I can't believe what you've just done, you idiots. What did he say?" I couldn't answer; I felt like a prat but I was still convinced that Mark had something to do with it.

Brian looked over at me before answering, "Well, it turns out that our vampire works nights as a security guard down at the warehouses."

"That's exactly what I mean. He'd have access to the warehouses to dump the bodies in."

"Leave it out, Jack, for God's sake. He told us that the police have been to ask him questions and they thanked him for his cooperation, don't you think it's time to drop this nonsense? We should be concentrating on trying to find Stella and Megan."

I was about to say 'no, I am not dropping it' when Kelly sat next to me and put her hand on mine. "Brian is right, Jack, we must look for the girls." I was still mad but I couldn't get angry with Kelly so I half-heartedly nodded.

Later, as the night crept in and the fog became thicker, I walked down Greenstone Street to our flat. I had been to Gemma's, a friend of Stella and Megan's, to see if she had heard from them. She hadn't. Panic for them was now setting in. Brian had gone to see some other people who knew them and Kelly was ringing the police. I entered the building and went up to my flat.

"Hiya, Kel, what did the police —" My heart almost stopped, the flat had been ransacked, chairs overturned, crockery smashed, the TV on its face still playing. I checked everywhere and Kelly was gone. I rang Kelly and Brian's mobiles but got no answer. I went into my room and got a baseball bat and shoved a knife down my belt; I then made my way downstairs, sweat trickling down my brow.

I knocked on Brian's door — no answer. I was about to try the handle but the smell was so overpowering that I hesitated. It seemed to be coming from below in the basement flat. I changed my plan and, using the spare key, I went and opened the door to the girls' flat.

The smell hit me; it was like rotten eggs and warm, rotting meat. I had to stop myself throwing up. Flies buzzed in front of my face. With my hand clamped firmly over my mouth I went deeper into their flat. I looked around but I couldn't see anything. The smell was ripping at my nostrils. I was about to leave when I remembered the little closet door that led to a makeshift wine cellar. I could feel my chest pounding as I reached out for the door. I slowly turned the handle. I paused. Then, with one deep breath, I pushed it open and entered.

I dropped to my knees, my body heaving. There, on the floor, was the white, twisted body of Stella, her long, blonde, blood-soaked hair covering her face. In the distance was Megan, her body practically in half, her organs everywhere, her ginger curly hair in pieces and her head almost ripped off. I ran out only stopping to be sick.

I took a long deep breath and steadied myself. My fear was turning to anger as I knew now that Mark had deceived me and could have already killed Kelly and Brian. I was filled with hope though at the idea that they might still be alive.

I ran upstairs, got to Mark's door, took out the knife and went in. It was dark. I went to turn on the lights but they wouldn't work. Instead, I opened the curtains but because of the thick fog outside this was of little help.

I crept into Mark's front room. On his table was his work torch. I grabbed it and took a breath, finding my courage. With the knife in my left hand, torch in my right, I burst into his room.

I dropped the knife on the floor at the sight that met my eyes. Mark's bed was covered in blood, his naked body on top of it, his throat ripped open. I rushed into the hall, trying to gather my thoughts. I was so confused. Then, from below, I heard a scream which sounded like Kelly's. I couldn't believe it, how could I have been so stupid? Brian had deceived us all.

I picked up the knife and ran down the stairs. Brian's door was unlocked. I made my way in, hoping I was not too late. I rushed into the front room and there was Brian's drained, white body in the arms of Kelly, whose fangs were feasting on his neck.

Depressing/Depressed Again

DEPRESSING

Mood in my mind is not good

Surely I have something to give

 I so down and low today

My head really hurts today.

My body feels numb.

Ya know I would love a bag of chocolate minstrels, even at this early time in the morning.

Is it my time to chat with my maker?

Police sirens surround my ears

What a miserable looking day

I could fair use a cuddle

Depression has got a hold of me today and how many more days to come?

I feel lost in a mind full of hopes, dreams, reality and confusion

NOW THE SUN'S BREAKING THROUGH THE CLOUDS.

I'd like to swim, drown, swim in the dirty city river

But my strength shines through, in the thought of my loved ones

I feel unable to fly today

Walking will be such a strain

I want the simple things that keep passing me by

I need to keep strong

It's all in your head, so they say

It is all good, just look around

*

DEPRESSED AGAIN

𝔐y head aches this morning — not as much as my teeth though

I feel life has been drained from me

I don't even want to answer the phone to loved ones

I wish I had a gun

Who's making that noise? I want to chop him up

WHY   OH   WHY   ?

do you think I will ever be happy *?*

it must be because I don't pray

It seems like today is just like yesterday and it sure resembles the other day

I WOULD LOVE TO HAVE A CIGARETTE

and I don't even smoke

Again the river looks appealing

I'm always there to be leaned on, but everyone seems to be gone when I need to lean

John AD Hickling

I wish I had *two* guns

I'M IN THE MIDDLE

If I jumped, would I land on the bottom?

I suppose it's time to get a grip

Brush myself down and carry on

BRING ON ANOTHER DAY.

Robert Hood

It was June 2014 and England had been in a state of despair ever since John Prince had become Prime Minister; which raised an a eye of suspicion right from the start.

People of all classes were disappearing; some were thought to have been locked away, others killed for resisting Prince's plans. People were losing their jobs and the poor, who couldn't afford anything as Prince had abolished the benefits system, were becoming homeless. Prince wanted worldwide domination; he thought of himself as being similar to Hitler in that he too wanted to build a superior race.

Prince had managed to trick his way into power by promising the things people wanted to hear. His original policies had included stopping all immigration, making a better future for the working man, having the NHS deliver on its promises and ultimately giving England back to England to turn it into an empire once again.

Upon starting his rule his view had been that the poor and weak be discarded while the rich, who could pay his high tax demands, would live well under his protection. If you didn't play by his rules you were bound in prisoner camps or, in some extreme cases, even disposed of. Some of the forces (police, army) had tried to stand up to him but they had been captured or killed, while many more had joined up with his madness. More and more MPs were coming over to his side too now they had realized that it was foolish to do otherwise.

Prince, alongside his dodgy chancellor, Gary Gisbourne, had struck up a deal with Russia as their corrupt leader, Peshiniv, shared much of Prince's vision for his own country. Peshiniv had been promised one hundred and twenty million pounds plus some land in England; a promise that Prince had no intention of honouring. Together they had assembled an army of Russian soldiers combined with mercenaries from all over the world and willing members of the British army and service personnel, including the police. It was an army that had come to be known as the Black Death Military; at least four hundred thousand strong and growing. The Black Death's only desire was to follow Prince's every whim. Dressed in black jackets, trousers and boots they were a formidable looking foe and this was enhanced by the positioning of a skull badge, emblazoned with the word 'death', on their right chest pockets. They had belts around their waists that carried water bottles, handcuffs, phones and ammunition. They wore black, full faced helmets with a silver face plate and black glass eye slots covering their real eyes. They had various knives on them including a three foot machete type sword and each of them carried a 656 AR machine laser rifle, black and silver in colour, with an eight inch bayonet attached. A button on the side of the laser rifle released a flexi-net, a sticky membrane like a spider's web that could snare a target. They had been drilled by their generals in hours of training to show no compassion.

Prince had by now managed to corrupt various members of all countries' governments with sham promises and the fact that when he finally took control of the world they would be able to rule alongside him, which ultimately meant power. America wasn't getting involved at this point in time as it was trying to sort out its own country's unrest. Civil war was upon the world.

England was falling fast and in London Prince was stood on the balcony of Buckingham Palace with his aides; they had just completed their operation to remove the royal family. That morning the Black Death had stormed the palace and were met with little resistance from the Queen's security detail. It was amazing how little power the Queen suddenly had when faced with a Prime Minister who could threaten the lives of her staff's family. Broadcasts of the Palace's seizing were being shown on the only channel in operation by order of Prince. Footage of the royals, Charles, William and Harry among them, being led away was being played on a loop. Not long ago Prince had received a phone call informing him that the family were now all securely locked away, under close watch, at Balmoral. Also being shown on the TV channel were Prince and his generals ripping the badges off the chief of police's uniform and taking medals off other senior security personnel and anyone with rank who would not play ball with him. It then showed them being led away to one of the camps. People looked on in horror as London was brought to her knees.

Prince stood looking out from the balcony at the masses of people, some supporting him, some not, who were booing and shouting obscenities at him. The sun was still shining as the Black Death and police jostled with the crowds. He was now deep in thought with a sly grin on his face. It wasn't long ago that he had been a happy family man and just a simple Conservative MP for Kensington. His policies had been fair: lower taxes, get the best out of the NHS, tackle immigration fairly, but he had started to get disillusioned with the Prime Minister. As he travelled the country he began to notice the ever increasing immigration, loss of jobs, the NHS struggling to deliver what it promised, more people begging, more out of work and some having no intention of getting work but just feeding off the benefit system.

The last straw had been when his wife had become ill and died suddenly a month later from mistakes made at the hospital. Prince blamed the Prime Minister for this as he believed he had let the NHS come to ruin. Prince decided to run for office himself and his campaign and ideas were met with a positive response. Prince eventually won the election and became Prime Minister; it helped that the previous Prime Minister had been murdered by a down and out heroin user who belonged to a hoodie gang. He had waited in a dark alley, near Downing Street, for the PM to return from an evening engagement. The man wore a greyish hoodie top to hide his face and, holding a handgun, he shot the two security guards then the Prime Minister in the face. As the murderer had gone to leave the scene one of the security guards, who was still alive, shot the hooded man in the leg; he was eventually given a lethal injection for his crime.

The events of his wife's death and the murder of the PM at the hands of a low life chav troublemaker had finally snapped him. He blamed the system and certain spineless people in the government for this; for letting people do what they wanted and get away with it. In his eyes, he wanted to stop giving benefit handouts that cost the economy billions and create jobs for these people instead. He believed if everyone worked and earned money, crime, such as robbery, would slowly disappear. His belief had been that if people wanted to keep their homes then they would find jobs to pay for them or join him instead so that he could put them to work as part of the Black Death.

The royals had backed Prince's leadership at first but had started to realize the change in Prince and his power mad plans, but they never fully realized what kind of man he would become. He started to corrupt the MPs by turning a blind eye to tax fiddles and money bungs. He relieved MPs of their duties if they didn't believe in him or his policies, while those that were faithful were rewarded with Prince turning a blind eye to their tax fiddles.

He then formed the Black Death army. He abolished the benefit system and made people pay for treatment at hospitals. He wanted to build a race with dignity and honour and for everything to run like clockwork. Immigrants were not allowed in unless they could pay and the ones that were here already and couldn't pay were being forced back to where they came from. Those that had nothing were eagerly volunteering to join the Black Death or other parts of Prince's bandwagon.

Prince looked down at the masses, knowing he was achieving his dream and people were beginning to toe the line. In fact, no one could now stand up to Prince and those that tried quickly disappeared. Times were desperate; who would stand up to him?

*

The answer lay in the city of Nottingham, which, at present, was a shell of its former self. Buildings and cars had been abandoned, violence and crime, especially theft to survive, was the new plague of this great city. It mirrored how it had all happened in London. John Prince had seemed to set out to have one elite rich society with no chavs or what he considered to be riffraff.

Any areas that had opposed him had now become rundown and, in most cases, Prince's plan to make things better was, in fact, making them worse; England was riddled with crime as people tried to survive. It was now Nottingham's turn and other cities in England were also facing the same fate.

The police, not the ones that had joined Prince's armies but the honest ones that opposed him (what was left of them), were doing what they could to help their towns and cities by trying to keep order and help people where they could. Some were trying to set up task forces to try to stop Prince, but there were too few to make a difference. Quite a lot of the shops and homes were in ruin in places like Sneinton and St Ann's, areas close to Nottingham's city centre. Some shops, such as McDonalds, all the travel companies and estate agents such as Martin & Co and Frank Innes, were trashed from people breaking in to see if there was anything worth taking. Some properties were now even boarded up.

Walking through the city centre of Nottingham, heading towards the river, was a man who was observing and thinking about his city. He was thirty years old with short, brown hair and a thin goatee beard. This former soldier stopped and looked at the boarded up Major Oak pub that he used to drink in. Robert shook his head at the sight and good memories of this pub filtered through his mind. He glanced up at the sky, thinking he felt a drop of rain, before carrying on his way.

With his job gone and the dire situation England was in he found himself wondering where his destiny would now lie. He didn't realize that soon England's destiny would be in his hands. This man was Robert Hood. He was wearing a grey/green Adidas hoodie top; he liked to wear these and wore it a lot with the hood up. It always made Robert smile when people referred to him as a chav and a no hoper when the truth was the total opposite. Robert cared about his fellow man and wanted to help; he would rather be dead than serve Prince.

In fact, he used to be a Marine and had served and fought all over the world, picking up numerous accolades along the way. However, all had changed two years back when he saw a mate get killed. He killed the murderers but had then had to go through a court system to justify his actions; he had felt like he was on trial. This had all made him angry towards the governments he had fought for and so he left the army. That was when he came back to his home town of Nottingham and found himself work in a garage as a mechanic for a while; that was until the reign of Prince had forced the garage to close, leaving Robert unemployed.

He couldn't believe what was happening to his home town; he shook his head at the rubbish that littered the square. Once-thriving shops were now either empty with no customers or shut down. The Black Death took poor people, who were begging, away. Robert was overpowered with anger as he watched well-off people sneer and ignore the needy. How could this be better for the people of England?

He made his way by a well-known public house that was built in the fourteen hundreds called the Bell Inn. This once well-maintained city landmark had now ceased trading and was boarded up and covered in graffiti. Over the past week Robert had been to a few areas in Nottingham and he couldn't believe the contrast he had seen in different places. Sneinton was a mess and Robert had stood in shock as he saw houses that were uninhabitable, burnt out cars littering the streets, dogs running wild and shops that had been robbed down to their last item. After seeing Sneinton he had made his way to Arnold and Mapperley, which seemed to be bearing up OK. There had been a handful of beggars and boarded up properties, but, on the whole, life had still been going on as normal as most people were in work and abiding by Prince's rule.

A couple of days ago, Robert had been to the areas of West Bridgford and The Park, which were both flourishing. Robert had observed that the people in these places were rich, sucked up to Prince and were ignorant as to their poor fellow man's fate. People were shopping and driving around in the best expensive cars; it was a world away from other areas. The rich and important such as Ian Sheriff, the MP of Nottingham and one of Prince's top aides, had now taken up residence at The Park, a top, expensive, residential area in Nottingham which was full of the rich and Prince's followers. It was rumoured that Sherriff himself lived in an eight bedroom mansion. The Park now had a wall around it and was guarded by the Black Death military.

Robert was deep in thought as he made his way by Nottingham Castle, avoiding the gaze of the Black Death soldiers who stood guard all around it, he didn't want any unnecessary attention from them. The castle was now being used by Prince and his army as a communications post. This once beautiful historic landmark had been turned into a games room; years of history had been destroyed or thrown into storage in the smallest room in the castle. People said it was now all full of screens, computers and all the top gadget wizardry which was operated by trained army personnel to keep eyes and ears on what was happening not just in London and England but all over the world.

Robert, avoiding an oncoming rich couple in an Audi convertible, had passed Ye Olde Trip to Jerusalem, the oldest pub in England, which had now ceased trading and was used by the Black Death for storage and their own alcoholic ends. Robert shook his head as he couldn't believe that a national historic artefact was being abused in this way. He crossed the road, witnessing a scuffle between some soldiers and a couple of men that had tried to rob a passing woman, then made his way down to the river.

After walking for a few minutes along the river he headed towards a couple of old, abandoned warehouses on the riverbank. They had once been thriving businesses but now they housed the homeless of Nottingham. On his arrival he was met with excited screams of "Rob!" as a handful of dirty, undernourished children, consisting of teenagers, younger children, toddlers and even some babies, cried out to him. The children that could ran up to him accompanied by some smiling adults. Robert smiled and cuddled the children but found it hard to contain his anger as he looked around at the homeless, which were becoming more every day. These people had all escaped, for the moment, from being taken to prison camps. These were people that had had to leave their homes as they had been repossessed because work and benefits had ceased.

He handed out a bag of sweets to the children that he had bought out of his dwindling savings. He passed an adult some apples, oranges and bread to share around. Robert didn't have to do this as he knew the adults would go and take what food they could, but it was his way of trying to help the people of his city; plus there were some familiar faces within these people. Robert smiled as a little girl of about eight came up and gave him a hug; he knew this girl. Rob looked down at her dirty face, she smiled and said, "Hey up, Rob, thanks for the sweets and everything."

Robert knelt down, facing her and, clasping her small, dirty hands in his, he smiled as he spoke, "Hello, Annabelle, that's all right, sweetheart, and don't worry, everything will be fine." They knuckle touched and Robert took a selfie of them both as Annabelle had always been obsessed with taking photos before she came to be here. She then went off to play hide and seek with the other children, while the teenagers just sat there, sullenly playing on their phones. Robert smirked at this and thought, *at least Prince's reign hasn't changed some things.*

He stood up and bid farewell to the homeless before taking his Samsung Galaxy phone out of his pocket and checking the time: 12.40 p.m. He needed to nip to his flat to get a little more money. He got to the Castle Marina retail park which had retail giants such as PC World and Mothercare among others and they seemed to still be trading. Across from the retail park was the Castle Boulevard canal tow path bridge; it was about twenty metres to the other side and its sides were flanked by four foot high barriers. It was made of wood and had a curved design like a rainbow. Robert's flat was on the other side and he could quickly nip across to his flat before going back into town to meet his mates Adam Dale and Bill Scarlett.

Halfway across the bridge stood a huge black man, looking over the edge. He was about six foot four and was as wide as a door with a shaved head and a scruffy appearance; his clothes were torn and dirty. As Rob neared him the man turned to face him. He stood in the middle of the bridge, legs astride and hands on hips. Rob went to push past him but the man pushed him back. Rob, confused, said, "What's that about, pal? Do I know you?"

The man took a deep breath as he stared at Robert and then said, "I'm hungry so hand over your money and there will be no need for you to get hurt."

Robert looked at the huge, desperate man. "Well, pal, I'm afraid I only have a little money myself and I need it in these desperate times. What little food I had I've just given to some homeless children." Robert took a deep breath and went to get past the man, who shook his head before landing a right fist full on Robert's face, knocking him on his back; he landed a good five feet away.

A dazed Robert got to his feet just as the man swung again. Robert ducked then let go a left right combination into his ribs;

the huge man staggered back. As Robert tried to squeeze past him the man picked him up and threw him back to the beginning of the bridge where Robert landed on some rubble on the ground. He dusted himself down, took a deep breath and charged towards the huge man. They met in the middle of the bridge, exchanging blows with their fists. The huge man swung down his right fist, Robert blocked him then Kung Fu kicked him, forcing him to hit the side of the bridge. He bounced back and grabbed Robert, taking them both over the bridge's barriers and into the river.

They were both submerged in the dirty river. Robert puffed out his cheeks; the water was freezing and came up to his shoulders. The big man forced a little grin at this as the water only came above his waist. It was so muddy that it was quite a bind as they made their way to the slippery brick built bank on the retail park side of the bridge. They were both sporting bleeding noses; the big man had a cut lip too while Robert had a bruise on his right cheek. They were both breathing hard as they raised their clenched fists to carry on the fight. That's when Robert caught sight of the guy's pendant chain that hung around his neck. His opponent seemed to have noticed the same thing dangling from Robert's neck. They both lowered their fists.

"You were in the Marines?" Robert asked, fighting for breath. The huge man nodded.

"You too?" Robert nodded. They both sat on the river bank wall, dripping wet, and started to laugh.

Rob put out his hand. "Robert Hood."

"Donald Little; nice to meet ya, Bob."

"Likewise, Don. If you wanna eat follow me." They walked off, laughing.

*

Not far away, in St Mary's church, the local vicar Frank Tuck had finished his midweek service. The church was packed with all ages and races and more and more people were turning up each week. People had found themselves turning to the church for comfort and hope in England's current desperation. Tuck got the feeling that people felt safe here with him. His parting message to them was always the same: to work together as a community and keep strong; God would help them.

Tuck was furious that Prince believed that people such as those that visited his church were rejects just because some were ill and poorer than the ones he wanted to keep in his superior England, despite the fact that they were actually good people.

His eyes filled with grief and anger as he bid farewell to the scared looking people. He, as well as others, just couldn't understand how and why this atrocity was happening in the twenty-first century. He smiled at a couple of young teenagers who were leaving; during the service he had had to tell them both to turn off their mobile phones.

With everyone gone Tuck bolted the main front doors then put on his jacket and scarf to keep his five foot five, chubby frame warm. He picked up some parcels of food to take to the ever-growing homeless population of Nottingham; the churches across England believed it was their duty to give hope and aid. He went out a small back door of the church, checking that he wasn't being followed, and scurried past the boarded up shell of McDonalds, making his way down to the river.

*

Tucked up safely in his mansion Ian Sheriff, the MP for Nottingham, had just come off the phone to Prince; they had been discussing the imminent takeover of Nottingham. Ian Sheriff had recently turned fifty. He was six foot in height with huge, stocky shoulders, short, greying brown hair and a thick moustache. He took a drink of whiskey; he loved the finer things in life. He ate and drank expensive food and drink and his house was fitted out with the most expensive and beautiful furniture and drapery money could buy. It housed an array of modern features, modern art and sculptures alongside all the top gadgets such as a home cinema and games room, which was full of arcade shoot 'em up games. The place had a good range of original features like fireplaces, sash windows and wooden beams across the ceilings.

Sheriff hadn't always had these luxuries and he only had them now because of Prince. He used to live in the rough area of the Meadows in Nottingham in his younger life and had had to work all hours as a miner. He and his ex-wife had never had a family until they took in Marion, Sheriff's niece. Sheriff had always been an honest, hardworking man; his belief had been that you had to work hard for your loaf of bread and he had been happy with his life. After a spine tingling speech over pay cuts that he once made at work in front of the bosses and unions he was persuaded to go into politics, which he did and he quickly climbed the ladder. When he first started he would never have agreed with the policies of someone such as Prince as he had been a good man, fighting for all things good.

The turning point had come when his wife had left him for a man Sheriff thought to be a money grabber and a lowlife; someone he considered to be below him. It made him change what he wanted to achieve through his politics; he too now wanted the dredges of society sorting out and had found his policies starting to align with Prince's mission. Although he would never admit it, Sheriff was also frightened of what the Prime Minister was capable of, but, as he always said, 'it's better to run with the devil than to go against him'.

His kind demeanour had become harder and he found that he no longer trusted anyone. His work ethic had changed too and his new belief was that hard work didn't bring you anything but heartache.

"Marion," yelled Sheriff. Upstairs, in her room, was Marion Fitzwalter, Sheriff's niece. Sheriff had taken her in after the tragic death of her parents who were killed in a car crash. Sheriff, who was Marion's mum's brother, had taken her in along with his wife when Marion was only ten years old. Sheriff had wanted to protect Marion from further harm and heartache and he thought he was doing it the right way by joining Prince and agreeing with him on everything. He thought that he and Marion could live well and unharmed under Prince's reign. Sheriff still believed Marion loved him and thought their relationship was as good now as it has always been; Sheriff was like a father to her and they doted on each other. He used to take her everywhere, holidays, day trips, help her with her education and take her to karate classes. The truth was, Marion still did love him but more out of duty and pity.

*

Upstairs in her room, lying on her bed, Marion wiped her puffy, red eyes. She had just read a news report on her iPad about homeless people in London being attacked by the Black Death. She could not believe what was happening in her beloved country.

She felt constantly miserable lately; it was like she was a prisoner and her uncle's excuses for keeping her locked up here were wearing thin.

At first, Marion had noticed that her uncle was getting a little possessive over her but she knew that he had never gotten over the pain of his wife leaving and guessed that he just wanted to keep his loved ones close. So, at first, she went along with his demands of spending more and more time at the house with him and informing him where she was going and who she was going out with. He had changed from a loving, caring uncle to a possessive father like figure. The demands had then gradually become more and things got worse. He kept asking her not to go back to London, then demanding it and now she was holed up in one room. His latest thing was even trying to stop her from having any contact with her friends through social media. He tried to cancel her phone contract and after that failed he had tried to disconnect her WiFi, but Marion was more tech savvy than him and had gotten it connected again with ease.

Marion and her uncle's love for each other had long gone; Sheriff had become bitter and twisted when his wife had left him. He had become disillusioned with politics and the simple things in life that he used to enjoy, like travelling, became a burden.

Marion was twenty-seven, had studied medicine at university and had travelled all over the world as an aid worker. She was five foot five with a very athletic build, shoulder length brunette hair and blue eyes. She considered herself to be a very loving and kind person and she was a great animal lover.

She had been living on her own, in London, but she had come to visit her uncle a few months back, and now, because of his paranoid state, he wouldn't let her leave in case something happened to her in these dangerous times.

At the sound of her uncle's voice resounding up the stairs, Marion started guiltily, quickly stuffing her iPad in her underwear drawer out of sight.

"Dinner is ready," shouted his voice. Marion breathed a sigh of relief, glad that she wasn't in trouble again for something.

She went downstairs to where her uncle was sat at the dinner table. The table was full of food. There was lobster, various meats, as many vegetables as you could name, potatoes, various puddings and champagne and wine of varying vintages.

Marion was placed at the table by one of the assistants and she shook her head as Sheriff ripped apart his lobster. "What is the matter, my dear?"

Marion looked disgusted at her uncle, stuffing his face. "Well, let me see...the city is starving to death yet we're sat here with too much food."

"That is how it goes; I have told you before, it is about the strong and the weak, my dear."

Marion kept sneaking bread and meat under the table when her uncle ate, looked away or checked a text on his phone. "What? In this day and age? It's the twenty-first century, damn it. You are supposed to be MP for Nottingham. It's your duty to help your people, yet you endorse this madness of John Prince, why?"

"Believe me; it is better to serve the devil than to cross his path."

Marion stood up, banging her fists down on the table. "But we should be out there, helping our people. It's madness, people having to rob to eat. I see Tesco's in Beeston was ripped apart last night; it took less than an hour to strip it of everything."

Sheriff flicked a bit of lobster off the sleeve of his expensive suit and scowled at Marion. "Marion, please eat."

"But, Uncle, haven't you listened? We should help."

It was now Sheriff's turn to bang on the table, causing some of his wine to jump out of his crystal glass. "Marion, you will do as you are ordered and that is the end of it. Now, please, eat."

Marion stuffed some food in a bag and put it up her top, not realizing her uncle had seen her do this. "I'm not that hungry; I'm going for a walk."

Sheriff wiped his mouth on his napkin and stood up. At that moment four soldiers came in, Marion slowly backed towards the door. "I am afraid, my dear, you are to stay in this house; it is not safe out there."

"Th-that is not fair, Uncle. Why do you keep me prisoner?"

"Prisoner? No. Like I say, it's for your safety." With that Sheriff nodded to one of the soldiers, who grabbed the struggling Marion while another took the bag from her. Marion shook her head at the soldiers, gave her uncle a stare, then resignedly sat back down at the table and carried on eating. She was angry at being stopped by her uncle but didn't show it as she wanted him to believe that she was willingly going along with his demands. But in truth she was hatching a plan of how to escape and where to go without being caught. She rubbed her arm where the soldier had grabbed her and gave him a nasty glare, wishing she could fight back and hurt him too. The soldier just looked straight through her, like he was trained to do.

*

At the Dragon public house there were only a couple of people in. The landlord, Graham Mutch, poured a couple of pints, his pub being one of a handful still trading. Business owners that could pay Prince were getting the help they needed to keep running, but those that couldn't pay were being stripped of their livelihood. The pub also now housed a secret meeting place in the cellar which ran so deep underground that it was like a cave; one of many that Nottingham had.

Mutch's eyes warily flicked to the window as two soldiers patrolled by. Mutch wasn't the tallest of men, coming in at five foot seven inches. He had a shaved head which made him look quite tough and his nose was thick and twisted from having it broken a few times in his younger days. He had a great sense of humour and used to be a policeman before he had had enough of how things were going within the force and became a pub landlord instead.

He was a good friend of Robert Hood's and had known him since secondary school. He had met and become friends with Adam and Bill through Robert. He thought a lot of all three of them but he had a soft spot for Adam; he loved to hear him sing. All afternoon Mutch had kept on sticking his head out of the Dragon's door and glancing down the street to hear Adam busking and singing the Olly Murs song *Troublemaker*. Mutch wiped around the bar area then looked through the window to make sure there were no prying Black Death eyes before going into the back and turning the cellar lights on. He stacked up the fridge with bottles of Budweiser and Corona while he waited for his friends to arrive for their usual evening get together.

*

Robert Hood along with his friend Bill Scarlett walked through the city centre. Bill was six foot in height with a very muscular build. Bill loved to run and he could do ten miles without breaking a sweat. He had brown hair shaved around the sides but cut short on top, his eyes were a piercing light blue and he was clean shaven. He was an honest and kind man with a good sense of humour.

Robert and he walked through Nottingham square and there, stood outside Primark, was their mate Adam Dale with his battered, old, Tanglewood guitar busking the Ed Sheeran *A Team* song to the busy Nottingham crowds. The town hall still lit up the square despite its littered appearance. The Black Death tried to keep the ever growing numbers of beggars away from the well-off, who were just going around doing their shopping like nothing had changed; ignoring the people that could hardly afford food never mind clothes, gadgets and whatever else these rich people were buying. Robert and Bill were clapping and whistling sarcastically at Adam, who had broken into an acoustic version of *Happy* by Pharrell Williams; Bill threw a penny in his case.

"Wow, you're being generous, Bill," joked Adam as he finished up, strapping his guitar on his back. Adam was twenty-nine, six foot in height with brown hair tied back in a ponytail. He used to be in the Territorial Army as well as being a kickboxing instructor. He loved to play his guitar and Robert always considered him to be as honest as the day was long. Adam had known both Robert and Bill for years, being from the same village — Beeston.

They all made their way to the Dragon pub together with Robert shaking his head at the boarded up buildings and people begging while the rich and privileged shopped and the Black Death, which were becoming more and more each day, patrolled the city.

They entered the pub and exchanged pleasantries with Graham Mutch and with the other two men that were sat at the bar. After Mutch locked the door, dimmed the lights and put up the closed sign they made their way down a doorway that had bookcase wallpaper covering it and boxes of crisps stacked in front to keep it hidden from the Black Death. It led to the underground cellar.

"I can't believe this is happening, Rob; what you reckon is gonna happen?" asked Bill as they sat down at a large, oak table. Mutch passed round a bottle of beer each.

"You saw it the other day, Bill. Prince has taken over London and it'll not be long before Nottingham is the same. There are more soldiers every day, signs all over about protection and tax money. The homeless become more every day while the cowardly rich turn a blind eye. People are pulling each other apart to survive; two poor beggars were shot yesterday for stealing a couple of Pot Noodles and some microwave meals. We are all down to the bare bones, food and money wise, and Prince will want his tax or he'll want us in his armies; joining in with his power mad ideas." Robert stood up and started pacing around, deep in thought over England's current fate.

"So what do you think, Rob? Evacuate abroad somewhere?" Mutch asked then drank most of his bottle. Adam looked at Robert, the two other men sat still, while Bill accepted another bottle from Mutch. Robert, who had been facing the wall, spun around to face his friends. "No, Mutchy, the airports are overrun by the Black Death; no one in, no one out. Nottingham is starving; so first things first we need to start getting food and lots of it." Robert sat down as the other men started to voice their opinions.

"And where are we going to get the food from like, eh Rob, ma duck?" asked Greg, one of the men.

Before Robert could answer, Bill chipped in, "Aye, he is right, Rob, where do you intend to get this food? Ring Gordon Ramsay to see if he will gi' us some? Plus, it will be big trouble if we get caught."

Robert smirked at Bill's Gordon Ramsay remark then took a swig from his bottle. "There are lots of places we can borrow food from, lads; the posh folk in The Park, their cupboards must be bulging at the seams. The Asda superstore in West Bridgford; I know it is guarded but there must be a way in — there will be lots of possibilities; we just have to sound them out."

Mutch nodded in agreement, Bill and Adam looked at each other and Robert knew that whatever he decided to do they would be there alongside him. The other two men seemed unsure and just stared down at their beer bottles. Mutch got some more drinks while Robert and the others bickered over the pros and cons and where they would try first.

*

It was still light outside and back in Sheriff's home Marion lay fully clothed under her duvet. She pretended to be fast asleep as she had told her uncle she was tired and feeling unwell. It was only just gone eight o'clock when her uncle poked his head in the door to check on her, making sure she hadn't left as she was always threatening to do.

She listened, holding her breath, as Sheriff made his way back downstairs. She then jumped up, grabbed her phone and purse and slipped on her trainers. She quietly opened the window and slowly shunted down the drainpipe, keeping a lookout for the Black Death as she went. The climb didn't faze her as in her youth she used to be a bit of a tomboy, climbing trees and walls and stuff with her mates. She wasn't bad at football either come to that. Her climbing skills were obviously a bit rusty, though, as she let out a muffled yelp after grazing her arm on the pipe. She dropped to the ground, rubbing her sore arm, before checking around her again. She then snuck up to a tree, climbing it, so that she could get high enough to drop over the top of the wall that surrounded the house. As she got to the top of the wall, ready and poised to drop down over the other side to freedom, she heard her uncle shout "Marion" and presumed he had gone to check on her again. She looked at her window to see Sheriff in her window, looking for her.

Marion didn't wait a second longer and, as she dropped over the house wall, she grimaced from landing heavily on her ankle. After a quick pause she set off once again and as she did she heard her uncle shout to the soldiers, "I want her bringing back alive. Now, go." She ran towards the main wall around The Park where she could climb a ladder that was used by soldiers as lookout points. She had to figure out how to get by the guards (if there were any around as they did roaming patrols) but she would worry about that when it came. At the wall there was one guard in the distance so she took a deep breath and sneaked towards the ladder, her ankle still hindering her a little. She thought the guard had seen her as he turned his head and her heart thumped. She couldn't believe her luck when the sound of some shouting from some passing youths filtered over the wall and the guard went to investigate. Marion took a deep breath and scaled the ladders. At the top, she checked it was clear before running as fast as she could in her quest to reach the city.

*

A little later, Robert, Adam and Bill had just left the Dragon and were walking back to their home, which was now a rundown, two bedroom flat on Castle Boulevard. It was a bit tight for space at times with Robert in the small room and Bill and Adam sharing the other but in these hard times it was a better financial arrangement. They walked straight across the city centre and were all deep in thought when a woman, five foot five with long, brunette hair, came running towards them wearing a black jacket, blue jeans and white Adidas trainers. She tripped and fell.

"Please help me," she yelled as she slipped. Robert immediately went running towards her just as one of the soldiers came round the corner, also slipping on some litter. The woman jumped up with Robert's help as he grabbed her arm to pull her to her feet.

The soldier ran to Robert whose instincts kicked in and he hit the soldier with his fist, knocking him to the ground. "Are you all right?" he asked her.

She brushed herself down and smiled at Robert. "Yes...thank you, my name is Marion, by the way," she said.

"Hi, I am Robert." Robert gazed at Marion. Women didn't normally turn his head at first sight; it was more about personality with him, but Marion was different as there was no doubting her prettiness. Robert just felt that there was something about her. He could tell she was a strong character and believed her to be a caring human being; like himself. He could see she was cut and bruised and a little scared and he found himself just wanting to help and protect her. He normally wasn't someone who would jump into a situation without knowing the facts, especially where the Black Death was concerned, but her worried face and smile had won him over and convinced him to help.

Robert was about to introduce Bill and Adam when Marion said, "There are some more on my tail; quick, follow me. I think I know where we can hide." And they could hear the soldiers' shouts as they all ran off.

They ran down a narrow street with the soldiers not far behind. By the boarded up NatWest bank they ran and past Saint Peter's church to Saint Mary's church. Robert couldn't believe he was running away from soldiers with his and his mates' lives in danger all over a woman he had just met and didn't know anything about. His head was telling him to get a grip and get out of this situation; while his heart was telling him to help her. As they made their way past the Galleries of Justice Museum, then to the church it was obvious Robert's heart had won.

"Quick, this way," Marion said, pulling at Robert's arm. They went round the back of the church and Marion frantically knocked on the door. The time was now 8.35 p.m. and it was still quite light outside.

*

Frank Tuck scurried towards the sound of constant banging on the church door; he looked through a spy hole to see a woman he had known from a child. Marion used to attend church regularly as a child but after she went to university and moved to London her visits had become few and far between. Behind her stood three men who seemed to be looking out for something or someone. Marion banged again and Tuck noticed for the first time how scared she looked, which prompted him to slowly open the door. "Marion? Is that you? What is wrong?"

"Father Tuck, please, we are in danger; please help." Frank Tuck cast his eyes over the party; Tuck observed one of the three men, sporting a green hoodie and a goatee, was cautiously looking all around.

"Quick, this way," uttered Tuck. They all ran in the church; Tuck nodded at the man with a guitar strapped to his back, who helped Tuck bolt the doors.

"Quiet," whispered Tuck as he looked through the spy hole once more. He could see soldiers standing at the front of the church, deciding which way to go. Then, suddenly, the soldiers, which there were now five of, ran off.

Tuck turned to the group of rebels. "They have gone. Marion, can you explain what is going on and who are these fellows?"

Before Marion could answer the man in the green hoodie pushed forward with his hand outstretched. "I am Robert Hood, Sir, and this is Bill Scarlett and Adam Dale." They all shook hands then turned to look at Marion for an explanation.

She cleared her throat and with a solemn look to Robert croaked, "I am sorry, Father, and I am also sorry, Robert, Adam, Bill for getting you all tangled in my mess." Marion bowed her head.

Tuck clasped her hands and smiled. "My dear, you are safe here and will always be welcome, I know it has been difficult to attend, with you living away. But at least you have attended, not like some, mentioning no names." Tuck looked at the three heroes who all looked at each other before sheepishly shrugging their shoulders at Tuck.

Robert stepped forward. "Please excuse my bluntness, Marion, but what is this mess you have gotten into? Can we help at all?" Adam and Bill nodded.

Marion smiled at Robert. "Thanks, I am sorry, but I have placed you all in grave danger. You see, my uncle is the MP Ian Sheriff. I live with him; he has been keeping me locked up, but the worst of it is he seems to endorse Prince in what he is doing to our country. He won't listen. Prince has him eating out of his hand. I couldn't take it any more so I escaped." She started weeping.

Tuck held her. Marion had always seemed to respect and have a fondness for Tuck as he had always been on hand over the years to give her advice, but more importantly it was he who had helped her cope with her parents' death. Tuck in turn also felt protective over her and wanted to make sure she was looked after. "There, there, don't cry, Marion; I'll have to clean the floor," Tuck quipped, bringing a smile to Marion's face. Tuck wasn't bothered about the predicament he could find himself in by helping her as he knew Sheriff had become a deluded man who only listened to Prince. Marion needed someone to watch out for her, and Tuck was more than happy to step up to the plate.

*

Robert stood was studying Tuck' and straight away felt like he was someone to be trusted; it was obvious how much he really cared for Marion.

Robert couldn't believe that just by being a good person and helping a woman in need he had put him and his friends in a dangerous situation. He gave a sigh. *No good in crying over spilt beer*, he thought. They were in this mess and now they had to find their way out of it. However, Robert could sense that the situation wouldn't be sitting well with his two companions as it had all happened so fast and without them having much of a say. His suspicions were confirmed when Bill finally piped up, yelling in exasperation, "Well, that's great — the firing squad."

"If we're lucky," quipped Adam. Adam and Bill, Robert knew, were happy to have helped Marion, as that was the type of guys they were, but because they had been trying to go undetected by

Prince's regime and live a quiet life for so long they were now obviously worried about being out in the open and hunted. They both now saw how much trouble their act of kindness towards Marion would bring for them.

Robert quickly stepped in to extinguish his friends' sarcastic quips and doubts as they were not helpful to anybody. "All right, lads, enough of that. The war of Prince is coming anyway; sooner or later we would have been in it, what's a few more days matter?" Robert grinned at Marion as their eyes locked together.

He thought that she was the prettiest thing he had ever set his eyes upon with her gorgeous, sweet, appealing smile. Everything about her seemed to captivate him and he admired her strength of character; even when she was crying he felt a pang in his heart for her. He felt deeply puzzled as he was very attracted to her and he was normally so clear and level headed, liking to focus on the task at hand. He could have stared at her all night but a loud bang on the door broke their gaze. He intentionally looked away from her so that he could concentrate on the matter of the Black Death hunting them.

"Open up this door, now," raged a soldier.

"Quick, all of you follow me," uttered Tuck and led them to a hidden passage that led to the vast underground caves that ran through Nottingham. "You all go; I will give them a false trail. Marion, where will you go?" said Tuck as he led them to the entrance. Marion shrugged her shoulders.

"She will be safe with us, Father," said Robert with a smile.

"Take care of her, Robert, and of yourselves; I will find you. Now go — go." And they all went down the tunnel, which would have been pitch black if not for the torch that Tuck had handed to Bill. It was cold and damp but they followed the directions that Tuck had hurriedly given them to lead them underneath the Galleries of Justice, which used to be a court house, prisons and workhouses in days gone by, but it was now a tourist attraction and museum. The cave came out at the backyard of the galleries and just a few yards from there was an old church that had been renovated into a pub called the Pitcher and Piano, which was still in use by the wealthy.

"What's your plan, Rob?" said Adam, checking over his shoulder.

"We will hide her at Mutchy's; come on." Then, from behind a wall at the side of the Pitcher and Piano, just in front of the contemporary Nottingham art gallery museum, came two soldiers. One stepped back to shoot as Adam smacked him with his guitar; Robert and Bill jumped on the other.

"Marion, run; the Dragon, go," yelled Robert as he snapped one soldier's neck. Bill took out his blade and stabbed the other. They were about to go in pursuit of Marion, who was at the crossroads on Weekday Cross, when they came under fire from about twenty soldiers who were stood at the top of Weekday Cross. Marion's screams filled Nottingham's murky air as two soldiers dragged her to a Land Rover jeep to be returned to Sheriff.

Robert grabbed a gun from the body of one of the soldiers they had just killed, Bill got the other, and they returned fire, dropping two of the enemy, but there were too many more of them to fight. It was getting on for ten o'clock now and night was drawing in; the streets were vaguely empty apart from a few people looking for food. A couple got caught in the gunfire, but Robert and the others couldn't get to them to see if they were alive or dead (even though one of them seemed to be moving) as the gunfire was too fierce.

"Quick, come on," yelled Rob. They ran down the steps at the side of the Pitcher and Piano leading onto Cliff Road, once a vibrant bustling street it was now rundown with only a handful of occupants hiding out there. They all watched in fear as Robert, Adam and Bill made their way across Canal Street towards the river.

Down at the river they made their way towards the arches under the bridges and abandoned buildings; the soldiers still giving chase. They hid behind a wall and exchanged fire with a few of the soldiers, but more came and on Robert's orders they split up to give them a better chance of escape.

Robert ran towards the Jury Inn Hotel that was on the river bank. As he went around the corner two soldiers were in front of him and he shot one to the ground with his handgun, using his last bullet. The other soldier was charging towards him so Robert threw his gun at the soldier, which hit him on the right shoulder, forcing him to stop in his tracks for a few seconds. They engaged in combat with the machete swords that the Black Death carry with Robert hastily grabbing a machete from the soldier he had just killed. Robert had just knocked his enemy to the ground when —

"Freeze, scum; drop your weapon. Hands in the air, hands in the air." Two soldiers with guns pointed at Robert were stood in front of him. Robert dropped the machete and raised his hands. One of the soldiers smacked him on the head with the butt of his gun, forcing him to drop to the ground. They put cuffs on him and led him away.

They had been walking up the river for a good few minutes now and a dazed Robert was weighing up his situation when a shout of "Aaahh" came from behind him and one soldier was thrown in the river and the other one fell to the ground, his head smashed in by some unseen weapon. Robert fell back. He looked up to see a big figure standing over him. "I can't leave you for five minutes, Bob."

"Ha, Little Don. Thanks." Shots were fired as a couple more soldiers came on the scene.

"Quick, Bob, come on," yelled Don as he pulled Robert up with one hand. A couple of men appeared from nowhere to aid them. Robert was wary of them at first as he didn't know whether they were friend or foe until one of the men said, "Quick, Don, hurry." They then made their way to some underground caves that you could access from an old warehouse along the river.

As they entered Robert was faced with a smiling Bill. "Rob, are ya okay?"

"Bill, Adam, thank God; what happened?"

"Some of these chaps helped us and brought us here." Robert turned to the three men.

"Hi, thanks a lot, my name's Robert," he said with his hand out.

"No problem, man. Winston."

"That's okay, mate. I'm Neil."

"You're all right, pal, no worries. Greg."

Neil was in his thirties and an ex-policeman who didn't want to join Prince. Winston was about twenty-two and was a black Jamaican who used to be a fireman, while Greg was a rather scruffy, undernourished fifty year old. Robert turned to the men and Don. "Thanks again."

Don patted Robert on the shoulder. "No worries, man; now stand still." And they freed him from his handcuffs with an old rusty hacksaw.

"What about the soldiers?" asked Adam.

"You're safe down here," uttered Neil.

"Yeah the soldiers and Sheriff know that some homeless have taken refuge in the arches and caves, but they don't know the full layout of the caves yet," said Winston.

Don wiped his brow with his hand then said, "Prince has ordered us to be left at the moment, that is the word from the decent police that are left, apparently Prince and his scum are setting up a prisoner camp at Wollaton Park. His plan is to make use of those people that he considers useful while God only knows what they would do with people that do not play cricket."

Robert threw down the cuffs. "But what about the people up there? There are children among them."

Don didn't have an answer so Robert began to pace around the cave. There were families there; some ill and most hungry. He turned to Don. "Prince and the soldiers are coming; most of these people will be prisoners for their cause. Men like us they will want for soldiers; God knows what he will do with the rest." Robert gave a young child a sweet that he had in his pocket. As he paced around all eyes were on him. "We need to find better shelter and food; we have to get food for everyone." Rob drank some water from a bottle that had been pinched from Tesco's. There were a few supplies in the caves that the people had managed to bring with them or nick from shops. "Get some water, lads, and have a minute," Robert then ordered, taking another sip of his own as he thought hard. Robert scratched at his chin as he said, "We need to find lots of these caves, make them safe. Then we will take food from the ones that have food coming out of their ears. Then we will go and find the people that are struggling and bring them to the caves; any that have been taken to the prisoner camps we will sneak in and break them out — that will give that idiot Prince and his brown noses lots to moan about. The only trouble is the caves are close to Sheriff and his soldiers; they even run under the castle, but it is the only option we have until we can find a better place or solution. Right who is with me on this?"

Robert looked at Don and the men, who looked at each other, and after a brief pause they nodded and Winston replied, "Why not, man? What have we got to lose?"

Robert carried on inspecting the caves, leaving the men to think about what he had said.

*

Bill knew Robert like the back of his hand. After all, they were from the same village, had served in the Marines together, watching each other's backs on numerous occasions; they were like brothers and had gotten into all sorts of capers over the years. He looked at Adam to see what he thought about the master plan. Adam shrugged his shoulders then smiled, which told Bill that Adam would leave the decisions to Robert and Bill; Adam would follow them to hell and back. Bill had a few doubts over this plan of Robert's; he agreed that something had to be done but he was a bit unsure about the safety of using the caves as he knew the punishment would be severe if they were caught. But Bill trusted Robert with his life and knew that if anyone could pull it off it was Robert. So of course he would be with him all the way, but he intended to have a face to face chat with him at some point to discuss the plan in depth.

Bill looked over at Robert, who was leaning against the cave wall while the others discussed places where they could get food from. Bill could see Robert was deep in thought about something which he suspected was Marion. He had never seen him like this over a girl; he never normally let himself get distracted. In fact, Bill thought hard about Robert's past relationships and couldn't even remember their names except for one, Sarah, who had wanted the full package with Robert: kids, marriage, mortgage, dog, the lot. But while Robert had liked her he didn't want all that as his career in the Marines was everything to him; so that relationship didn't end up lasting long.

Already, though, Bill could tell that with Marion it was different, she had bewitched him. Bill knew that Robert would want to do something about these people in need and about Prince thinking he could do what he pleased, but he could also tell that Robert couldn't help but worry about Marion and would have to attend to that matter first.

Bill smirked as he watched Robert try to sneak away. As Adam drank water and talked with Don and the others Bill watched Robert slowly make his way to the entrance, trying to go unnoticed.

Bill followed suit and snuck up behind Robert, placing his hand on his shoulder. "And where do you think you're going, pal?" he said.

"I'm going to the flat to get some things before the soldiers find it. Then I will look for better shelter for everyone."

"You think we're daft, Rob. Not thinking of looking for a certain Marion, are you? Well, we are coming with you; no arguing," said Bill. Rob smiled.

"Who's Marion? And count me in," said Don, walking over after overhearing their conversation.

At that they left for the flat with Bill explaining the eventful time they had spent with Marion to Don.

*

Marion wiped the tears from her eyes as she looked out of the jeep window as it arrived at her uncle's house. She was in a bit of pain from the cuts and bruises she had collected on her escape attempt, but she was angrier with herself for getting caught and involving Tuck, Bill, Adam and Robert in her mess. As soon as she thought of Robert she couldn't help but break into a smile. He had seemed so good looking and mysterious as his face peered out at her from beneath his green hoodie top and she caught sight of his gorgeous blue eyes and warm smile. His whole presence had made her feel safe. She thought he was so kind and brave for aiding her, especially as other people she had asked for help on the way down had simply turned a blind eye, not daring to stand up to the Black Death. She wondered if she would see him again and hoped he had gotten away, which she was sure he would have done.

Her smile soon vanished as the jeep pulled up outside Sheriff's mansion. Sheriff was stood in the doorway, his face awash with anger, but Marion also detected in her uncle a bit of relief at her safe return. She got out of the jeep and gingerly walked towards him; she put her head down, hoping to walk past without anything said.

Her uncle blocked the doorway so Marion couldn't get by. "Marion, why do you do this? I want to protect you; like I always have, that is all."

"And protecting me is sending me to my room, is it, Uncle? Locking me up? I am not ten! I want to go back to work in London."

Sheriff's smile had become a scowl. "I worry about you in these times, that is all, and London is unsafe at the moment. You'll be fine here. I could get you a job here instead. There are plenty of injured soldiers to tend to. Why don't you get some food? I have to go somewhere."

It was clear to Marion that her uncle wasn't listening and was becoming more deluded by the minute. So as not to make him more suspicious that she was up to no good Marion thought it best to play along with him. "Okay, Uncle; I am hungry," she replied courteously and walked on past him.

"Just a minute, sweetheart; these men that helped you, who were they and where did they go?"

Marion's heart nearly stopped, she knew her uncle would hurt anyone for trying to take her away. "I don't know, Uncle. I ran into the market square and I fell, they helped me up. I only got one of their names, which was Richard. Then your goons showed up and tried to kill them so we ran. They were just passers-by who were in the wrong place at the wrong time."

Sheriff looked at her with such a distrusting expression. "Well, these passers-by killed a few of my men."

"It was self-defence, they were getting shot at. Can I go for some food and a lie down please, Uncle?" Marion yawned and rubbed her cut arm.

Her uncle nodded. As Marion started to walk off Sheriff summoned one of the soldiers and she heard him say, "I want these men finding and bringing to me alive if you can, and make sure you lock her room and keep an eye on her." He then went to get in the jeep.

Upon hearing all of that Marion's legs nearly buckled but she managed to make her way in without drawing any attention to herself, trying to hold back the tears as she thought of Robert.

*

A week later Prince was due to arrive at Nottingham Castle while at the same time hundreds of soldiers were due to take residence at Wollaton Park and set up prison complexes there. These camps were being set up all over the country in unused airfields, farms, heritage sites and now it was Wollaton Park's turn. They were very tightly run by a general and the Black Death. People that wanted to join the Black Death would be trained at the camps and people who disobeyed were imprisoned there. Old, rundown Portacabins that were full of bunk beds with dirty mattresses and bed linen filled the complexes. Food was good if you had joined Prince, while it was very scarce if you didn't abide by his rule.

Robert, Adam and Bill had gotten their weapons and clothes from their flat just in time as soldiers had found it and destroyed it. They had tried to locate Marion but couldn't get near. Robert had found out about Prince's arrival from a soldier that they came face to face with the night they set off to the flat. He wasn't a Black Death soldier, they would rather kill themselves than give away information, but someone who used to serve in the British army before joining Prince. This made him easier to question.

Robert and his men had tortured him into giving this information by, at first, dunking his head in the dirty river water. Robert wasn't happy about having to act in such a way but he knew it had to be done for their survival; they had to stay one step ahead of their enemy. He had watched Bill punch the soldier constantly in the face to no avail, and then, when all looked lost, Don (who was armed with the biggest axe Robert had ever seen, its long handle had been taped up with black sports tape and the huge head had the word 'enjoy' written on it) had pushed the soldier to the ground, swung his axe over his head before bringing it down, cutting a big branch (that was laid on the side of the river) in half. He had then swung the axe again and smashed it down, missing the soldier's head by centimetres. As he swung again the soldier had told them everything: how they were using places like Wollaton Park as camps to train people who wanted to join Prince's revolution and those who refused to join were to be treated like animals. With another swing of Don's axe the soldier had then told Robert that Prince was coming to oversee things and the castle was being prepared for his arrival that very moment. After Robert had squeezed all the information out of the soldier he had felt conflicted as he didn't want to kill him in cold blood, but he also knew that the soldier now knew their faces. Bill pulled the soldier to his feet and was about to cuff him when the soldier pushed Bill and went to make a run for it. That time Don's axe didn't miss.

Currently, Mutch and Tuck were in charge of helping more homeless into the labyrinth of makeshift cave homes that they had developed underground; continuing the work they had been doing for the past week.

Robert and the others had spent the majority of the week approaching the homeless that were hiding in boarded up properties and taking them out of harm's way. Some were reluctant at first, as trust was becoming a hard to come by quality these days, but after they were shown photos of food and comforts on Robert's men's phones they were quickly won over. The word was soon spreading that a gang of men, led by a chav in a green hoodie, were providing safe havens for the unfortunate people of the city.

The rest of the week was spent putting up alarm and CCTV camera systems at every entrance and nook and cranny they could find. They had acquired all the gear from a B&Q that had recently closed with its entire stock still inside, and having a few electricians among their ranks had come well in handy. Don, Winston, Neil and Greg had set up booby-traps such as trip wires and nail bombs which were set like mines, buried or hidden in the floors, so that if some poor soul walked over them their body parts would be everywhere.

Adam had been in charge of disguising the ways in and out of their hideout. On Cliff Road there was an archway that led to some caves under the (now abandoned) Broadmarsh Centre and Adam had camouflaged it with an old, wrecked, unused lorry. He had even put a door into the caves through the lorry itself. Bill had been responsible for organizing his group of men to bring in beds, electrical gear, generators and whatever else they had pinched, found or brought with them.

*

It was now Monday 14th July and three weeks had passed since Robert had tried to help Marion. Darkness was setting in and Robert and his men were lying in wait in an abandoned house across from the roundabout near the A60 and A614 routes. They were waiting for a lorry that had food and supplies on it bound for Wollaton Park; information they had gained from Prince's soldier, thanks to Don and his axe. Robert was in his green hoodie with hood up and a bulletproof vest underneath, holding the machete and gun he had taken from a Black Death soldier. His men were similarly attired except Don, who had his trusty big axe as well as a revolver he had bought on the black market.

Screech, who was a very skinny and lanky lad with a face covered in freckles and long, ginger hair, was the gang's newest recruit. He had lived in Clifton with his elderly father before he had died, leaving him homeless with no other family to care for him. Robert and the gang had taken to him as he was brave, honest and in Don's words 'a good kid'; he was also a very fast runner. He was sixteen and when he spoke it was like a high pitched piercing sound; earning him his nickname. Screech had been hiding around the corner from the abandoned house. He rang Robert. "They're coming; a jeep at the front and a lorry behind. Looks like four soldiers in the jeep; two in the lorry."

"Okay, Screech, nice one; come back to your position — and be careful." Robert hung up and ran to the top of the stairs in the abandoned house, looking at the targets through his binoculars.

"Right, lads, there's a jeep, a lorry, six soldiers — positions."

*

About an hour later Mutch and some other men who resided in the caves were pacing up and down at the Cliff Road entrance; they had expected Robert and the gang to have been back long ago. Mutch began to think to himself, *what happens if Rob and the others have been caught or even killed? Who would take over?* He knew deep inside that he would try, but he wasn't a natural leader. *Would it be the end of everyone? Would people be forced into joining Prince to save their lives?* Mutch knew he would rather be dead than join him. All these thoughts and questions started to scramble his brain and worry him, but his worry soon turned to relief when he heard the screech of Don's battered, old transit van coming around the corner.

Robert and his men jumped out with boxes of food and passed it to Mutch and his companions, who took them into the caves. The caves were now full of people that had once possessed every type of employment imaginable; from plumbers, electricians, builders, even people with medical experience to help everyone keep a clean bill of health. The caves were vast and quite damp but they were very well lit thanks to the electricians who had put lights up all along the walls. But it was starting to get cramped in there and such a large number of people in one space was causing problems from time to time with clashing of personalities along with people's resentment at having their homes, way of life and pride ripped away from them; but as a whole they worked and existed together in fear of what could happen to them.

There was a big room with food and supplies. There was even a room with a big screen TV and DVD player (that was powered from one of the generators), which kept the children entertained. Robert and his men, thankfully all in one piece after the hijacking, walked through and began to recount their adventure.

Mutch took another box of food from Robert; he had a quick look in it and licked his lips at the sight of various biscuits and cakes. He then passed it to a woman whose job it was to store it properly. "Where you been, Rob? You had me worried, mate. I take it it wasn't as easy as we hoped?"

Robert put his hand on his mate's shoulder. "You worry too much, Mutchy; but yeah, they put up a bit of a fight."

"Was it easy to get in the lorry then? How many men were there?" Annabelle, who came up and high-fived Robert walked with him and Mutch to help sort out the supplies and looked as intrigued as Mutch to hear Robert recount the story.

"So, there was a jeep, with four soldiers in, and a lorry with two in the front, right? And they came round the corner of the A60, well, you know them houses across from the garage?"

"Yeah, I know where you mean, the roundabout where you turn left onto the A60, right onto A614?" Mutch replied.

"Yeah, that's it. Well, we were hiding in one of the abandoned houses for what seemed like an age — Adam read a month old edition of the *Mirror* twice." Robert and Mutch laughed.

"Well, I shot at the jeep in front, killing the driver, which brought the lorry to a halt. We eventually shot the others after they had hidden behind the jeep, firing at us; it turned into a bit of a battle. Then I shot the one in the passenger seat just as he was about to shoot Screech; it was close. The driver was a big lad, but Don soon sorted him out. Anyway, we were high fiving and that, Don even did a bit of a dance — we thought he was having a fit." Annabelle laughed and Robert rubbed her head while Mutch opened a stubborn box that a young woman was struggling with.

"Anyway, let's just say it was a good job Bill was on the ball. It took Don a good five minutes to get the doors of the lorry open and as he pushed them up, as luck would have it, he stumbled to the ground. There were four soldiers in the back and I thought we had had it, to be fair, Mutchy, as we had put our weapons away. Just as the soldiers cocked their guns there were shots fired and the four soldiers were laid slain. There, stood behind us was Bill holding his rifle, which was smouldering."

Mutch shook his head, Annabelle gasped. "It's a bit too close for comfort, ain't it, Rob?"

"We got away with it today, mate, thanks to Bill. Now we know we have to keep our eyes on the ball at all times."

"Here you go, Annabelle," said Robert as he passed her some food. Robert had known Annabelle and her family for a few years now as he used to live on the same street as them. Mutch watched Annabelle's eyes well up as she was overjoyed at his safe return; she had always loved Robert and he her. He had been in her life as far as she could remember; she loved to play with him and was grateful for what he had done for her family, especially since they had become homeless. She gave him a peck on the cheek and a big hug before running off to watch *Frozen* with some other children.

*

The next day, at Nottingham Castle, Sheriff was at the gates, waiting for the arrival of Prince. The castle was now set up for Prince to use as an operations outpost; it had all the technology needed to achieve this. Prince would be arriving with his generals and some valued MPs.

Sheriff checked the time on his watch; he smiled at a few rich people who were having a drink in the pub across from the castle, but Sheriff's smile quickly turned into a frown as a couple of men, who were very scruffy in appearance, caught his eye. Sheriff then started to feel angry as he watched the rich people, who made him proud to be their MP, being harassed by these two men who seemed to be begging from them. Sheriff told a couple of his soldiers to bring the men inside the grounds of the castle before making his way inside himself.

A couple of minutes later the two men were dragged into the castle grounds. One of the men dropped at Sheriff's feet. "Why are you bothering those people out there?" Sheriff asked.

"Please, Sir; food — I need food," croaked one of the men.

"Where do you live and why haven't you got your own food?" Sheriff said as he scratched his neck.

The man, still on his knees, coughed. "I haven't got a home or money since the benefits system was abolished."

Sheriff clicked his fingers at one of the soldiers and yelled, "Take him away." The man screamed as two soldiers dragged him off. Sheriff then turned to the other man, who was on his feet, flanked by two soldiers. "And is your story the same as his?" Sheriff asked.

"Well, Sir, I had my own business as a builder and paid my way, but I lost it all as work dried up with Prince's rule." Sheriff's eyes widened at the man's remark over Prince.

"So is that a yes then?"

The man gulped. "Yes, Sir; I have nothing."

Sheriff smiled. "Take him away as well."

The other beggar dropped to his knees, his hands clasped. "Please, Sir, spare me, spare me."

Sheriff smirked. "And why would I do that?"

"Because I can lead you to the man who takes your food and protects the people."

Sheriff turned round. "Wait," he yelled at the soldiers.

"Who is this man? You know where he is?"

The beggar stood up. "His name is Robert Hood, and no, Sir, I am not sure where he is; but I will find him."

Sheriff grabbed the man by his coat and looked him up and down. "What is your name? And how do you know of this man?"

"Billy Knox, Sir, and people, well, the poor are talking about him."

Sheriff let go of him and turned to the soldier. "Give him a phone." The soldier reached into a pocket bag on his belt and brought out a Samsung Galaxy Mini mobile. The soldier gave it to an anxious looking Knox, who looked back at the angry face of Sheriff.

"Now listen, Knox. As soon as you locate him send a text to my number, which is in the contacts, then we can locate you as we can track the phone. Now, tell me, why exactly would you want to help us? What is it that you want?" Sheriff urged Knox to stand.

"Just to eat and live well, Sir, but I would also love to serve your army," replied a smirking Knox.

Sheriff, with his hand on his chin, looked Knox up and down then glared into his eyes. "We will see, Knox. You have three days to locate this man or we will locate you and feed you bit by bit to the pigeons. Off you go." Knox struggled to his feet, nodded and ran off. Sheriff watched Knox as he disappeared around the corner just as Prince and his posse in black hummers (bullet proof glass, small canon guns on the side) came up the road and entered the castle.

Sheriff, wearing his biggest smile, walked up to Prince's hummer. Prince stepped out of the vehicle; straightening his tie.

"Welcome, Sir." Sheriff shook Prince's hand.

"Thank you, Sheriff; let us go for a walk." And they both went off on a walk around the gardens.

"Is everything okay, Sir?"

"Not really, Sheriff. The country in some corners is fighting back. Some people are still not paying their way; we have to stop being soft. The prison complex at Wollaton Park is complete so now we will take the people of Nottingham. If they're not willing to be in my army or to serve any purpose that suits me then I think we should banish them out of our country." They both came to a sudden stop as Sheriff thought he had heard a rustling in the bushes behind them. They turned to see a bird fly upwards. They leaned on the wall looking out over the city, but unbeknownst to them there was someone watching and listening in the bushes.

"I agree, Sir; when do we start?"

"The day after tomorrow. Gisbourne is coming with supplies tomorrow by helicopter. Which reminds me, Sheriff, I hear some scum robbed our food; what are you doing about it?"

"At this moment we are trying to locate his whereabouts, I have recently found out his name is Robert Hood; we are checking his details now, Sir. He will be another thief, an ex-benefit grabber, nothing more."

Prince squashed a bug on the collar of his twenty grand suit and said. "Whatever he is I shall not have people doing what they please; I want him caught, Sheriff."

"Yes, Sir, he will be." They spoke for a few minutes then they made their way into the castle, unaware of the spy in the bush who climbed down the wall and made his way past the Olde Trip to Jerusalem and across the empty road to the river where Adam Dale was waiting.

"Did you find anything out, Screech?"

"Did I! We need to see Robert." And off they went.

*

Once inside the castle, Prince and his party were shown the operations room, which was operated by personnel of both sexes, working the various computers and communications. After Prince had given his seal of approval they made their way to the dining room; the long wooden table was set with the finest of home ware. Marion was already in there and Sheriff introduced Prince to her. They sat down as food and drink were brought in.

Tucking into his steak, Prince looked up at Marion, who was looking a little red eyed; he knew that this was because Sheriff wouldn't let her leave at the moment. Sheriff had told Prince that he loved her very much and wanted to protect her as the world had become so unpredictable. Prince agreed with Sheriff, it was a dangerous place out there.

Prince took another bite of rare steak, telling himself that he didn't want to get involved in this family's politics as he had far more pressing matters to attend to such as how to get everyone on his side. It was Sheriff's duty to deal with his own niece. Prince wiped his mouth and, looking directly at Marion, he said, "So, Marion, your uncle tells me you are an aid worker and you work abroad a lot? It must be interesting."

Marion swallowed her food and looked at Prince. "Well — err — Prime Minister, I did, but I haven't done much of late." Prince grinned as she looked at her uncle, who was going red. Prince guessed that this was because Sheriff didn't want her saying too much.

"Please, call me John, and why is that?" replied Prince as he helped himself to more wine.

"Well, for some reason, my uncle has decided to keep me homebound, which has kept me from my work."

Prince watched in some amusement as Sheriff, redder faced, said, "Marion that is enough, I do apologize, Sir," he said to Prince.

"Well, it's true, Uncle, you keep me locked up like an animal," retaliated Marion.

"I said enough," shouted Sheriff.

"That's enough, Sheriff; please, both of you, calm down," interjected Prince. "Sheriff, please explain to me why you won't let her go back to her work." Prince knew why, but he liked to see people of importance squirm, it fed his power thirst.

Marion smiled while Sheriff looked shocked at Prince's question. "Well, Sir, it is my duty to protect her and, as you have said yourself, it is not safe in some parts of the world at the moment; especially in England."

"Well, I can see your point. As things are you are safer here at the moment, Marion." Prince smiled. Prince tucked into more food; enjoying this argument he had set up.

Prince could tell Sheriff looked relieved at the thought of Prince backing him up. Whereas he watched Marion as she got angry. "Excuse me, Sir, but surely that should be my choice? And if it is unsafe out there then that is surely your doing, making people do things against their will. I thought it was your job to protect them?" Sheriff stood up but Prince waved his finger at him.

"It is all right, Sheriff; I admire her honesty. And that is my wish, to protect the people; I just have a vision that our race can become a complete one, all on the same page, so to speak. So that means everyone contributing and if that means people can't pay then they can be given jobs to aid me in getting the country as one. We are setting up camps at Wollaton Park for the homeless and bringing in food for them, and those that oppose our rule are educated and drafted into our workforce." Prince smirked to himself as he thought it best not to mention that people would be killed or shipped abroad if they didn't comply. Prince could tell Marion didn't trust him.

"Well, that sounds fair, I suppose. But I feel I am doing very little to help as I used to help at a church I attended, but I haven't been allowed to go much. Please, Sir, please, Uncle, could I go to the service tomorrow? We could tell everyone of your plans." Prince watched Sheriff shake his head while Prince sat there wondering if she really did now trust him. He then realized that Marion's idea could work out in his favour.

"I tell you what, we will go along with you to the church as you say, Marion; it will prove I am trying to help."

"That would be great, Sir, thanks, and thank you, Uncle." Prince nodded with a smirk on his face as he watched Sheriff glare at her. Silence then filled the room as they all continued eating.

*

The next day five jeeps, full of armed soldiers, surrounded a lorry full of supplies to protect it from thieves as the lorry was bound for Nottingham Castle. In one of the jeeps was James Crabbe, MP for Birmingham, who had decided to join Prince's rule. He was on his way to the castle with gifts including a couple of £500 bottles of champagne, truffles and a lot of money. Crabbe was clearly hoping to get his tongue brown. He looked up at the noise of three helicopters, with Gisbourne in one of them, making their way to Wollaton Park.

Crabbe's convoy went past the old Nottingham Home Ales brewery building, which was now a shell of its former glory, most of the windows boarded up and apart from a few homeless people the building was not as occupied as in its days of old. Crabbe looked out of the windows at the empty littered streets, burnt out cars and dogs running wild. They all came to a sudden halt and a soldier got out of the jeep in front and approached Crabbe's jeep.

Crabbe wound his window down. "What is it? Why have we stopped?"

"There is a burning lorry in the road, Sir." Crabbe stuck his head out of the window and sure enough, as well as a couple of overturned cars, there was an old abandoned Asda 7.5 ton lorry which had been set on fire.

"Well, go and see if we can get round it, you buffoon." The soldier walked up to the lorry and was about to wave Crabbe and the jeeps on when a man came from behind him and threw him into the burning lorry. Crabbe thought he was going to be sick. He didn't care about the burning soldier, he felt sick because he didn't want to miss his lunch with this distraction. He was concerned enough, however, to wonder, *who would do this and go against Prince?* Because, in his eyes, he thought everyone in these times was like him — a coward. He never really liked Prince, but he wasn't going to tell him that, he just wanted the best foods and wines, the best everything really. He couldn't give a damn about Prince's policies and the suffering that England was enduring as long as he maintained his good pampered life — that was all that mattered. And if that meant shoving his tongue as far up Prince's behind as possible to achieve this then that is what he would do.

*

Don shot the driver of the lorry that was carrying the supplies while Robert had sneaked to the open door of one of the jeeps, stabbing a firing soldier. Another soldier jumped at Robert, knocking him to the ground. Robert then found himself staring at the barrel of the gun. He was about to accept his fate when a sword slid through the soldier, skewering him from back to belly. The soldier dropped to the floor and Robert looked up at a man who he didn't recognize. The man pulled him up. "Thanks, stranger."

"No problem. The name's Billy Knox."

"Robert Hood."

After five minutes of fighting they had killed all the soldiers, except for Crabbe and his driver, who now had Bill Scarlett's gun to his head. Robert had lost two men, which had left him feeling upset and responsible. He had known one of the men, Steve, for over six years. Robert shut his dead friend's eyes before their bodies were put into one of the jeeps.

Robert opened the door to the final, remaining jeep to see what he believed to be a snivelling worm of an MP who was gulping, sat up with his right hand on a briefcase. Robert took it off him and threw it to Adam who opened it. "Wow," he said as he showed everyone the contents of the case. None of them had ever seen so many banknotes.

"Don't kill me please," pleaded the snivelling MP.

"Oh, I am not going to do that. We're just gonna take this money and food to the people of Nottingham, pal. Right, lads, move out." Robert said with a wide grin. His men took occupancy of the vehicles and he made Crabbe and his driver get out of their jeep. "The castle is that way." Robert pointed out to Crabbe.

"The Prime Minister will not be pleased."

"Good, I am glad of that," Robert replied.

Crabbe, pulling his coat over his shoulders, replied, "Who are you?"

Robert, whose face was partly covered by the green hood of his hoodie, pushed it off his head and grinned at Crabbe. "Robert — Robert Hood." And jumped in a jeep's passenger seat while

Don clambered into the driver's seat. Knox climbed into the back seat. They sped off with the others. "Thanks for saving me, Billy. This man driving is Don Little. Don, Billy Knox." Don, looking at Billy in his rear view mirror, nodded.

"Hi, Don, and not a problem; glad I was walking by."

"Is that where you live, Billy? Around there?" asked Robert.

"I don't really live anywhere. I just wander the streets for food and try to keep myself out of the clutches of the Black Death." Don swerved to miss a couple of roaming dogs.

"Why don't you come back with us, Billy? We have shelter, food...you seem a good man to have around — eh, Don?"

"Aye, the more the merrier."

"That would be great. Are you sure?" said Billy

"Absolutely — put ya foot down, Don; it'll be night before we get back," Robert chuckled while Don shook his head. Both were unaware of Billy looking out the window with the biggest sly grin spread across his face.

*

Later that evening, Robert was showing Knox around the caves and introducing him to people. Knox was impressed with the hideouts and the happiness of the people there and found himself getting caught up in it. He had to force himself to snap out of it and remember his mission to tell Sheriff of Hood's location, but Knox now had a bigger ambition: to take Robert to Sheriff himself. However, this new plan posed a couple of problems; how to get Hood there and, more importantly, how to get him on his own as he was very rarely without one of Don, Bill or Adam. Robert then took Knox to show him his sleeping quarters; Knox was barely aware of where they were going as he pondered the stumbling blocks of Robert's capture.

Knox came from a well-to-do background and had once been happily married with his own successful business, but a messy divorce left him not being able to pay his way and under Prince's regime he had been left an outcast from the superior race mould. The old him would have never even contemplated giving Robert up and at first he had felt a twinge of guilt and wished he wasn't in this position as Robert had been good to him so far. Knox, however, was in a desperate position and blind to what men like Sheriff and Prince were really like. At first he had thought about whether he should team up with Robert instead as he was impressed by him and what he had achieved, but ultimately he believed that Sheriff would make him rich beyond his wildest dreams. That was it, his mind had been made up: he would have to betray Robert.

*

At the castle a red, dirty, out of breath Crabbe had just explained the earlier events to Prince and Sheriff. He had told Prince of how Robert Hood and some other men had ambushed his men and that even though the soldiers had been killed they had still killed loads of Robert's men. Crabbe also added that he had beaten four of Robert's men up before more had overpowered him, taking the money and the top of the range champagne. Prince grimaced as he heard the tale. Crabbe then said, "I think this Robert Hood is just a chav, even though he was very good, well trained. It's just a shame I was busy sorting his men out or I would have probably had him for you." Crabbe nervously whistled as he avoided Prince, making his way to a huge table that was set up in the back room with food and drink.

Prince was pacing around the room when a soldier came in. "Sir, we have his files." Sheriff and Prince went into the operations room. A soldier saluted then pressed a button; on screen was Robert Hood's picture and his impeccable service record in the Marines. Prince shook his head as he read it; Sheriff was quiet.

"Another thief? A benefits dodger hey, Sheriff? This Hood has an untouched service record; he has been awarded various medals for successful missions." Sheriff was about to answer when Crabbe, who was still stuffing his face, said, "*Chomp* — a Marine? That don't surprise me; he was good." He went to pick up a chicken leg. Prince took out his gun and shot Crabbe between the eyes. He fell, chicken leg in hand, landing face first on the table.

A worried looking Sheriff cleared his throat. "We will find him, Sir; I have someone called Knox locating him as we speak."

Prince took out his phone and rang Gisbourne, whom he had known for years; they had both attended the same schools and universities and entered politics together. Gisbourne, who was six foot one inch with muscular build, a balding head and a brown goatee, wasn't really interested in Prince's policies. But Gisbourne trusted Prince and knew what Prince was capable of; plus Gisbourne had been made chancellor and been given wealth beyond his wildest dreams so whatever Prince did was OK by him.

"Hello, Sir."

"Gisbourne, are you set and ready to go up there?"

"Yes, Sir."

"Good. In a couple of days I want you to start the clean-up of this city. No mercy, understood?"

"Yes, Sir."

"If you come across a man named Robert Hood — I will send over his file — I want him alive. I will be over to oversee the camp after church." Prince hung up and patted Sheriff's shoulder. "Right, Sheriff, tell me about this Knox."

*

A couple of nights had passed since Crabbe's escapades. It was the night before Prince and his party were due to attend the church. Down in the caves Knox had been learning the cave system as best as he could. For a couple days now he had been learning all the ways in and out, how many people they held, the equipment they had, every detail to try to help him.

He had thought about hitting Robert over the head with a club or something then just simply carrying him out over his shoulder, but he soon dismissed this idea as Robert was always with someone and he would get quite heavy. Also he had to bear in mind that the camera systems were everywhere; to which the only plan he had on that at the moment was to try to sabotage the camera set up, by shutting them down somehow. Knox settled down to sleep, thinking of a way to pull this mission off.

*

Sunday morning was a warm, peaceful morning considering what was to come. At Wollaton Park Gisbourne's troops were getting ready for their assault and Prince, Sheriff, Marion and a handful of guards had arrived at Saint Mary's church. Frank Tuck smiled at Marion as they entered the church, but was confused at the attendance of the Prime Minister and his party; he welcomed them all the same. They took their seats for the service amidst some dirty looks and scornful whisperings.

*

Meanwhile, the Black Death had started to march around the Wollaton area. It was carnage; people being taken or killed. A few tried to fight back with guns, knives and whatever else they could get their hands on; even stones. At first the people of Nottingham seemed to hold their own, but as more Black Death and better fire power arrived the men who opposed the Black Death were dwindling. While the two sides were involved in heavy gunfire one man hid behind the shell of an abandoned car, took out his phone, typed a message and pressed send.

*

In the caves, Don ran up to Robert. "Bob, it has started — look," yelled Don, holding his phone up to Robert's face.

"Right, get geared up. Mutchy, I want you to stay here to protect everyone; sort the men you will need, mate, and get the children into the hideouts." Mutch nodded. "Right, let's go, men. Knox, you can travel with me and Don." They all got their weapons; a collection of machine guns, revolvers, axes, swords, knives and clubs which had all been taken from the Black Death. They then made their way to their jeeps they had taken from Crabbe and his soldiers and set off towards Wollaton.

*

At the church the service had finished. Tuck went to speak to Marion but Prince and Sheriff approached the two of them. "A fine service, Father Tuck," sneered Prince.

Tuck reluctantly nodded and was biting his lip hard so as not to say anything, but he couldn't bite that hard. "Tell me, Sir, I am a little confused. You are using us as slaves, if we are lucky, taking every penny you can; that is why most of these just own the dirty, ripped clothes from Primark on their backs." He indicated to the congregation now leaving his church. "And you are here in God's house like nothing has happened."

Tuck smirked at Sheriff, who was furious with Tuck's outburst. "How dare you, Tuck?"

"That is enough of that, Sheriff. After all, he has his opinion. You have me wrong, Father. I am only trying to build a stronger race and offer protection against outside forces. I want to protect these urchins — I-I mean people." Tuck scowled at Prince as he watched him turn and pretend to lovingly pat a young girl on her head. Straight after he tried to surreptitiously wipe his hand on his suit.

Tuck looked at Marion and he could tell she was desperate to talk to him, but knew she couldn't with her uncle there. He tried to force a smile, when Sheriff wasn't looking, to reassure her.

"So that is why you have blessed this church on this fine morning? To help these fine people? Financially perhaps?" Tuck said with a teasing smile.

Prince, gritting his teeth, forced a smile. "That is correct, Father Tuck."

Tuck looked at Prince, wondering whether to believe him or not. He was about to reply when Prince's phone rang, to the annoyance of Tuck. Prince walked towards the church organ to take his call and Tuck pretended to go and sort some hymn books when really he had both ears trained on Prince's phone conversation.

"Sir, it is Gisbourne; we are engaged in combat with some rebels and Hood and his men have shown up." Prince pulled his phone from his ear and even from his vantage point Tuck could hear a grenade explosion and piercing screams.

"Right, I want him alive; we are en route," roared Prince. "Sheriff, Robert Hood and his chavs are on the scene at the battle — let's go." Marion gasped and looked at Tuck. Prince turned and knocked the young girl, whose head he had patted earlier, over.

Tuck was furious at Prince showing his true colours in church; he now had his answer to whether to believe him or not. Tuck felt helpless as he heard Sheriff yell, "Take Marion back to the castle; it will be more secure there than at The Park." Then he, Prince and two soldiers, who were escorting a reluctant Marion, left among the panic and screams.

The young girl's parents picked her up off the floor while Tuck went to see if she was OK. "Are you all right, Annabelle?"

"Yes, Father." She smiled.

Tuck waited until Prince, Sheriff and the soldiers had driven away then led her and a handful of others to the secret cave path that led to the underground hideouts. He turned to a young man. "Screech, follow Marion and locate her whereabouts, but be careful." Screech smiled and left while the others made their way to the hideouts to take shelter from the coming war.

*

The battle was intense; injured and dead rebels and Black Death littered the streets. The noise was deafening with constant gunfire and grenades going off. The once quiet streets were besieged by burning vehicles. This was the sight that met Robert and his men as they pulled up in jeeps and old vans. They engaged in battle with the Black Death, but they were heavily outnumbered.

"Don, let's get as many of the survivors as we can and get out of here." Bombs, smoke, gunfire and screams filled the air. A helicopter came overhead and Bill Scarlett jumped up and fired a machine gun, blowing up the 'copter, which came down on a lorry, in turn blowing that up.

After the explosion, Gisbourne and his soldiers, who had taken shelter behind a wall, stood up, but Robert and his men were already gone.

*

As night fell Wollaton Park was full of activity with the bringing in of prisoners caught from the day's fighting. Soldiers were taking children away from parents by placing them in separate complexes; Prince hoped this would make the parents swear their allegiance to him; plus he could educate the children to join him away from the influence of their parents. Some cowardly adults had already agreed to join Prince's madness. A few that had opposed had already been shot.

If you joined him then the camp could be like being at Butlins; if you didn't then the caves that Robert Hood's homeless were housed in would seem like a five star hotel by comparison. The areas people were kept in were unclean with dirty water and minimal food.

Gisbourne was overseeing these activities. He sniggered to himself as he watched children scream as they were torn from their parents. If it was left to Gisbourne he would torture and kill them all; he was always annoying the soldiers by asking if he could shoot the uncooperative. He was never into politics, but had always worked and couldn't stand benefit cheats; so, in his eyes, what Prince was doing was right. He loved to shoot things and had always killed defenceless animals. Gisbourne pulled a crying girl of about ten from her mum then handed the girl to a soldier, who took her to the children's complex. At that moment, his phone rang; it was Prince.

*

At the castle Prince had just got off the phone to Gisbourne after expressing his anger at Robert Hood escaping. He was even more displeased because he had to return to London to attend to the matter of a couple of MPs rebelling in his absence and he had wanted the Hood matter to be resolved before he left.

"Right, Sheriff; you and Gisbourne know what is expected. When I get back in a couple of days I want Nottingham in my pocket and Hood captured or killed."

"Yes, Sir; it will be done." A soldier walked in to inform Prince that his helicopter had arrived.

Prince shook Sheriff's hand.

*

As they walked to the helicopter they were unaware of Marion's activities. There were a few rooms at the top of the castle that were used for sleeping. Marion had been put in one, 'for her own safety' her uncle had told her. She realized her uncle had lost the plot and that their relationship would never be the same again. The room was small but clean and comfortable. The door had been locked and soldiers would walk past about every twenty minutes to half an hour.

She had been listening intently at the door until she heard the soldiers walk past before running over to the window and opening it. She puffed out her cheeks as she realized that the drop was too far and the drainpipe was a few metres out of reach. She was holding her head in defeat when she saw a young, ginger lad in the bushes.

Marion jumped back inside and the ginger lad lay low as a patrol passed a few yards from them. Once it was clear that they couldn't communicate through talking, in case anyone heard them, out of desperation, Marion, who had learned sign language at university, signed 'who are you?' with her hands and, to her astonishment, the lad replied.

188

He told her he learned it as his dad had been deaf. Marion eyes and face lit up when Screech told her Robert was looking for her. Marion then watched him disappear; feeling reassured he was going to tell Robert of her exact whereabouts and the problems they faced in trying to free her.

*

In the hideouts the people with medical knowledge along with others were trying to help the injured, which ranged from minor cuts and bruises, to broken bones, to having arms and legs blown off. Also there had been a lot of innocent people killed that day. Knox looked on, partly horrified and partly glad that Sheriff's plans were in motion.

Knox was becoming more and more pressed for time to get his plan in motion as they had just been informed that everyone in the caves was to be moved to a new secret camp that Robert and his men had located. For the past month they had been leaving in secret to get it all ready, to Knox's annoyance he had not been included in these plans. Bill, Adam and some other men were there now, making sure that no soldiers had located it and that it was all ready to start relocating people to.

Father Tuck was currently getting people of all sizes, races and ages organized with Mutch, while some of Robert's men loaded a lorry with supplies and stuff like food, weapons, blankets, medical supplies and whatever else would be of use.

Knox had volunteered to stay behind with Robert as Robert had wanted to make sure that he would be the last to leave; to ensure that everyone else had left safely. But Knox still had one problem: Don was also staying behind as Robert's plan once everyone had left was to go with Don and finally get Marion.

One of Robert's men came in amongst the chaos of people getting their stuff. "Rob, there are a few Black Death patrolling around, but they are round the castle side. Bill has rung me; they are ready, what shall we do?" However, while no one had been looking, Knox had taken a syringe with a knockout drug from amongst the medical supplies in the caves. As people around him gathered up all their earthly possessions Knox sent a text to Sheriff, informing him that he was with Hood at this moment; he knew Sheriff would then be able to locate his whereabouts by tracking his phone.

Knox was with Robert as he gave out instructions. "Okay, Pete, start taking what and who you can and go to Broadmarsh entrance; Bill and Adam will meet you all where we agreed. Take Annabelle and be careful, pal." Knox watched the affection he had for this young girl as they knuckle rubbed. Knox waved at her as she left and then the operation finally got underway. Knox was deep in thought as he helped people get their stuff; he wondered if Robert suspected him. *Would he be able to follow him without him being rumbled?* But Knox's question about him wondering if he was suspected was answered and an opportunity arose as well when Robert said, "You stay with me, Knox, if that's okay? Help get things sorted here."

Knox tried not to show his joy too much. "Yeah, course it is, Rob, pal; whatever you want." The main problem Knox had though was how to get rid of Don. He had thought of capturing them both, but he knew that this would be too much for him. Just then, as if God was on his side, Don said, "Shall I go and help at the other end, Bob? If Knoxy is gonna help ya?"

"Yeah, good idea."

Knox had his back to them, pretending to pick stuff up, wearing the biggest smile. Knox then went to help Robert get his stuff and followed him into the cave that he slept in. Don had already gone to help with the evacuation. Knox pretended to be busy picking up some of Robert's clothes and then, while Robert was bent down on his knees, rolling up his sleeping bag, Knox took a deep breath, ran in and jumped on Robert, sticking the needle in his neck.

"Aaah, Knox, what you doing?" They struggled for a few seconds then Robert dropped to the floor.

Knox looked up as he heard an explosion go off at the boarded up Broadmarsh entrance. He heard shouts and screams and gunfire and he could see smoke. He smirked, knowing this was the Black Death and Sheriff responding to his text message.

Knox tied Robert's hands and put him in a wheelbarrow that had belonged to one of the men in the cave: a builder who had left it behind in his hurry to escape. Knox paused for a few seconds as he looked at Robert, knocked out in this battered old wheelbarrow. Knox felt a trifle guilty and questioned if he was doing the right thing. Robert had shown him nothing but kindness. He couldn't go back now though, the text had been sent.

So, with a deep breath, he pursued his plan to deliver Hood to Sheriff.

He stopped and looked over his shoulder as he thought he heard a scuffling and the sound of someone breathing. He glanced around the cave but it looked clear so he grabbed the wheelbarrow's handles to push when...

"Aaahh," Knox yelled as he felt a pain in his leg. He swung round to see the needle stuck in his left calf. "Nooo," he tried to grab at his attacker, but he couldn't see anyone. He started to drop slowly to the ground, his body already starting to feel numb. He yelled then fell at the feet of a scared Annabelle. His mind was telling him to do something, but his body was paralysed. Knox, who was in a semi sedated state, realized that Annabelle must have been scared of the explosion and come back to Robert. After all his planning he had been thwarted by a child. Knox watched as she went over and patted Robert, who didn't respond, she then ran back out of the cave, presumably to get help, it was the last thing he saw as he blacked out.

*

Annabelle had found Tuck, who was helping evacuate the caves. "Quick, Father, Robert has been attacked, I think he is dead. That man called Knox did it," yelled Annabelle. Tuck felt furious that Knox would do this; after all the help Robert had given him.

Tuck gave her a reassuring hug. "Which way, Annabelle?" Tuck said, he then smiled at the young girl's bravery as she pointed him in the right direction and off they ran to help Robert.

Tuck bent down and shakily checked Robert's pulse at his wrist. He felt a twitch beneath his fingers and sighed with relief; Robert was alive. His gaze shifted to Knox on the floor. He looked up at God for forgiveness before giving Knox a swift kick in the head. "Do forgive me, Lord. Come, Annabelle, quick." Tuck then took the handles of the wheelbarrow with Robert in it and they headed towards the passageway to his church.

*

A couple of hours had now passed in which hundreds of the people of Nottingham had been captured, a few had escaped and well into a couple of hundred had been killed. Sheriff and some soldiers had been checking the cave system for Robert when they came across a half dazed Knox who was sat up in a chair.

"Well, well, Knox, and where is Hood?" sneered Sheriff as he slowly paced around Knox, who rubbed his head.

"Sorry, Sir, I had him; I drugged him, put him in a barrow to bring him to you when —" Knox bowed his head.

"Do go on, Knox."

"When someone drugged me."

Sheriff went up to him so that they were now face to face. "What someone, Knox?"

"Erm…a small girl, Sir." Knox bowed his head while the Sheriff stood up shaking his. "Sir, I will make up —" *Bang.* Knox slowly fell back with a smouldering bullet hole between his eyes. Sheriff stood, arm outstretched, with his pistol in hand.

He put it away and turned to a soldier. "If Hood is half dazed like that idiot," he pointed to the now dead Knox, "then he can't be far. I want everywhere searching now." And so the soldiers began their search for Robert.

*

Not far away a dazed Robert had now come to at the church with Tuck and Annabelle explaining to him what had happened. Tuck was giving Robert a drink of water and some paracetamol.

"Thank you, Father. Ouch, my head; what happened exactly?" Robert forced a smile through his banging head as he shook Tuck's hand.

"Well, it turns out Knox is a traitor; he knocked you out with some sort of drug. My guess is, he was going to take you to Sheriff." Robert was furious, he wanted to punch something, but his tired body wouldn't let him. "I can't believe it. You think you're helping people." Robert shook his head and then looked up at Tuck. "Thank you, Father, for saving me."

"Don't thank me, son; it was Annabelle who went back for you and stabbed Knox with the same thing he got you with."

Robert laughed, even though it hurt his head to do so, and Tuck and Annabelle joined in. He shook Tuck's hand again, knuckle touched Annabelle and said, "Thanks again, both of you."

"It was our pleasure, Rob, especially after what you have done for all of us. You have done wonders for the people," replied Tuck as Robert gave Annabelle a cuddle.

"Wonders? You mean I have failed them," moaned Robert.

"Enough of that talk, my lad, you have given us hope in the midst of this madness — and that is a miracle in itself." Robert smiled as Tuck patted him.

Robert sat with Annabelle for the next few minutes, trying to regain some strength. Annabelle, who had now calmed down from her ordeal, was playing *Candy Crush* on Robert's phone. Robert lovingly patted her on her head, then stood up. "What is the word, Father? Have you had any news from the lads?"

Robert watched Tuck take out his phone and scroll through it. "Yes, lad, a lot made it to the camp, but there were some fatalities and a lot have been captured. Mutch is missing, but Don, Bill, Adam and Screech are on the way here." Robert felt a mixture of sadness and relief.

It didn't take long for Don, Adam, Bill and Screech to arrive at the church and they were pleased to see Robert was alive; and the feeling was mutual. They were dirty and tired from the fighting as well as shocked and choked up over all the friends that had been killed or taken. They still couldn't believe something like this was happening in the twenty-first century. Don lifted a smiling Annabelle up in the air; she too looked thrilled to see them all.

"Our little heroine, hey?" smiled Don.

The men all smiled at her. Robert patted Bill and said, "What's the word, mate?"

"There are soldiers everywhere in the city, but we managed to get people to the camp without being followed. So, for now, the camp is secure and unfound."

Adam coughed then said, "We think they have Mutchy, Rob."

Robert rubbed his chin. "Yeah I heard, do we know where they've taken him? Or if he is even alive?"

Bill stepped forward and said, "He was alive when he was captured by soldiers; we presume they have taken him to Wollaton Park, but we're not sure on that."

Adam, who had been checking his iPhone to see if there was any word about where Mutch and the others had been taken to, then spoke. "You do realise, that if he is alive they will torture him to get to us and bring us down. What we going to do about it?"

Don put Annabelle down and said, "Sheriff and his men are looking for you, Bob. It'll only be a matter of time before they come here; we have to go to the camp."

Robert nodded. "We must get out of the city and then we have to locate Mutchy and the others and get them out somehow. What about Marion? Any news on her?" asked Robert.

"She's still held in the castle. I know where," said Screech.

"We have a couple of men waiting in the abandoned McDonalds building ready to take Tuck and Annabelle back, Rob," said Bill.

"What about transport back?" asked Robert.

Bill replied, "Yeah we have a couple of the jeeps we borrowed hidden in the old *Evening Post* building, close to the castle."

"Right, Don, would you be kind enough to get Annabelle and Father Tuck to the men who can then take them to the camp? When that's done, come back and meet us at the castle; we are going for Marion."

Don smiled and said, "See you in a mo then; are you ready, Father? Annabelle?" They said their goodbyes for now and Don and his party left.

Robert had a drink of water to wash down some more paracetamols to soothe his aching head. He felt like he could just drop to sleep any moment and his body felt like it had been hit by a bus, but he knew he had to find the strength for his friends and Marion. Ten minutes later, after the others had gotten away OK and Robert had gotten himself together a bit more, he and the others left for their mission.

*

At the castle Robert and his men had already snapped some soldiers' necks and managed to climb the walls. Screech explained to Robert that Marion was in a room on the east side of the castle; her window was the one next to a drainpipe. Robert patted him. "Thanks, Screech; I want you to wait at the bottom of the hill, at the back of the castle, to keep an eye out for soldiers or any danger." Screech nodded and left. Rob, Adam and Bill climbed up the wall at the side of Ye Olde Trip to Jerusalem, checking for more soldiers' whereabouts before making their way into the castle.

Two soldiers patrolled the dining room; Bill and Adam grabbed them, cutting their throats. Robert checked his watch and was a little worried; Don should have re-joined them by now. But they couldn't really wait any longer for him so Robert, Bill and Adam went to look for Marion. There were only a few minutes into the search when they were stopped by two soldiers pointing guns at them. "Hands up," one shouted. Adam and Bill slowly raised their hands and Robert had just started to do the same, wondering how they would get out of this predicament, when the soldiers' heads were suddenly banged together. They fell to the floor with a smirking Don behind them, Robert went over and high-fived him. "Talk about good timing, Don, mate."

"Bob, Sheriff has just got back," Don said as he knuckle touched Bill and Adam.

"Right, we must find her and get out of here," replied Robert.

Robert and his men were sneaking through the museum part of the castle, where there were numerous displays showing various points in Nottingham's timeline. There were glass cases full of military uniforms and weapons through the ages as well as different displays on life in Nottingham; going as far back as Roman times.

It was as they passed a display of old coins and pots that Sheriff and his soldiers opened fire on them, smashing a couple of the glass cases; spilling thousands of years of history all over. Robert ran through to a bit of the museum that had uniforms and weapons from Roman and medieval times. He had no bullets left just the Samurai sword on his back. His men were engaged in fighting with the Black Death soldiers.

Robert was hiding behind one of the display cases, waiting to pounce on Sheriff, who had walked in with his pistol in hand.

"Where are you, Hood? I only want to talk to you," said Sheriff, grinning.

Robert ran between some of the display cases of uniforms and weapons. Sherriff shot about six bullets, smashing some of the glass cabinets, spilling some old swords, helmets and other weapons to the ground. A mannequin, sporting Roman attire, hit Robert, knocking him to the ground.

Sheriff walked up to Robert, who was facing Sheriff with his bottom and hands on the floor, and Robert started slowly shuffling backwards. "Well, well, scum; trapped like the rat that you are," said a smirking Sheriff. He shot Robert, nicking the top of his shoulder.

"*Aaahh* — I thought Prince wanted me alive?" Robert said, squirming as he looked to the right of him at some old clothing and weapons.

"If you come across a cockroach you don't keep it as a pet — you crush it." Sheriff smirked as he took aim at Robert's head. *Click, click* — he had ran out of bullets. "No," yelled Sheriff. He picked up a sword that was amongst the debris on the floor. Robert took a deep breath, jumped up and rolled to the items on his right. Sheriff ran at Robert, who had a bow and arrow in hand, it was a very old one from medieval times. He let the arrow fly, hitting Sheriff and taking him off his feet and into a glass cabinet.

At that moment, Don, Bill and Adam ran in. "Rob, come on, more soldiers are coming," Bill shouted. Robert ran after them as they set off to find Marion; trying to follow Screech's directions. With all the chaos and gunfire surrounding them it felt near impossible to navigate the castle and get to Marion. Then, as they ran up a staircase, they heard Marion shouting. Adam and Bill threw a grenade at some soldiers to keep them at bay while Don and Robert followed Marion's voice and arrived at a locked door.

"Marion, it's me — Robert, are you okay?"

"Robert? Thank God you're all right; yes I am fine."

"I'm gonna shoot the lock on the door, stand back, jump on the bed," Robert said as he took aim at the lock.

"Okay, I am clear," Marion yelled. Robert then shot off the lock to Marion's door and rushed into Marion's room. He was overjoyed at seeing her again; she was as beautiful as when he had last set eyes upon her.

"Hello again. It's funny, but every time we meet you're always in some kind of trouble," Robert chirped, wearing the biggest of smiles.

Marion rushed to him. "I know, it's just a knack I seem to have; I bet you're getting fed up of it." Marion smiled back at him as they embraced

"Well someone has to save you, might as well be me." Robert smiled. They were about to kiss and Robert felt a mixture of emotions. He was incredibly attracted to her but the relief at finding her alive and well seemed to heighten the situation and just made him want the kiss even more. He went to instigate the move and reached out for her.

"I hate to be the party pooper, but don't you think we ought to get a shift on?" said Adam.

"Yes, let's go, Bob," yelled Don.

Robert tried to hide his disappointment but he knew that his friends were right. He grabbed Marion by the hand and they all made their way out to the castle grounds.

They had managed to dispose of most of the soldiers by this point, but they knew others from Wollaton Park would soon arrive. They climbed down the wall into the courtyard with Adam slightly twisting his ankle after landing on a disposed Coca Cola can. They went to Screech who was waiting with their getaway transport: one of the jeeps they had taken from Crabbe. Don took the wheel and the others jumped in. It took two attempts to start it before it finally chugged into life, throwing out a cloud of thick black smoke.

"Let's go, Don, pal," yelled Bill as a few soldiers came running down, firing, with a couple of the shots hitting the back of the jeep, making them all duck for cover. Robert and Adam clicked their rifles, jumped up and fired back. Bill threw a grenade, sending a couple of the oncoming soldiers flying through the air, Don smashed the jeep into gear and they sped off.

Don's foot was almost pushing the pedal through the floorboards as they drove past the river and made their way out of Nottingham. Robert was sat in the back with his arms around Marion, who had her head on his shoulder. Like the rest of the company they were silent as they took in the recent events. Robert looked out of the window at the wounded, but not beaten, Nottingham. He thought about how he was going to defeat Prince and put an end to this madness. But his first priority was the captured people and his true, good friend Mutch; he knew he would have to rescue them soon.

He looked out of the window again and Nottingham was behind them; he just hoped that the camp they had set up would be safe and remain undetected as there would be a lot more people that would come and need his protection. He pondered how he would rescue Mutch and the others, then how he would eventually defeat Prince, which had become his destiny.

His thoughts were broken as he looked down at Marion, who smiled then closed her eyes. Robert rubbed his hand gently across her forehead then looked up and looked out of the window to see a sign that read: *To Sherwood Forest.*

Lightning Source UK Ltd.
Milton Keynes UK
UKOW02f0601260716

279237UK00002B/14/P